The Ghosts of Riots Past

The Troubled Conflict in Derry Through The Eyes of a Volunteer First Aider

Jude Morrow

www.judemorrow.com

ISBN: Paperback
9798842187638

Front cover image by
Spiffing Covers

First printing edition
2022

www.judemorrow.com

Contents

In Loving Memory Of

Bernard Bonner and Captain Leo Day K.M. Order of Malta

INTRODUCTION - BEFORE YOU ALL START!

The year 2022 marked the fiftieth anniversary of the Bloody Sunday Massacre, which occurred on the 30th of January 1972. Being born in 1990 in Derry, I didn't know much about local history. Given the huge press coverage of the Bloody Sunday 50 programme of events, I decided that I should learn more about it.

I started to read books written by those present on Bloody Sunday and contemporary analyses of it. When looking at the pictures, I saw what appeared to be young people wearing officer-type uniforms and white medical coats. They seemed to be everywhere and were the Order of Malta Ambulance Corps volunteers, also known as the "Knights of Malta". I found them interesting immediately and wondered what it was like to be a teenager going into the line of fire to render aid to those who were wounded. I thought, *surely one of them wrote a memoir, or somebody wrote a book about them that I could read.* I was stunned to find that no such book then existed.

Being autistic, I feel like I have to know everything there is to know about a topic. I looked at various sources, like the Savile Report of The Bloody Sunday Inquiry, and I knew the Knights of

Malta were heroes, and that their story needed to be told. They were present at all the major historical events of the Free Derry period. With the benefit of hindsight, I could create a reliable witness who could be in the right place at the right time, or the wrong place at the wrong time, to give a more expansive view of events. Nobody was present at every event, which is why Martha was created. I could place her as an observer within the Order of Malta Ambulance Corps and capture emotions and feelings rather than simple factual occurrences. Martha is not based on anybody! I made her up.

Martha's addresses are fictitious because I have a fictional person in a real place. I didn't want to take anybody's actual address, so I know that Mura Place in the Rossville Flats didn't have the number 73, for example. I wanted to place her in block two of the high flats to compliment the story timeline and not the later built block three, where the higher flat numbers would have been.

The Order of Malta Ambulance Corps wore mostly grey dress uniforms up until 1971, but the white coat and kitbag are what people would most associate with the Knights of Malta of that period. The white coats and white linen kitbags were brought into wider use among all the first-aiders around the end of 1971. Given the "ghosts" concept of the book, and the fact Martha isn't a real person, I have kept her in a white coat and kitbag even before 1971.

In my early meetings with staff and volunteers of The Museum of Free Derry, I realised that re-traumatising is a sensitive issue and that many people in my local community live with the trauma of Bloody Sunday. To address this, I have written the narrative so that the reader can skip over the Bloody Sunday section of the book if they wish and not miss any major plot points within the narrative. Some summary points are raised in the following chapter without reliving the fundamental elements of that murderous day.

Martha's first-aid journey is a fictional narrative that resonated with the actual first-aid volunteers of that time that I met whilst developing and writing this book. Martha's experiences are entirely fictional, but the events she finds herself in throughout were shaped by Leo Day's reports, and statements the Order of Malta volunteers made to public enquiries. I invited the first-aiders to tell their authentic stories if they wished, which I have included as appendices at the back of this book.

Part One

"Watching days go by you get the notion in your head.
You're going nowhere.
I'm sure you've felt that way too!
Don't the good times fly?
They say you'll be a long time dead."

Eamon Friel

One

Foyle Road

"Martha, I am sorry to tell you, but your brain scan has shown changes indicative of the early onset of Alzheimer's ...."

I shut down. I am only fifty-nine! My Mammy is still alive and has all her faculties at eighty-four. Even though my eldest Joanne held my hand, my mind switched off, and I didn't take in much of what was said after that; I just stared at the penholder on the Neurologist's desk. I always hated the old Gransha hospital. The place smelled the same as when I was last here in the late 1970s. I heard some words here and there, but I didn't look at the doctor's bespectacled face. I knew he was talking; I just nodded to pretend I was taking everything in.

... I will show him! I do have a good memory! I know it is the 12th of June 2013 because my brother Derek's birthday is today. If only the nurse had done the wee questionnaires on an important date! So what if I can't recite a recent news story or who the prime minister is? Or that I can't count backwards from one hundred in multiples of seven, or was it eight? When you were born in Derry and lived through the 1960s, 70s or 80s – the news was the last thing you wanted to watch! I don't even buy the papers.

Joanne squeezed my hand and brought my wandering mind back into the room.

"Mammy, they have good memory drugs now, and sure you are good at remembering things from years ago."

I was too stunned to speak. I was still embarrassed at yesterday's "incident". I was sitting in my living room and saw Joanne's black jeep entering the parking square in front of my mid-terraced house on Foyle Road. Joanne got out of the car followed by her eldest Rosie. Rosie reminds me of my younger self, with curly brown hair and is an absolute firecracker. When Joanne was carrying in the baby seat, I became agitated. What is our Joanne's newborn called again? I tried to remember wee Lola's name before they came in my front door, but I panicked and failed. It wasn't the first time either.

When older people started losing their marbles, I thought they didn't know what was happening. When I hit eighty or ninety, I believed I would return to my childhood in the Rossville flats, live in eternal happiness, and not know one day from the next. During this time my family would look after me until somebody came to take me to the other side.

I assumed that older people forget what they forget. Somehow, I can remember what I forget. I still have enough marbles to know that part of me is dying every day.

Eventually, I piped up, "I can remember things from fifty years ago, no problem. When it comes to recent things, I am not always so sure."

Take it from me; I know doctors don't always have kind faces. They become desensitised after years of telling people that they are dying or have a new life-limiting illness. This one seemed nice, but don't ask me what his name was.

"That's how it goes with Alzheimer's. I have seen patients who can recite their entire childhood and forget yesterday. I think a good thing to do would be to look at old photographs – reminiscence is very effective with many of my patients. We can start on Donepezil, ten milligrams; you don't take alcohol, do you, Ms Bradley?" the doctor asked.

"No, doctor. My drinking days are long gone. By the way, I'm not breastfeeding or planning on getting pregnant if that's your next question."

A hearty laugh filled the room, and our Joanne went bright red, "Mammy gone stop it! You can take her nowhere, Doctor! Mouthy Martha strikes again."

I know doctors aren't exactly the laughing type, at least not in this region. This one laughed, though. So much so that his glasses nearly fell off his face. That is me to a tee! If feeling sad or powerless, I crack a joke to save face. As Lord Byron said, "Laugh when you can; it's cheap medicine."

We left Gransha hospital, and it was a beautiful, warm, and still day. We don't get many of those here. I was shocked at the number of cars in the car park and that Joanne had to park her big, mucky jeep on a path beside the entrance. My two younger boys, twins Frankie and Sean-Paul, are twenty-seven. They live and work in Dublin and seldom come back up to Derry. Joanne does all the looking after me. God love her. She has enough on her plate! She just turned thirty, two wee ones under six, walking the roads to shift the baby weight, dying to get back to work in the bank, and having a tight farmer husband.

We left the hospital and detoured through the city to return to my house. We passed Rossville Street, and every time I do, I am still shocked that the "high flats" – my home in my teens – are gone! In the Bogside, there was a housing crisis in the 1960s, so three massive tower blocks of flats were built slap bang in the middle of the estate. The blocks had three street names, Garvan

Place, Mura Place, and Donagh Place. Our flat was number 73 Mura Place, in block two on the fifth floor of the Rossville Flats.

The flats were knocked down when our Joanne was about six or seven, at the end of the 1980s. When approaching Free Derry Corner, I sometimes expect to see the long-gone houses attached to the white gable wall monument. The gable wall is painted with big, bold black letters; YOU ARE NOW ENTERING FREE DERRY.

As we passed, there were American tourists taking photographs beside it. You always know the American tourists, with their New York Yankees hats, big cameras around their necks, and generally thinking they own the place. If the Brits couldn't own Free Derry – the Americans won't hold it either. Funny, I remember the Battle of The Bogside riots in 1969; somebody hoisted an American flag onto the roof of the flats. I remember that vividly.

The flats were the epicentre of the madness that was the city of Derry back in troubled times. I am glad my wee ones grew up when the worst of it was over us. Two good things came through in 1998, the Good Friday Agreement to end the violence on our streets and my divorce from Mickey Davidson. Everybody knew me as Martha Bradley anyway. Mouthy Martha from the flats!

We finally reach my house on Foyle Road, but "HM Prison", Rossville is still my home in my head. Joanne bids me farewell and tells me she will get my prescription because I might forget to get it. She was lucky the wains were with her. Otherwise, I would have told her to piss off!

It is just me here now. I never got used to living on my own. Not out of neediness, but I remember when all our front doors were open, neighbours walked in and out, and we all helped each other. Since Mrs Doherty's bungalow was robbed six or seven years ago a few doors down from me, none of that now.

I hate seeing my car parked outside. I also drove an ambulance for years, but now I am a prisoner in this house since the doctor told me I am not allowed to drive. No more wee trips to Buncrana, and I can't go and visit my Mammy in her supported living place in Creggan. I just have to accept my position as Derry's youngest geriatric invalid.

Like any Derry girl in distress, I plonked myself down on the armchair beside the window in the living room and lifted the phone to Mammy. Even though Mammy is in her eighties, everyone says to me, "jeez, Bridie can still fairly walk the roads". I don't even see her as a little old lady; even though her hair is white now, she is still as fit as a fiddle. She stood at 5' 9" in her prime, but she shrunk to about 5' 7" in her old age.

Jesus, I bawled my eyes out. "I have fucking Alzheimer's, Mammy; the doctor told me today."

I was stuttering, stammering, and as our Joanne would say, "proper ugly crying".

"Don't be worrying, wee love", my mother said to me, her fifty-nine-year-old daughter. I am still "wee love" to her. "Sure, they have medications and all that; sure, a couple of the dolls I go to bingo with on a Thursday are on it too!"

As if that was supposed to cheer me up? I thought I was a million miles away from Strand Bingo, lunch clubs and bus trips to Lourdes.

She continued, "apparently, the best thing to do is look at old things from the past. Sure, you had brilliant days, a great group of friends, and the Order of Malta was the making of you. You always kept things; everybody knows you're a big softie, Martha! Do you not know that everybody knows that, and you fooled nobody? I think it is time to dig out the old memories from the suitcase, even write them down so that the grandchildren can know who their Granny was. Sure, you always like to write stuff anyway."

With her mystical motherly powers, my ugly crying stopped. "I am not sure, Mammy, some bad times too, us cooped up in the high flats. The vertical ghetto. I'm not sure if I want to return to that; there's a lot of pain too. I can still remember everything I saw as clear as if it all happened yesterday. Sure did you hear I couldn't remember wee Lola's name?"

"Aye, Joanne was up yesterday. She called in when she was picking Rosie up from school. She was telling me you are losing the plot! I had to quickly remind her that this was absolutely nothing compared to what you were like before she was born."

We had a good laugh at that; she was on her own for a long time. She raised Derek and me pretty much on her own. No matter what age you are, you will always need your Mammy. Being a busy body, Mammy had to hang up because she had somewhere to go. I never took an interest in where my Mammy had to go, but now I can't remember where it was; I am dying to know.

In her sign-off, she said, "Everything will be okay, love, and don't let me tell you again, Martha, don't swear in front of your mother, you hear me?"

I gulped and said sorry before hanging up the phone.

There's never anything on TV during the day. Everything combines to make the same programme. Panel shows and chat shows where people air their dirty laundry and think they have problems. Thoughts creep into my head and disappear. Often, I am left wondering if the ideas were important. One remained - to look through the old suitcase in the back of the wardrobe. Mammy had planted a seed that refused to be forgotten.

When I left the flats in 1979, I put all my old stuff into an old leather suitcase belonging to my late father. In the years since,

I never considered opening it and never considered throwing it out. Who knows? The fairies could take me away at any moment, so writing everything down may not be a bad idea. Typically, people have old photos in their house; I never did.

I went up the stairs toward the suitcase at the back of the wardrobe in my bedroom. Twice I turned around and retreated to the living room.

The notion was in my head; there are things I haven't told my children. Things I didn't even discuss with my ex-husband or anybody else. I have enough first aid experience to know that, eventually, I will lack the capacity to make decisions for myself. If I wasn't hasty, those stories might be lost forever. I decided that I wasn't going to let that happen.

Maybe it was my older age, but the bloody suitcase was heavy. The thing weighed a ton! I dragged it along the floor and used my hands to lift it onto the bed using the old Knights of Malta training – lift with your knees, not your back! The suitcase made a big dent on the bed and sunk about five inches into my mattress.

Like ripping a plaster off, I just opened the damn thing. Surprisingly, the mould didn't get at any of my things inside; as I took them out and laid them across my bed, everything flooded back. At the top were all my records! Mammy bought a record player that stayed in the living room in the flat. She bought me records, and the one immediately staring me in the face was Cher's album from 1971! I remember that record so well; she did a brilliant version of "He Ain't Heavy… He's My Brother"! Nostalgia is powerful; my soul lifted, and I just felt happy.

I associate music with certain times of my life; I can remember songs on the radio or Mammy's record player when certain things happened. Funny how the brain works, or like in my case, doesn't work. Then the photos. Wee blubbery tears started when I saw a picture of my Daddy, my first love, a lovely photo of us standing out the front of our house. Although looking at this photo with the benefit of hindsight, I wonder how I didn't see the true extent of his agonising pain.

When I look in the mirror now, I expect to see the curly brown-haired and freckled firecracker I once was. Instead, I get the image of a greying wrinkled stranger. Derek hasn't changed a bit. He still has a smug smile, a tight haircut, and looks younger than his age. I suppose that is one of the perks of never marrying or having children.

Then my heart felt happy again; I saw a photograph of Hugh and me; his little smile was one that I couldn't help but smile back at.

The smiling was short-lived whenever I pulled out an old gas mask and first-aid kit. It was in a white linen kit bag with a red cross. The bandages inside it were slightly discoloured, then an empty green bottle that would have had water in it. The scissors were rusted somewhat and made a strange squeaky sound whenever I clipped them open and closed. I wasn't sure I could feel every emotion at once, but then I did. I don't care how far the fairies take me; I will never forget how I felt when I unearthed my past that day. I immediately started smiling when I held my white coat aloft with the red Maltese Cross on the left breast pocket. I had it close to my face and inhaled in the memories. It still smelled like the flats! Although a lot happened in our family before we moved there in 1967.

Two

Wellington Street

My Mammy's name was Moran before she married my Daddy, Francis Bradley, in February 1950. Mammy was the youngest of seven; her parents, my grandparents, were too old to take in my newlywed parents. Mammy was pregnant with Derek when Daddy lost his job on the railways, forcing them to live in the back bedroom of my Granny Bradley's house. My Daddy's twin brother Damian was also unemployed, and his family had set up in the front room.

It was cold, cramped, dark, and miserable in that two-up two-down house on Nelson Street.

My Daddy was never called "Frank" or "Frankie", as was customary with almost every boy called Francis. Even my son gets called Frankie. He was always Francis or Mr Bradley. Tall, thin, with the most giant puppy brown eyes God ever put on a face, he was always immaculately clean, quite a nervous man by nature, but I can't remember his voice now. He had black hair and a smooth, clean-shaven face.

On the other hand, Mammy is a force to be reckoned with. Always a powerful woman. Not loutish like myself, but a lady who knows her boundaries and exudes decency. She was taller than most women I know and taller than me. People always told me she had a brisk and purposeful walk, and my poor wee Daddy used to do a light jog to keep up with her.

In Derry, one doesn't "become" pregnant; one "falls" pregnant. Mammy fell pregnant before Christmas of 1950, and the pregnancy was horrific. Never one to exaggerate, Mammy tells me it was thirty-six weeks of pain. She had spotted several times. The midwives said either the pregnancy was failing, or the baby was already dead.

Derek was born on the 12th of June 1951 and wasn't expected to live. He was roaring hot to touch, refused feeds, and squealed the house down. It was meningitis. The priests came out to pray over him, and Daddy was the one being comforted by Mammy. People came in and out of the house with holy water to pray, and eventually, the doctors and midwives stopped coming. This went on for a couple of months, and suddenly Derek started to giggle and laugh as a healthy baby should. It was a miracle! Mammy says her rosary daily and thanks Our Lady that Derek was allowed to live. They all called him "wee Lazarus Bradley" in Granny Bradley's house.

The pregnancy experience was so brutal that my parents waited a while before having me. Daddy had just started work again for the Great Northern Railway in mid-1952 when the north and south of Ireland nationalised the railways. Two miracles in two years, Derek survived, and Daddy found work again.

Mammy discovered she was pregnant with me at the end of 1952. I was a walk in the park as far as pregnancies went. I burst onto the scene on the 7th of August 1953. Mammy was delighted to have a girl as she had six older brothers. So was Daddy; he only had a twin brother. What would they call their new baby girl? Mammy was always very religious and wanted an appropriate name for me. In the Bible, Martha was the sister of

Lazarus, so that's how I got my name. This isn't memory related - but I haven't the faintest idea where the story of Lazarus is in the Bible. Probably in the book of Jonah, somewhere.

With two children, Mammy and Daddy could get a house from the old Londonderry Corporation, the snarling, shapeshifting gatekeepers who decided who got a roof over their head. If you were a Catholic in Derry in those days, you were beat. Protestant and unionist communities got housing much quicker. Most property owners were Protestant and got as many votes as they had houses! It was complicated to get accommodation, but we got lucky because Daddy worked on the railways. He knew somebody who threw in a good word for us to a landlord who could house us.

We moved to 98 Wellington Street in late 1954, after my first birthday. Our very own two up and two down house. We lived at the end of the street, with a big lamppost outside the front door. The lamppost didn't always emit light, and because we were in the end house, it was dark all the time. The fire in the living room was the only natural light source, and I can still smell the tea in the pot. As a treat, Daddy used to bring home jam for our toast. They don't make jam the same anymore. It isn't as sweet and joyful.

The house had an outside tap in the backyard and an outside toilet. There was no central heating and very little space, and it was a nightmare to heat. Some families in Wellington Street had up to fifteen people in their tiny houses. Daddy used to go out with Derek and a couple of other boys in the street and kick a big leather football. My Mammy always tells the story of the day I wobbled out the front door wanting to join them. I was only four or five at the time and kept looking at the big brown leather ball. Derek shouted to me, "kick it, Martha!"

Mammy always does her snorty laugh when she gets to this part, I took an enormous run-up to the ball and kicked it with all my strength, and the ball didn't move because it was that heavy! I walked over to Mammy with my eyes welled up with tears, but I didn't cry. Daddy came over, hugged me, lifted me on his shoulders, and walked me to the sweet shop. I try hard to remember what my Daddy's voice sounds like, but I can't hear it.

I always had a soft spot for fudge and still do. Daddy gave me the fudge inside the magical kingdom of the sweet shop, and his big innocent eyes smiled back at me. This is the most vivid image of him still in my head. When I think of Daddy, this is what I see.

We had lovely neighbours; I remember people saying to my parents – "hello Bridie, hello Mr Bradley". Everyone loved Daddy. He used to take me for walks, sometimes to places he shouldn't have. Whenever Mammy would go into town, Daddy would be sneaky and meet a couple of his friends in the Greyhound Bar at the bottom of Nelson Street. He used to take Derek and me with him, and some of the other Daddies were very naughty boys and brought their wains with them too!

Sometimes Daddy used to take me to the Brandywell Stadium to watch the greyhound races. I innocently used to dote on the greyhounds, and Daddy smoked his pipe. Even at six or seven, I figured out that Daddy got a bet up if I got the fudge on the way home. One evening, we returned to the house, and Mammy and Derek were standing inside the front door. Derek was sheet white, and Mammy had that look on her face. She was raging! Francis was in the bad books. Mammy roared, "what do you think you are doing taking her to the races?" I remember him sulking and saying sorry, but I don't know how his sorry sounded. He was sentenced to a few nights on the sofa.

***

I made a wee friend in the street, or a "mucker" as we call them here. Caroline McLaughlin lived in number 37 with her family. She was the eldest and had two brothers and two sisters. She had chalks, and we used to draw pictures on the pavement outside her house. No cars were in the street, so we made grander artworks that covered most of the road when our creative juices started flowing.

The most extensive work of art I ever saw was on my fiftieth birthday when I went to the Museum of Modern Art in New York in 2003. I saw the Reflections of Clouds on the Waterlily Pond by Monet. I can safely say my and Caroline's pictures were better.

As the neighbours got to know each other better, we were all in and out of each other's houses. There were many other children my age, and Derek made a gang with other like-minded wee brats. A couple of times, Derek was hauled up the street by the ear for stealing milk bottles or throwing stones at windows and running away. Mammy dealt with him. She was the disciplinarian.

Miss Anderson was a bitter old spinster who hated children and lived in number 60. Caroline and I were at our creative height when our drawings became so large that they crept to the front of her house. She never kept her door open, but she burst through it one day, demanding that we go away and draw in front of our own houses. This was when the first recorded "mouthy Martha" incident happened. I told her, "But if I draw in front of my Mammy's house, she will get cross and scold me. Sure, you wouldn't know, you don't have any children."

Caroline gasped, and Miss Anderson had a big vein in her forehead that almost burst through the skin. She was seething, grabbed my curly locks, and marched me to Mammy. I can't defame my mother, but I can say that she "taught me a bit of manners".

Risk-taking was something I did too much of in my lifetime. It started by wondering how close I could draw to Miss Anderson's house without being marched back up to Mammy again. With every drawing, I would go a bit closer. Now and again, she would beat the window and gestured for me to go further up the street. One morning she came out to go to mass when I was drawing outside number 56 with Caroline. Needless to say, I shat myself and ran up to the house again.

The winters were Miss Anderson's saving grace because we didn't go out to play much in the cold winters. Our house was freezing. We used to pour milk bottles of water on the road the night before so that it would freeze, and we had a slide in the morning. Just as well there weren't many cars in the street. The only day I remember being warm in the fourteen winters in that house was Christmas Day. The fire was always on all day on Christmas Day. Poor Daddy worked himself to the bone on the railways and always gave us sweets and treats, often without Mammy knowing. Mammy fondly remembers him as more of a third child than a husband.

One of the biggest days in the Derry calendar is Halloween. Nowadays, Halloween is a huge carnival attended by tens of thousands of people every year. Tons of people go out in their costumes and enjoy the festivities, but Halloween of 1961 brings back a sad memory for me.

It was lunchtime, Derek and I were off school, and I remember a thunderous thump on our front door. Mammy threw her tea towel on the floor and stamped to the door.

"Mrs Bradley, you have to go to Altnagelvin; Francis was in an accident," I heard from the front room. I remember Derek shrieking, "Mammy, is Daddy alright?"

"Just come on, Derek, Martha, get your coats on. Go and ask Mr Carlin if he can drive us over to the hospital, please, Martha."

So, in shock, I ran to number 68 and asked if we could have a lift to the hospital as my Daddy had an accident. Marty Carlin would have been friendly with Daddy and gone to the greyhound races with him now and again. We crushed into the car, and it was a white Volkswagen Beetle. Bizarre that I remember this detail and can't remember what I had for my lunch earlier today. Derek and I asked Mammy if Daddy was okay, and she tried to reassure us, but her big glaring eyes told us she was concerned.

Altnagelvin Hospital had been open for less than a year. Because Daddy was working in the Waterside railway station in Derry, and Altnagelvin was the nearest hospital, that was where he was taken.

We all ran through the door to the desk; Mammy just blurted out, "Francis Bradley!" and the nurse nodded nervously. Derek and I were crying at this stage and feared the worst. The nurse bowed, and we walked silently behind as she led us to him. I ran ahead, and Mammy didn't stop me. I got to the end of the long bright hall and saw an open door to my left. It was him! It was Daddy, sitting upright on the bed. I shouted "Daddy!" but he didn't turn around.

I shouted to Mammy and Derek, "look, he is in here, here he is okay!"

I looked in at Daddy again; I remember the sound of him crying. He had a bandage on his head, but it wasn't soaked with blood. Thankfully the nurses had cleaned him up before we came in. Mammy threw her arms around him, and Daddy looked startled and distressed. We thought he was dead before we got there!

A man wearing a suit and shiny shoes was there; Mammy knew him to be Alexander Nutt. He was Daddy's boss, and he had driven Daddy there. Mammy asked what happened, and he invited us to sit beside Daddy. Three chairs were waiting for us beside his bed.

"Francis was servicing a steamer engine on the line when a water leak caused the engine to dry up and burst. Luckily, the lads got off the train before she went up. He was bleeding badly from his ears and screaming. I took him here, and the nurses tended to him," he said solemnly.

Mammy asked Daddy if he was okay and rubbed his back, but all he did was stare. A wide-eyed and shocked stare. A doctor with a lit pipe came in with a notes folder; whilst my Daddy survived the explosion, he was bleeding profusely from his ears. I remember his following sentences word for word, "there appears to be perforation of both of his eardrums, and damage to the bones of the middle ear."

We looked at Daddy with his eyes welling up; I had never seen Daddy cry before. Our world became sadder the day that Daddy lost his hearing.

THREE

KNIGHTS OF MALTA

After a few days in the hospital, Daddy got home. He wouldn't be able to work again, and our house was completely silent. Derek and I couldn't understand the gravity of what had happened, and we pleaded with Daddy to talk to us. We used to think that if we shouted louder, Daddy would hear us and respond to us. He never did again.

We used to ask, "Mammy, why can't Daddy hear anymore?" "Mammy, why can't Daddy talk to us?" "Will Daddy ever laugh and be happy again?" As sharp as Mammy can be, she always smiled at us and became gentler toward us. She would say that Daddy was magic and knew what we were saying.

Even Miss Anderson didn't stop me from drawing outside her house. The neighbours were constantly leaving groceries, spare bottles of milk, and coal at our house leading up to Christmas that terrible year, 1961. Everyone wanted to see how we were, and the children in the street invited us to play with them more often.

Wee Caroline and I used to have an old rope and ask any tall man to tie the rope around the lamppost so we could swing around it. We had tons of fun, and because the lamppost was outside our house, it became known as "Martha's lamppost". A few girls, Caroline and I, were skipping and swinging around the lamppost when Mammy and Daddy walked toward Leo's grocery shop at the bottom of our long street. Daddy looked pathetic. Mammy even slowed down her mighty walk to accommodate him, a shell of his former self. He didn't look toward us once.

It is pretty ironic that in Derry, we have a famous fireworks display on Halloween night, and videos of them can be seen on the internet. It is a huge spectacle, and I always loved taking the children to see them. Even though a loud boom took my Daddy's hearing on Halloween, I developed more positive memories with my children on the 31st of October. When we stand along the River Foyle, I can see over to the train station where he worked, and I smile when I think about him.

Mr Nutt wasn't the worst in the world, and Daddy got a pay-out when it couldn't be determined who was at fault for what had caused the steam engine to explode. Mammy told us many years later that he got £920, which was quite the sum back then.

In the usual fashion, anything Daddy got was spent on us. Derek got a great bicycle, and I got lots of toy dolls and a few boxes of chalk! He must have bought one of everything in the sweet shop. He bought Mammy a lovely necklace that she still has. She keeps it "good" and barely wears it.

The streets were disgusting; there was shite everywhere, as there was an outdoor cattle market on Rossville Street before the high flats were built. To make matters worse, there was an abattoir where Little Diamond in Derry is now. A gentleman in our street kept pigs, cows were walked to Rossville Street on market day, and the place was filthy.

As we walked to school, Caroline and I would try to shove each other into the cowpat. One day I got her! I pushed her as hard as possible, and she splurged into a mound of fresh dung! Right in the middle of it, in her good school shoes.

She was raging! I cackled at her, and she took her shoe off and threw it at my head; there was shite all over my hair, and we both laughed as we were clattered from head to toe! When wee Caroline got home, her Mammy battered her.

***

Wooden cattle trucks would bring the livestock to the abattoir to get slaughtered. The rumble of the trucks was a constant feature, but one day, a wee pig decided it had enough and escaped from the truck. The pig ran around our street, and we were all cheering for it while the truck driver and his young fella ran around after it!

Derek and I went to different schools, he went to The Christian Brothers, and I went to St. Eugene's. I smugly laughed at him as he had to walk further to get to school. My teachers always asked how I was, and genuinely cared. Academically, I was always good. I enjoyed school, and none of my friends believed me when I said I was barely slapped!

As for poor Derek, he was constantly slapped for mixing up his letters. One of his teachers was so mean toward him that he caned Derek on the back of his hands instead of his palms. Daddy used to look at the back of Derek's palms and pant in anger; he abhorred corporal punishment, whereas Mammy didn't.

Now and then, the priest would pray with Daddy. He wasn't as religious as Mammy, and we often wondered why. When we went to mass every Sunday, he never seemed interested.

Then again, why would a loving God take the hearing from a thirty-one-year-old family man? I asked this to Mammy, too; she would always say, "these things are sent to try us". I didn't think so; I felt Daddy was being unfairly punished. I believe this is where my faith started to drift and eventually evaporated.

As a fifty-nine-year-old, life has taught me that bastards never suffer. Further evidence of this observation is Mickey Davidson, living in a villa in Mallorca with his significantly younger mistress, whilst I'm stuck in Derry with a rotting brain.

After Daddy's accident, he tried to be as affectionate as possible. He would sit me on his knee by the fireplace, hug me tightly, and smile at me. He learned to lip read a wee bit, and when he knew I was asking, "can you hear me, Daddy?" he would frown and shake his head from side to side. He was at home all the time now, and he would sit in the kitchen looking at Mammy putting our clothes over the washing line in the kitchen. Eventually, our eternally open front door had to remain closed. When people came into the house, as was customary in our street then, Daddy kept getting spooked. The neighbours understood, and everybody respected it. Some neighbours came and took him out for walks into the town to get out of the house. Some other men in the street took him to the pub, but he got fed up and walked home again as he couldn't follow conversations anymore. I think he only went to give us a break from looking at his sad face.

***

Daddy's birthday was on the 22nd of January 1962, and we had a birthday party for him in the house. Mrs McDaid, from number 75, baked him a cake - and I have never had a cake like it. I've been to some very fancy bakeries, darling! But no baker in the fanciest French patisserie could match Daddy's thirty-second birthday cake. Many people came to wish him well, and all he could do was nod his head and mouth thank you.

Mammy was cleaning frantically that evening and told us we would have a visitor tomorrow.

At breakfast, I asked Mammy who our visitor was. She told me a "Knight of Malta" was coming to help Daddy communicate. When I heard this, I spat my watery porridge out. Derek and I were so excited.

Daddy communicated using a notepad and pen, and “Knights of Malta coming at four o clock” was written on it.

When Derek and I thought of a Knight, we thought of a knight in shining armour, a sword, and a white horse with a feathery plume on its head.

I asked Mammy if this mythical knight would help Daddy talk, and she said, “sort of. They will help Daddy communicate and for us to communicate with him.”

Our prayers were answered. I think we waited to see if we could hear hoofs through the thin pane of glass that was our flimsy living room window.

Instead, we got a wee heavy-set girl blonde girl. She was about eighteen, was wearing a fancy grey uniform and cap, and had a few books under her arm. She introduced herself as Marie from the Order of Malta and told us that she would teach Daddy sign language.

One of the priests in St. Eugene’s Cathedral had asked at mass to see if anybody knew sign language and if they could help someone who had recently been deafened. Marie came forward and was directed our way.

I know from later experience that the Order didn’t do this as standard, but she told us her wee brother was born deaf. She reassured Mammy and us that it was easy to learn and that Daddy could have a better quality of life if we could communicate with him. She didn't bring a sword or a horse, which disappointed Derek. She came every day, and to say Derek and I were dying about her would have been the understatement of the century. We loved seeing her come in, and we were picking it up quite quickly. She came every other day from four until five, except for Saturdays and Sundays. We all took it seriously, and Derek and I were keen to impress. She always heaped praise on us.

It was hard for Mammy and Daddy; they kept looking at each other while their hearts ached. There were times Marie had to end the lessons early because Daddy kept breaking down. He would get frustrated, fold his arms, and look away from Marie and the rest of us. Marie always kept upbeat and held a sign to him saying, "you are doing brilliant, Francis!"

Sometimes, Daddy stormed upstairs and slammed the door. Mammy ushered us outside to play as quickly as possible when his sniffles could be heard downstairs. We knew he was crying. Sometimes I hear those sniffles in my dreams and nightmares. Sometimes he came down and engaged when Marie came in, but as time passed, he stopped engaging completely.

We were still keen to learn, and she still taught us. I was pretty good by the time I was nine. Derek was great at it too. The worst was the person who was supposed to be the best at it, Daddy. Children do pick up languages quite quickly; they are adaptable wee things.

Caroline always knocked at the door, and we would roam the street together. We loved going to buy sweets, and it distracted me from the tension inside our house. There was another wee shop halfway down the street; the lady's name escapes me now. She had a shop in her front room, and there was a window cut between her back living room and the shop so she could see who came in. Sometimes when we went to the window, we saw the shopkeeper eating dinner or doing her housework. If she was busy, we had to wait until she was good and ready.

Mammy said that Marie had suggested getting Daddy St. John's Wort to try and "ease his melancholy". She went to Maginnis' chemist and dragged Derek and me with her. The man working in the shop was Mr Ferguson, the boss man, who told us it was the oldest chemist and apothecary in Ireland. He gave cough medicine to the Prime Minister once. It is still a chemist, but I am unsure who has taken it over now.

When we returned, Daddy was in the foetal position on the sofa. He looked at the bottle, and Mammy wrote, 'for your sadness' on his notepad. He never had a violent or raging temper, but he slammed the bottle on the table beside the sofa and started panting. Mammy was growing more and more frustrated. He didn't take Derek or me onto his knee as much anymore, and he just became more distant and withdrawn as the weeks came and went. He never took the St. John's Wort, but he seemed happy to see Marie when she visited him. It was a fresh face for him, and it was as clear as day that she was fond of him. Everybody was. If you didn't like Francis Bradley, the problem lay with you; that was the kind of man he was. I haven't met many people like him, universally loved. Part of me wishes I was as loved and patient as he was. Sadly, my big stupid mouth got in the way all the time.

Mammy was always trying to tell us that Daddy could hear us, could relate to us, and we innocently thought those things were true. We held him in mythical regard, almost like a blind seer. He could still read our body language, and his smiles were not as frequent. We knew he tried his hardest.

***

On the first of October 1962, we came home from school, and Daddy greeted us with a big hug at the door; he was in great form! He hadn't taken the St. John's Wort, but he seemed to be back, like my Lazarus brother. He had fudge for me, brandy balls for Derek, and Mammy smiled. He took both of us onto his knee, and I remember him saying "I love you," in his very nasal tone, to each of us. It was barely understandable, but we got it! My heart sang, and Derek was as excited as I ever remember him. "Told you he was magic, didn't I?" Mammy smirked, and we both shouted "yes!" in unison.

We sat on the sofa, looking at the photographs. We had plenty of family photographs, believe it or not. My uncle Damian had a camera and was happy to take our pictures when he visited with Granny and Granda Bradley. The photo I am looking at now, languishing in the suitcase, was taken on the 1st of October 1962 when Damian came up to visit.

Mammy always took the lead when bedtime came, but not that night. Daddy waited by the back door while I went to the outside toilet and walked me up the stairs. He tucked me in, kissed my forehead, and closed the door. I just felt so content and cosy in my bed. So did Derek in the other wee bed beside me.

Later that night, I heard the sniffles coming from downstairs. They were so loud that they woke me out of my sleep.

I crept downstairs because the sniffles sounded different. They weren't Daddy's sniffles; they were Mammy's. There was a clock on the hall table near the front door, and I could see it was a quarter past four in the morning. Derek was still asleep and didn't hear me leave the room. The living room door was ajar, so I decided to crawl and peek through the door.

The sniffles moved on to proper sobs, and I knew there would be bother if she saw me, so I made sure to be quiet. The door was only open about three inches, but I could see Mammy sitting on the chair beside the kitchen door with her head in her hands.

At that time, I was confused as to why she was crying. I saw that Daddy was magic from my innocent nine-year-old eyes, as I could see him levitating about eight inches off the kitchen floor.

Four

Longtower Chapel

Mammy closed the kitchen door as Derek came down the stairs.

"Don't go into the kitchen, Derek!" Mammy roared at him.

I was only nine when Daddy died by his own hand. He had enough, and he must have felt the pain to be insurmountable.

McClafferty's funeral directors were down the street and had a telephone. This is where the ambulance was phoned, and where Daddy would go after the hospital to prepare him for his wake. It seemed like an eternity until the ambulance came.

Mammy told us to go out into the street while the ambulance crew cut him down. Caroline and I were sitting outside on the kerb when Daddy was carried to the ambulance on a stretcher, covered by a blanket. After the ambulance drove down the street, neighbours left stuff in our house for the wake. The shops nearby also sent supplies: milk, bread, tea, fags, snuff, and sandwiches.

Granny and Granda Bradley came to the house, and my Granny was seething with rage. I could hear her from across the street shouting, "how dare he. That life was not his to take!" My Mammy's biggest worry was if he could be waked and buried by the chapel.

There was a horrible suicide epidemic in Derry not so long ago. So many young people seemed to decide to go in a short time, bringing back so many memories. Daddy left us behind because there was little to no support for suffering young men and women like him. Fifty years on, there still doesn't seem to be much support. Trust me; I know what it's like to feel there is no other option. I never resented Daddy, but Derek did. I asked Mammy why Daddy was laid out wearing a scarf that wasn't his; how innocent was I?

He was so well beloved by his neighbours and the local community that the Catholic Church granted a funeral. Not long ago, local churches of all denominations would not permit suicide victims to be buried in their churchyards. I don't think Daddy would have given a fiddler's fart if he was buried by the Catholic Church or not.

Mammy said that he used to joke that if anything happened to him, "sure, just put me in the dustbin. I will be grand". The house was jammed. I remember Granda Bradley and Uncle Damian rubbing his head and talking to him. It was very comforting to see everybody. Granny and Granda Moran were there too, but they were pretty old. I don't remember my two pairs of grandparents being in the same room before this.

Around this time, it was starting to become apparent that Granny Moran was "doting" too. I remember being told that she was beginning to get senile; if somebody called me senile now, they would get the hairy side of the hand! She was around sixty-five when her memory went, and she ended up in a home a couple of years later. Granny and Granda Moran died within two years, before we left Wellington Street for the flats.

Granny Bradley was consumed by anger; she snapped at people apologising to her for her loss. She pointed to my Daddy in the coffin and said, “he should be the one that is sorry, not you.” Rotten old bitch!

There must have been a few hundred that filed into the house. The railway boys all came, and they were heartbroken. They regretted not visiting very often. Or even at all.

It wasn’t unusual for the Protestant and Catholic staff on the railways to resent each other, but there were visitors to our house from the Protestant areas, including Mr Nutt. This is what surprised people, the cross-community aspect of Daddy’s wake and funeral.

The railroad men told a brilliant story about Daddy. He and a colleague Davy Thompson came in early one morning, catching a couple of thieves trying to steal copper. When my Daddy looked at them with his big brown eyes and told them to stop taking their things, they immediately put it all down and said sorry!

The wee thieves went down the next day looking for work, and Daddy took them under his wing. He never touted on the young fellas to Mr Nutt either! When those wee boys came over, they wept when they saw Daddy in the coffin.

Mrs McLaughlin let me, Mammy, and Derek sit in her house for a while during the wake. It gave Mammy a breather and let me see Caroline. She didn’t know what to say to me, and she just looked at me with her big green eyes and a frown.

The house got quiet the night before the funeral when our “knight in shining armour” turned up. It was Marie! She wasn’t in her grey officer-type uniform, but we were happy to see her. Daddy was so fond of her and she was part of the furniture in our house in the months before he died. Little did I know she would play a more prominent role in my life later. She hugged us, brought us sweeties, and Mammy erupted in tears when she saw her. Mammy was so thankful to her.

We stayed up all that night: me, Derek, and Mammy, in the candlelit wake room. Daddy just looked like he was sleeping. We knew he was being buried the following day, and we didn't imagine what life would be like after that. Anytime I did a night shift later in life, I always had a creeping thought about me, Mammy, and Derek sitting around Daddy's coffin. He was a beautiful man in death like he was in life.

The funeral morning came, the hearse drove up the street, and all the neighbours stood outside their houses. The men had their hats off, with straight postures and interlocked hands. Every neighbour was out and then joined the procession when it set off. Such was their conviction; the Protestant railroad men asked if they could do a "lift" when carrying Daddy's coffin to the chapel. Mammy was okay with it, and so too was his twin brother. But of course, Granny and Granda Bradley took issue. The final word was that of his wife, and Mammy agreed. After that, his parents never spoke to her again.

I followed slowly behind, holding Mammy's left hand and Derek her right. We were all dressed in black. Groups of men came forward to carry Daddy to the chapel; we stopped every twenty or thirty paces. I could barely see because I was so small.

I will be the first to say it. Catholic funerals are shite! It is the same requiem with an "insert name here" at the top of the priest's sermon page. Every single funeral is the same, but Daddy's was very different. When Mammy reflects on it, she expected the priest to call Daddy out for his "mortal sin" and that he was going straight to Hell.

It was pretty personal, and the priest called him "the much-beloved Francis Bradley". I looked over and saw Marie at the chapel too. I was happy to see her, and even though she couldn't get near us if she tried, her presence there that day meant the world to nine-year-old me. If I could have had a poster of Marie in my bedroom, I would have!

After the chapel, Mammy took my hand and walked me home without Derek. So, I never saw my Daddy buried. Derek did, and when I asked him about it later, he said, "it was no big affair. We put the coffin in the grave, kicked the soil over him, and that was it."

It wasn't considered a place for girls and women to go to the cemetery back in the dark ages when I grew up. I wish I had had a mouthy Martha episode and went to see my Daddy buried.

***

Mammy tried to keep busy, but we didn't return to school before Christmas. We went back after the Christmas break in January 1963. There was a massive void in the house, and Mammy took the washing line down from the kitchen. Instead, our clothes were dried by the fire on a rack, which made the already damp and dreary house much damper.

Mammy tried to replace Daddy's quirk of buying me fudge, but it didn't taste the same. Of course, it was the identical product from the same shop, but Daddy's wee smiling face made it taste nicer. Derek's bike just sat outside beside the coal shed, gathering rust. He became angry and was getting into fights with the other boys.

I can't remember what our birthdays and Christmas were like that year because it was just a blur. The trauma and shock propelled us forward; we had to keep moving forward. The neighbours came to check in now and again, but as time passed, everyone just got on with their lives while we were still stuck in the grief-stricken void.

I would love to write about Derek and I starting "big school", or secondary school. For both of us, it was uneventful. I went to St. Cecilia's College near the new Creggan Estate, and Derek went to St. Joseph's. I am not in contact with any friends or acquaintances from school now. Derek's time at school was a bit more eventful. Derek was a "wee hard man" in the street, but when he was indoors, he was much more effeminate as he entered his teens. Derek would put on a different voice, but God love him, me and Mammy always knew he was as gay as a mountain goat. His favourite music at the time was the West Side Story soundtrack. He has the worst taste in music, but I adore him!

As ladylike as Mammy is, she was always a bit forward-thinking. She asked me if I had any wee "boyfriends" on the scene to try and embarrass me. It didn't work. Although when she asked Derek if he had any "girls" on the go, he would turn into a human tomato, lie his arse off, and say, "aye, I do". She knew the score. She would say, "it's alright, Derek, if you don't have a girlfriend, you know?"

***

Mammy was starting to get fed up with the house. So, she decided to go to the Londonderry Corporation's lair inside the Guildhall to try and get us a new home in the new Creggan estate. We were at school, so she went down herself. When she explained her circumstances, a clerk told her, "Your husband killing himself isn't our fault. We have nowhere to house you, so you may stay where you are."

The house was falling into disrepair; we didn't have the money to fix it. The living room window developed an awful draft, the stairs were creaking and on the verge of collapse, the roof would leak and trickle onto my face sometimes when I was sleeping at night, and the interior wall plaster cracked. Poor Mammy tried to patch things up herself with Daddy's tools.

All we could do was sit in the house and hope it wouldn't fall on our heads. Mammy told us we could only have tea in the morning because the steam might seep into the bricks. I turned twelve on the 7th of August 1965 and was told I couldn't have a party in the house because some men were coming out. In the spirit of getting our hopes up, Derek and I thought the house would be done up, and we would live in a miniature version of Versailles. Of course, that didn't happen, and the men who came out condemned the house. No repairs, no reassurances, fuck all! We just had to shrug our shoulders and hope for the best.

I went down to Caroline's house, and I felt comforted. Their house was an absolute death trap. A hole in the living room ceiling left all seven of them in one bedroom. The weight of everybody in one room was causing even more damage. Caroline had a big mop of black hair that her Mammy always put bows in and a soft feminine voice, and I was always jealous. Caroline was a beautiful child, and when we were in our teens and early twenties, all the boys fancied her.

She had the most beautiful skin, big green eyes, petite, and a slim figure to die for. Wee bitch! I had wiry, curly brown hair, dark brown eyes, a mischievous freckly face, and was described as "solid" by Mammy. My tone would be described as "rough and ready".

More telephone lines had been installed in the street, and Mammy bought a phone. She was desperate, and I remember her sitting in the hall phoning everyone who would talk to her. She had wanted out of that house from the day we buried Daddy nearly three years earlier. Mammy never marked his anniversary and never took us to his grave. I didn't visit him until years later.

There is a saying here in Derry, "if you had brains, you would be dangerous". I certainly had brains that turned out to be incredibly dangerous. I came up with a good idea when Mammy cried beside the phone. I told her to ring the boss man of the railway where Daddy used to work. Her face lit up, and she got on the phone with him. He promised her to do everything he could to help.

We didn't hear from him in a while and knew there were plans for three new flat blocks down in the Bogside along Rossville Street. Mammy wasn't overly keen on living in a flat but knew that's where we would likely end up because our houses would be knocked down. We walked down to Rossville Street near the city centre and saw this massive complex being built. A mile-high structure of rectangular blocks that about one hundred and eighty families would call home. I saw New York and Chicago in magazines and picture books and thought the Rossville flats would grow higher than the Empire State Building.

***

We got our first television in 1966, and one of the first things I remember watching in our living room in Wellington Street was England winning the World Cup at Wembley. The English haven't shut up about it since! It was a small black and white TV, and Mammy even let some other children in the street come in and watch it.

We were told we would move in the autumn of 1966, but there were delays. We initially thought we were moving to block one of the flats, but many other families got in before us.

Caroline, the wee Judas! Her crowd got a flat before us. At least I was happy that Caroline would be there too. She didn't tell me she was moving until I saw them all standing in the street with suitcases one day. I remember hugging Caroline in the street; you would think she was going off to Vietnam or something.

Mammy phoned the Corporation when she heard block one had been filled. She was terrified that she would not be re-housed; she was fed up with our house and at the end of her tether. Derek and I could see it too. Although I felt a bit sad that we would be leaving Daddy behind, I'm not a spiritual being, but I felt him in the house.

April of 1967 was the time to go. Mammy got the call and was told to pick up the keys to our flat; it was time to abandon ship! Mammy had trunks, some neighbours donated more boxes, and Damian knew a boy who had a van and could help move us from Wellington Street down to the Rossville Flats. We emptied the entire house, and I even got to miss school so we could move.

Daddy had done a couple of stints in England in his late teens and had a couple of old leather suitcases. We filled those up, Derek had one, and I had the other. Mammy asked Damian if he wanted to keep Daddy's tools, but he declined and insisted we hold on to them. They came in very handy later.

For a family of three, it seemed like we had a ton of stuff — a television, beds, furniture, and pictures on the walls. After his accident, when Daddy got the pay-out, Mammy got good furniture and kept a wee chunk of money aside for a rainy day. Trust me; we had more than enough rainy days. I wish we only had rainy days, as opposed to the fiery, blood-spattered days not far from us at that point.

Of course, the flats weren't as grand in size as an American skyscraper, but they would have far more character, far more history, and far better craic.

Part Two

"If life's for living, it's up to you.
Let's Dance!
Romance!
Find El Dorado.
Beyond the mountains of the moon."

Eamon Friel

FIVE

ROSSVILLE STREET FLATS

We were dropped off outside block two of the Rossville Flats, and all the contents of our house were taken out of the van with my uncle Damian's help. The flats were so grand! They were huge and dominated the skyline of the 1960s Bogside. When we approached the ground-floor entrance, a friendly voice shouted down to us from a second-floor window.

Caroline's Mammy called, "Sorry, love; the lift isn't switched on yet. Let me send these boys down to give you a hand." I seldom remember the lifts being on when I lived in the flats. They may have been on one day, broken the next, and even be out of order for months at a time. Caroline's brothers Charlie and Peter ran down the stairwell on the far-left side of the flat block with a third wee boy running behind them.

I looked over at block one, facing onto Rossville Street. Our block was to the left, at a ninety-degree turn. A sheet metal canopy covered a row of shops underneath block two; grocers, chemist, butchers, a fish and chip shop, and a hairdresser's salon. I can still recall the irresistible smell of frying chips. Gallery access flats, darlings! We were elected! Brand new, lap of luxury, and we were thrilled.

Derek, Mammy, and I delegated trunks and furniture to the three wee boys who came down the stairs. Up and down they went, quick as lightning! Up and down the nine flights of stairs to where our flat was and they stacked everything neatly outside our door. Even the thought of it has me on the verge of an asthma attack.

Charlie, Peter, and their friend came downstairs, and I excitedly asked where Caroline was. They told me she got a wee job in Finn's hairdressers up the town. The third little boy introduced himself as Hugh.

I learned later that Caroline was sent to cut everybody's hair. The wee boys all had buzz cuts then. There is a hilarious photo of Caroline's family from the late 1960s or early 70s in the flats; they all had the same hairdo, even the fellas! Caroline could only do two styles, hippie hair or a buzzcut. She expanded her repertoire to include a Mullet, which all the Top of The Pops stars had.

I remember the sound of Mammy yelping when one of the young fellas reached for one of my Daddy's leather suitcases and insisted on carrying them herself. I will never forget Mammy turning sheet white at the sight of two skinny wee runts and Damian taking her good wardrobe up the outdoor stairwell of the flats while Hugh had the handy job of directing them to avoid hitting the stairwell walls.

Every time they had to turn the wardrobe to get up the next flight, they would argue over who had to turn.

I looked through the toughened Perspex sheet and was almost level with the Derry walls. The wee boys were shoving and straining this wardrobe up the stairwell while we followed them with the easy-to-carry stuff - cushions, mattresses, bags of tea towels and the like.

I started singing to them, "Right said Fred, have to take the wall down, that there wall is going to have to go. Took the wall down, even with it all down, we was getting NOWHERE!" They were absolutely raging, but Hugh laughed and smiled at me.

Hugh and I sang the last line together, "and so we had a cup of tea!"

The wee boys on either end of the wardrobe and Damian were sickened, and Mammy was dying to laugh even though she told me to stop tormenting these lovely wee boys, who were being absolute gentlemen and helping us with our stuff.

The big reveal was upon us, Mammy turned the key to our new flat, and we stepped inside. Let me give you the grand tour! As the flats were split-level, there was a staircase on the right just as you entered the door. There was a large entrance hall perfect for dancing in, with two bedrooms directly in front of you and a small toilet to the left. The two lower-level bedroom windows faced out to where Free Derry Corner is now.

There was an indoor bathroom upstairs, with a bath in it! No more having to bathe or wash my curly locks in a tin bucket in the living room beside the fire. We had running water inside the flat and gas central heating, and we felt unbelievably posh. The floors were covered in grey linoleum, and the walls were painted cream. There was even a dining room upstairs, but Mammy used it as her bedroom. The other bedroom upstairs was Derek's room.

I took one of the lower bedrooms, the one on the left beside the wee toilet. The bedrooms had built-in wardrobes too! The bedroom next door to me was spare, so Daddy's clothes and possessions went there. This became Daddy's room, a comfort to all of us. It was like we brought his spirit with us from Wellington Street.

Underneath the flats, everybody had a storeroom. Even though our flat was number 73, our storeroom was number 201. None of us could stomach the idea of Daddy's things going underneath us. He was already six feet under us, so any way we could keep him with us was our preference.

There was a massive airing cupboard about six feet long and storage space everywhere. An exciting feature existed in Derek's bedroom, an extra door that had an asbestos sheet behind it. As a safety feature, if your flat caught fire, you could stick your boot through this sheet and get into the flat next door.

Our upper-level sitting room looked out toward where Free Derry Corner would be now, and from my bedroom, I could see for miles, which was shocking. Dozens of derelict buildings, crumbling houses, waste ground, and poverty-stricken misery.

A television mast and a telephone aerial were on the roof of the flats. Mammy put the TV in the sitting room and even connected the telephone. The gas meter was also in the sitting room, and our tiny kitchen was just off the living room.

That new home smell is still with me from when we entered our flat for the first time. The fresh wood, paint, and linoleum excited us. We were marvelling at our new home, and the wee boys were still hauling all our stuff up the stairs; it took them nearly two hours to get it all up.

Our first night in the high flats was the first time I slept in a bedroom on my own. The walls were very thin, and I knew from night one that I could hear everything the couple next door was saying.

"Marty, when will you get off your arse and get another job?"

"Sure, there's nothing going here at the minute."

"You have been saying that the past year!"

"Sure, there are no jobs for boys like me here."

"You're a pipefitter, and they are building another block right beside us!"

"Aye, but they're not looking for anybody."

"How do you know?"

"I went over and asked them."

"When?"

"Yesterday."

"Liar!"

***

The following day, a familiar voice came through the door and shouted, "hello!" it was wee Caroline! She came in and gave me a hug, and I hugged her back, even though she was a betraying Judas who left Wellington Street before us. We were reunited! I was over the moon to see her, and Mammy was happy to see her too.

She wanted to show me her flat, so she took my hand, yanked me off the kitchen chair and dragged me out the door before I could say bye to Mammy. We went out the front door to the balcony of our flat block and nearly collided with a woman pushing a pram; we were moving so quickly!

Block three was still being built, and the wee boys around the flats were using it as their playground. The boys who helped us with our bags were down there, cheering on one who was making his way up the scaffold! Wee Caroline and I stood and looked on.

"Go on Gilly!" they shouted, as the fearless boy ascended fifty feet worth of scaffold in what seemed to be a matter of seconds. He pulled, shimmied, and swung around the scaffold poles, and the group of wee boys below him could only stare upward in awe and trepidation. It was Hugh, and when he reached the top, he held his arms aloft as his friends cheered him on, and some frightened girls, his sisters, were roaring at him to climb back down. Laing Construction flags were flown around the construction site, the Rossville Flats' builders. At the top of Everest, colourful prayer flags are strewn around the place to wish the climbers a safe journey up and down the mountain. For Hugh, these blue triangular Laing Construction flags were his best hope.

Did he climb back down? No. As the flats in block three were hollow rectangular blocks under construction, some gaps existed between them. When Hugh stood on what would become the roof of block three, I looked at him turn to his right. There was a five-foot gap, between the next section of the roof and the one he was standing on.

I thought, *he is going to listen to his big sisters and climb back down.* He walked over and looked down at the sixty feet or so drop in between these two sections of the incomplete roof. He took two paces back, and I thought, *oh fuck!* He ran up, and I closed my eyes as his feet left the ground. The cheers below told me he made it, but my heart was in my mouth. I can't imagine how his sisters felt.

After taking a bow for the adoring crowd below, a sharp whistle rang around the courtyard. When I peered down over the edge of my fifth-floor balcony, the man of the house was standing on the second-floor balcony, staring at his son, Tarzan Gilmour, who decided to rush back down the scaffold.

Our street within the flats was Mura Place, which occupied the fourth, fifth, and sixth floors of all three blocks of the Rossville Flats. The suddenly forgiven Caroline, lived in Garvan Place, which was floors one to three only in blocks one and two because block three didn't have Garvan place, as it was built on the upward slope of Fahan Street. Donagh Place was the street that had floors seven, eight, and nine across all three. We had to walk downstairs to get to her balcony in Garvan Place, on the same block as us.

Mrs McLaughlin always made an amazing stew; as children, Caroline and I used to sit at the table and have this incredible stew. I could smell the stew from the balcony; it felt like old times!

Recently, local chip shops and cafes mash up the stew, which isn't as nice. I love a whole spud, chunk of beef, and whole bits of carrot, and not everything all mashed together. Caroline's flat was the same as ours, and they all fit in well. The boys had their room, the girls had their room, and Caroline had the dining room to herself.

Caroline and I loved a good gossip, "did you hear the craic about my cousin?" she said to me eagerly.

I leaned in intently, and my eyes widened, "What Caroline?"

"Our Mairead got married and had a wee baby."

"That's lovely; I didn't hear; you disappeared! You left me in the last street."

Then Caroline got into a whisper and waited until her Mammy left the room, "she got married in September, so she did, then wee William was born in November. We don't have a phone so I couldn't tell you. I was waiting for your crowd to move down here; I thought you weren't coming."

At thirteen, I wouldn't say I had an in-depth knowledge of the human gestation period, but I knew it was longer than eight weeks.

"Thank God they got married then," I said to her.

"Her Mammy and Daddy weren't too happy, but the wedding was nice, and we had a nice meal down in the Northern Counties Hotel, dead fancy! Did you know that Amelia Earheart gave her press interviews in there when she landed here before the war?"

I didn't give a monkeys about Amelia Earheart. I was more interested in the scandal that Caroline was on about, I know when somebody is deflecting, and I wasn't letting her get away with it.

"Jeez, your Mairead is lucky, getting married and having a baby that close together. To be fair though Caroline, that's a photo-finish if I ever heard one!"

Caroline dropped her spoon, "Jesus Martha!" We laughed so hard that no noise came out. Actual belly laughs, tears tripping us. Caroline's Mammy and Daddy ventured into the town, and we brought her record player from the living room down to the entrance hall of the flat. Caroline put on "These Boots are Made for Walkin", and we danced around her hall for most of that afternoon. When we played records or had Radio 1 blaring out, Caroline's Daddy used to escape to the kitchen on a Sunday night with his own transistor radio and listen to the "Sing Something Simple" show on Radio 2.

***

We got settled in over the next few months and became accustomed to our newfound luxury. Mammy often sent me down to Molly Barr's shop on the ground floor of our flat block to buy a pint of milk. Every time Derek or I went to the shop for Mammy, we were always allowed "a wee something" for ourselves.

I always walked down to Caroline and we went to the shop together. It was lovely walking down to Caroline's in the rain without getting wet. The balconies were all well covered, as were the stairwells because the lift barely worked!

I was up the town one day on my own, and when I came back, I decided to go up to the flat in the lift because the usual "out of order" sign wasn't on it. Inside the lift in the flats, there was another set of double doors at the back of the lift that only the caretaker's key could open. This accommodated larger loads in the lift and the internal electrical systems.

When I got into the lift, I was soaked to the skin and pressed the button to go up onto the fifth floor when I felt a hand grab my ankle! I squealed and jumped so high that I nearly smacked my head on the lift's ceiling. It turned out that Hugh learned to pick the lock, hide inside the back doors of the lift, and frighten people like me who got in! It was an absolute belter. I was got!

At the front of the flats were six three-foot high hexagonal walls that were intended to be flower beds. I don't recall any flowers being in them, but everybody called them the threepenny bits, pronounced "thrupenny bits". They were a focal point at the bottom of the flats and a popular meeting place. They were right outside block two, and everyone would gather there. All the older boys would buy their cigarettes in Molly's shop before going to the local bars. They all stank of Brut aftershave and were talking about football and horseracing. The place was bustling, and wee Caroline would sit and drool at all the boys. We met other girls from the flats; the Rossville Flats community was alive.

One of my favourite past times is people-watching. I can sit for hours and watch the world go by with a cup of coffee in a café or in my living room. Back then, Caroline and I sat on one of the thrupenny bits, taking everything in, the laughter and the hopeful atmosphere. We were all in the same boat; nobody acted like they owned the place because they had lived there for sixty years (like Miss Anderson did in our old street), and everyone was happy. More local men got work, and the cranes were up. The third block was under construction, and another ninety-degree turn to the left of block two, leaving The Rossville Flats in a "U" shape.

We had a lovely Christmas that year, except I didn't get a record player for Christmas. I was disgusted, I really wanted one, but I think most of Mammy's money went into doing the flat up over the course of the year. She got the whole place wallpapered and got tiles for the bathroom. We were on top of the world. Mammy's décor taste was quite plain. Wee Caroline's Mammy put pink wallpaper with swans on it in their bathroom. Ghastly!

***

Mammy and Caroline's Mammy pulled together to have Christmas in our flat in 1967. She got a big dining room table, and her bed was moved into Daddy's room for the occasion. The dining room table was brought into the living room, as was the kitchen table, to make it long enough because they always had a crowd for Christmas dinner. Because the kitchen table was lower, the legs had to be propped up on books, and the whole thing was covered in a white sheet as a tablecloth. We didn't have a tablecloth big enough.

That Christmas was fantastic, and I loved it.

I left school at 14, and wee Caroline left the year before. She was a year and a bit older than me and had already started a part-time job in the hairdressers; Mammy hinted at Christmas Dinner that it was my turn to start working soon.

All the neighbours looked out for each other, everyone got to know one another very quickly, and there would even be sing-songs on the balconies at night in the summer. The odd time, Mammy would even let Derek and I stay up late and join. One night a boy playing the guitar asked my Mammy for a song.

She took a deep breath, blasted out Molly Malone, and by Jesus, there wasn't a dry eye in the house when she was finished! She was so loud, and the flats so silent, that she could even be heard from every balcony. Derek was a great singer too, and he was a dancer! As for me, I don't have a note in my head, but it never stopped me!

After months of begging Mammy for a record player for my fifteenth birthday in August 1968, my wildest dream came true. I was thrilled when I opened my birthday present and saw my new record player. I screamed the place down, and somebody actually came in to see if everything was okay!

"Martha, I know it's your birthday present, but you have to let Derek play his records on it too from time to time," Mammy said to me with a wry smile.

"No chance Mammy, he can take his Cilla Black records and piss off!"

"MARTHA! LANGUAGE!"

During that summer, I had my first job interview. It was for a café in town, and I didn't give the first, fourth, fifth, or final fuck if I got the job or not when I went in. The owner was a lovely man, and we got on quite well. When he offered me the job, I was happy to take it.

Just as I walked out the door, he said, "sorry, love, where do you live?"

"The high flats in Rossville Street," I told him.

"Sorry you can't work here," he snapped back at me.

I was taken aback, and I went home to Mammy, confused. That was the first time I felt discriminated against. I was genuinely hurt, I didn't know what that feeling was at the time, but it was hard to take.

I should have known; when I went into the café, I noticed sausages and mash were on the menu. The interview was on a Friday.

As the autumn of 1968 came to us, Caroline and I sat on the thrupenny bits as usual when I saw a group of seven teens wearing fancy officer-type uniforms walking down Rossville Street in front of block one. Five girls and two boys. They wore the same grey uniform and cap as Marie used to wear when she came to see us! Marie wasn't with them, though, which disappointed me.

They looked so proud, with their immaculately crisp uniforms and smiling faces, and everyone greeted them with a smile as they passed. I was mesmerised by them as they went in and out of the shops in front of me and came out with groceries and bags of medications.

I leapt off the wall and followed behind them at a distance as they went up the stairwell of block two. I could only pick up some words here and there, but I picked up enough to know that they were delivering medications and groceries to elderly tenants with mobility issues.

As our flat was at the end of the fifth floor, I stood outside my front door and could see the grey uniforms walking around the balconies below me and on block one - two hundred yards diagonally to my left. I could see them going in and out of people's flats. The lift was fucked, as usual, it was out of order more than it worked, so it left the poor seniors trapped in their flats if they couldn't make it down the stairs. They must have felt how I feel now, helpless because I'm not allowed to drive my car if I want to get anything. The thought of needing carers soon is scary because Joanne can't visit me every day, although if those Knights of Malta I saw that day came to me now, I would be happy.

There were covered walkways between the three flat blocks so you could cross from block to block. I saw the Order of Malta volunteers venturing into block one. I asked Caroline, "have you seen the Order of Malta going in and out of people's flats?"

"Aw Martha, there's a good-looking one that goes into the flat a few doors down from us. Gives in medication, some messages, and the like." Messages is our word for groceries. Don't ask.

"Is that right, Caroline? What does *she* look like?" I quipped. Wee Caroline was mortified, and I cackled in her face. She was always easy to blush, and I took full advantage every time the opportunity came.

The next morning, Mammy went downstairs while Derek and I were sleeping and brought us buns to have with our tea. It was a Saturday morning, and buns are a tradition on a Saturday morning here - probably to soften the blow because we were never allowed meat on a Friday in Mammy's house.

"Mammy, why are we not allowed meat on a Friday? What's that about?" I asked her curiously, scoffing at my cream bun while we sat in our cramped kitchen.

"It's a sin, an evil one, straight to Hell," Derek casually replied to me.

"Pfft, don't you start on sin, Derek!" I told him with my trademark sarcastic but loving smile. When I said that, Mammy nearly choked on her chocolate gravy ring.

"Martha!" she shouted. Poor Derek just sat there stunned with a wee red face. He knew we knew his obvious secret. Derek was trying to land a job at a clothes shop in the town but had little success. He gulped his tea and escaped. Martha one, Derek nil.

"Count yourself lucky wee love! When I was wee, your Granny and Granda used to stay away from meat on Wednesdays and Fridays!"

"Why but?" I couldn't understand this. I couldn't imagine the Bible restricting anybody from eating on certain days; I still don't get this even at fifty-nine. At least now I might have an excuse; I could say, "sorry, Mammy, I had a bacon sandwich this morning because I forgot what day it is."

***

On a windy October morning, Caroline and I were scoffing chocolate at the thrupenny bits, and the Order of Malta volunteers were coming down Rossville Street again. This time Marie was there! I shouted over to her and waved. When she came over, I instinctively hugged her, and she asked how my Mammy and Derek were. I was all star-struck; I was so happy to see her,

"Marie, I have missed you so much; thank you for everything you did for Mammy, Derek and..." I stopped dead when my lip started to wobble. She gave me a big hug and brought me back down to Earth.

"That is what we are here for, Martha, to help anybody who needs us. You might enjoy it yourself, you know?"

"Absolutely!" I blurted out, "Caroline will love it too." I pretty much enrolled Caroline without asking her. Thinking on my feet, I knew that she would eventually say yes because there was a boy that she fancied. Caroline's wee green eyes stared back at me with her mouth full of chocolate.

Marie told us, "there is a course of first aid lectures starting this Monday night at half eight at Ozanam House on Bridge Street. I think you will both be brilliant. I must make sure everyone is alright, but I will see you then. It is good that the two of you will come along, so nobody is coming on their own."

We waved her goodbye as she disappeared up the stairwell of the flat block. After that fateful conversation, I was unbelievably excited. Getting to be around Marie again, my actual hero. Caroline was just bewildered at the fact I had signed both of us up for the Order of Malta, and the rest, as they say, is history!

Six

Ozanam House

Monday evening came, and I was excited to become a hero and save lives like Marie. We were told to go to Bridge Street to have our first-aid training. The directions I got from Marie, after our chance meeting, were quite vague, go to the second last building on the right at the bottom of Bridge Street and go up to the second floor.

The Order of Malta Headquarters for the Derry Unit was down the street from where Fitzroy's Restaurant stands now. It was about fifty or sixty yards down the street on the right, just before the road bends.

My first task of the day was to go down and get Caroline. I raced down the stairwell from the fifth floor to the third floor and skipped along the balcony to wee Caroline's door at 27 Garvan Place. I hope you can imagine my face when wee Caroline opened the door, with a face full of slap on her and a smell of her Mammy's perfume!

"Are you mad wee girl?" I asked her!

"That nice-looking boy might be there; I have to look the part, don't I?"

"Naw Caroline, you look like you're about to start your shift in Foyle Street twelve hours too early!" I was a very streetwise fifteen-year-old. Mammy always told me that being "blissfully unaware" was a gift. In hindsight, she was right. I was always too aware. Nothing passed me, ever!

Caroline didn't listen and grabbed her coat to march to Bridge Street. We ran down the stairs to the row of shops so we could buy pencils and notepads to write in. Back then, we called a notepad a jotter. I asked my granddaughter recently if she had a jotter to draw in, and she looked at me like I had sprouted a third ear. I was amazed that she didn't know what a jotter was!

We turned to our left outside the shops, through the concrete jungle between Joseph Place and the High Flats, up the concrete steps, and onward to tackle Fahan Street. We had to walk up the hill of Fahan Street, which for us was very steep. Given the altitude, wee Caroline started sweating like a horse, and her makeup started to run down her face.

"Martha, gone stop at this wee pub so I can go in and wash my face?" she panted at me.

"Naw Caroline, we are going to be late. I'm not letting Marie down, serves you right for being a wee hussy, so hurry up!" I couldn't do it to her, I thought. I should take the opportunity to let my good friend Caroline maintain her dignity in front of the Knights of Malta boy she had her eye on.

Psychologists debate constantly. Some say people are born evil; the rest believe people become evil. I don't know what camp I fell into, but I didn't let her wash her face.

We finally got to Bridge Street and were relieved to see some downhill for the final part of our journey. We were a bit out of breath, I walked briskly to have the chance to sit in a room with Marie, and Clown Caroline rushed down for her own reasons.

"Martha, do I look alright"? Caroline asked me as she was adjusting her ridiculously backcombed black mop at the window of Ozanam House. Her hair was so massive that she needed a lightning rod on top of it.

"Of course you do, wee love, you are an absolute picture, and I promise your hair and makeup aren't that bad." That was the last day wee Caroline believed a single word I ever said to her.

When we walked in the door, a staircase met us directly ahead. It was an old manky building owned and operated by the Catholic Church for years. Mammy was able to tell me where it was because St. Vincent De Paul used it for some of their meetings and activities in her youth.

If we mastered anything as teenagers, it was a good lurk. So, we lurked in Ozanam House's hall until Marie came down and met us. We saw posters with the red Maltese Cross and bulletins on the cork notice boards. There was a room to our left just in front of the stairs. Inside were a couple of trophies and a poster about a first-aid competition. I wondered, what is a first-aid competition?

Marie, in her eternal gentleness, tried to hide her coughs when she got a good whiff of Caroline's Mammy's perfume after descending the staircase. Marie always greeted people with hugs, an endearing trait.

When Marie hugged Caroline, she hugged her like one would embrace a leper. She didn't want to walk away with half of Caroline's face on her beautifully crisp grey uniform and white leather sash belt.

The stairs groaned and creaked as the three of us went upstairs, and a hall that seemed huge opened itself to greet us. There was a mixture of uniforms; young people our age wore grey shirts, grey trousers, red ties, and grey berets. The longer-serving first aiders wore full dress uniforms with officer-type caps. It was all very formal.

The floral smell increased in pungency when Caroline whispered to me, "Jesus Martha, what have you got me into? This better not be like that new fucking Scientology crowd in England!"

"Awk, wise up, wee girl!" I whisper shouted back at her, "all we have to do is help wee old dears in their house, put the odd plaster on, and sure there are handsome men in uniform. If anything is your cup of tea Caroline, this is it."

Caroline's bottom lip turned downward when she said, "aye, but the one I liked had a wedding ring on him."

All I could do, was sympathetically pat her on the back and say, "hard lines love!"

I don't remember feeling nervous, everybody was friendly, and even though Caroline's heart was broken, there was a friendly atmosphere. Caroline seemed to know a couple of the girls and introduced them to me. Attracta, Robert, Eiblin, Antoinette, Majella, Hugh Deehan (who isn't just Hugh, he is Hugh Deehan), his eventual wife Cecilia, Jim, Maureen, Rosemary, Pauline, Alice, Kathleen, and the two Charlies (McMonagle and Glenn).

I am sure the rest of the Unit were there, but those are the ones I remember seeing and meeting on the first day. We were all quite innocent, excited, and happy to be part of something bigger than ourselves. There weren't a lot of jobs for Derry Catholics, and I assume there was a mutual feeling that this was as close to meaningful employment as we were going to get.

In the pre-lecture chit chat, a couple had brought up the trouble on Duke Street that had happened forty-eight hours before, on the 5th of October. The RUC had battered and baton-charged peaceful demonstrators gathered by the recently formed Northern Ireland Civil Rights Association (NICRA).

To be honest, I didn't know who NICRA were before entering Ozanam House. I hadn't even heard that there had been trouble! Mammy certainly knew but didn't tell me. Caroline and I spent that Saturday by the thrupenny bits being teenagers and eating chocolate. That might sound surprising given how historically significant it is now, but it wasn't significant to me back then. It was the catalyst that would bring a group of teenagers, who didn't know each other that day, together forever.

We all entered the hall, there were wooden chairs, a top table with a skeleton dummy, and two men were at the table in front of the hall. One was in a long white doctor coat, and the other in full dress uniform. The older gentleman in the fancy uniform called the room to order and introduced himself as the Captain of the Derry Unit, Leo Day.

A straight-postured and purposeful man, very passionate about the cause of helping others. He wore thick-rimmed glasses and a grey moustache. I am writing this from the same jotter I brought that night. I will quote directly from that notebook, "Captain – Mr Leo Day – moustache and glasses – teacher in Waterside Boys School". He spoke with a soft southern accent, hailing from County Roscommon.

He gave a history of the Order of Malta and an overview of our mission to serve the Lord's sick and the Lord's poor and emphasised, "regardless of background and life circumstances". He had some foresight as to what would eventually befall us; of course, he did, in his scholarly wisdom.

The ranking officers of the unit also said a few words to us, Eiblin's father John Lafferty, Leo Doherty, Joe O'Kane, Thomas McKinney, George White, Jim McDaid, Alice Long, and Judith Doherty. The Order is structured like a military unit, with cadets, volunteers, corporals, adjutants, sergeants, and then the unit captain.

The Order's full name is The Sovereign Military Hospitaller Order of St. John of Jerusalem, of Rhodes, and of Malta. Say that one five times fast! It started in 1938 in Galway and spread to have units throughout Ireland. In the early 1950s, it was only for Catholic Men, but in Derry, under the guidance of Mr Day, women and girls were encouraged to join in the mid-50s.

After Mr Day gave the outline of the heritage, which we would all be joining, he made a very significant point that I have always remembered and requoted, "it is the duty of all to learn First Aid. When an accident or illness occurs in daily life, First Aid knowledge may save life or limb for family, friend, or neighbour". His accent was quite hard to place, him being born in County Roscommon, then growing up on a farm in Donegal.

The Order is quite a ceremonial entity; the first class was constituted as an Order of St. John Class, and we all said a prayer, but I can't remember what it was. If I have blank spaces in the jotter, we were either praying or doing a practical activity. The doctor took the lead, Dr Domhnall MacDermott, a well-known local family physician.

The first lecture was about the basic principles of First Aid, symptoms, signs, history, diagnosis, and treatment. These were words I hadn't heard before. I found it a bit hard to understand, and I am usually the type to give up on something if I don't take to it immediately. I stuck at it; I had to for Daddy.

We got the first definition of our duty as a First Aider: To provide for medical aid. To arrange transport to a hospital if required. To restore breathing if it has stopped. To control all bleeding, immediate priority should be given to bleeding threatening life. To immobilise all fractures by splinting or other methods. To treat the condition of shock early. To make a concise report to the doctor if required. The first aider's responsibility ends when medical aid is available.

Even wee Caroline was interested in it! She was writing away; her pencil was nearly on fire. At the end of the lecture, first aid books were at the front of the room for five pence. I got one for me and one for Caroline. I still have that book, Elementary First Aid. It was another of the bits and pieces from Daddy's leather suitcase that I kept and opened to refresh my memory in writing.

We all said our goodbyes, and I looked forward to attending the following week: one lecture down, seven lectures and an exam at the end to go. I got home that night, and Mammy was waiting for me in the sitting room of the flat. I sat on the sofa beside Mammy's armchair, and she looked toward me. She knocked the television off and told me abruptly,

"The Melville Hotel phoned today; they are looking for waitresses in the Irish Kitchen. I told them you and a friend would be around tomorrow afternoon at five o'clock. Mrs McLaughlin knows the craic, and sure you can walk down together. I gave the manager our phone number up the town a couple of weeks ago." Then she just turned the television back on again.

"Aye, Mammy, I got on well at the First-Aid class; thank you for asking," I snapped back at her. Just as I thought I was getting into something good, a stupid part-time job came up. I was no more interested than the man on the moon, but Caroline would be with me at least. She had become fed up with working in the hairdressers and left.

"So, you went up the town, and gave my name everywhere, was that it? Why would they phone you back looking for me?"

"There were probably no Protestant wee girls that would work in The Irish Kitchen, that's why!" then we had a big, loud, cackly laugh among ourselves. Even though Mammy was a disciplinarian, she knew how to make me laugh when she wanted.

I was mortified at starting a new job; I had to walk down to Caroline's flat and go inside. Mammy had even bought me a nice new bright green coat to take with me. I hated it. Peter, Charlie and Hugh were sitting in the living room, and it was the first time I awkwardly said hello to Hugh. It was the first time we had spoken properly; he said to me, "There's King Brian from Darby O'Gill and The Little People!" it disarmed me, and I laughed. The whole room did. Wee Caroline said I went bright red; I say I didn't!

Wee Caroline was in a wee red dress and looked stunning in everything she wore. Her beautiful figure, big piercing eyes, fine legs, and flawless smile. She would look good in a bin bag, or anything for that matter. Caroline made that wee cheesy red frock look like fine Italian designers had made it.

We bid our goodbyes, and off we went to the Melville Hotel, at the corner of Orchard Street in the city centre. There was a sign saying Irish Kitchen, with the words in the shape of a cross. The second letter, 'I' in the horizontally lain word 'Irish', was the same 'I' used for the 'I' in 'Kitchen'.

The main hotel entrance was up a dozen steps, and the Irish Kitchen was essentially the main hotel cellar that had been converted into a pub. We had to go down a few steps beside the entrance steps and open the door at the bottom. When we went in, there was a big cloakroom and a large wooden archway leading to the dancefloor and bar area. There were two big fireplaces, no windows, and both fires were roaring. Even though I was only a first aider for two hours the previous night, I was concerned about how safe this was.

A gentleman, Patsy, was the manager and our interview was as follows,

"Good afternoon, girls, what are your names?"

"Martha Bradley."

"Caroline McLaughlin."

"Right. You will get ten shillings a night and a pound for a late night. Are you alright to come in on Friday night?"

"Aye, no bother," said I.

"Certainly," said she.

"Cheerio," said he.

That was it. So, we went home again.

Back then, many women married at twenty-one or even younger if they had permission. Many other girls would have worked in the shirt factories, which obviously left hospitality venues stuck for staff. We weren't even asked what age we were. Both of us looked older than our age and easily passed for eighteen.

I came home and told Mammy I was starting on Friday night. She was delighted and banged on the wall beside her sitting room armchair, the wall that separated the sitting room from Derek's room, "you hear that, Derek?! Your little sister has a job, get a move on!" He couldn't hear anything because he had the record player in his room and was blasting out "Yummy Yummy Yummy" by Ohio Express.

"Sure, that boy can't work Mammy, he might break a nail!" Mammy lunged out of her armchair, wielding the back of her hand at me, so I ran down the stairs to my bedroom before she could get me. I cackled behind the door and swear on my grand-wain's lives – Mammy was sniggering upstairs.

Mammy confessed years later that she and Mrs McLaughlin told the Melville Hotel that we were both eighteen, and then went to confession! It was okay to lie in those days if you went up to the Cathedral afterwards and told the priest about it. I told Mammy she was the fourth little piggy who made her house out of lies!

I kept my First Aid book beside me and was genuinely interested in it. I made lots of notes in bed at night. I had a lamp beside my bed in the flat and read the whole book cover to cover multiple times.

Mammy had my bedroom window open, and hanging on the door handle on the other side of my bedroom door was a white blouse, a long black skirt, and a thin green scarf. She was keen to get rid of me and send me out to work. She had it all prepared and planned out with military precision.

We had our first night in the Irish Kitchen that Friday, and we both turned up in our wee uniforms and scarves. Time for the grand tour of the Irish Kitchen!

Inside the door was a cloakroom on the left, and the décor was dark wooden beams everywhere. All the tables were made from the bases of Singer sewing machines, and it had a very rustic feel. Not old and dated, it was intentionally done, and it was a tourist hotspot. The bar was about four feet high, and there were benches where people would sit. There wasn't a stage in it, but three men and a fiddle played in the corner to the right of the bar.

All the girls in the bar smoked, and around this time was when I started to smoke. Wee Caroline never smoked and always hated it. It took me thirty-seven years to stop. As time went on, there was a storeroom where we would all go to smoke and gossip. After the bar management noticed that we were going missing off the floor, they took the lightbulb out of the room. It didn't deter us; we smoked our fags and gossiped in the dark.

On our first night, we did a late night. The craic was brilliant; a lot of tourists and those staying in the hotel were in the Irish Kitchen. A very multicultural gathering and we met people from England, America, and even China. When wee Caroline and I went to the bar to reload our trays with drinks, we laughed at the fact tourists even came here!

The roaring turf fires and the cigarette smoke would have choked the best of us, but the three men and a fiddle blasted out music and I loved it. Wee Caroline knew from day one how to work the barflies, she could give the eye, and it made us both a fortune in tips. We left the place just after one o'clock in the morning of our first shift and had a pound note, and three shillings in tips. One night, the Canadian Navy came in, and we made a small fortune in tips.

We had saucers on our trays, each with a pound float. Believe it or not, you could get a whole round of drinks for under a pound. When we went to the bar, we paid for the order, and then you had the correct change for the customer. Very often, they would say, "that's grand love, keep it" Music to our ears. Although not the locals, they never tipped.

I knew every trick in the book too. I am currently writing the book! If I ever did a stint behind the bar pulling the pints, there was a dish where the change would be. When taking the pint to the customer, one would "accidentally" drop a drip of beer onto the dish. Often, the customer said, "don't worry, you keep it!"

Lesson for the young people, never tell the person you are living with how much you make. When I scuttled up the stairwell to go back into the flat, I opened the door and Mammy was standing in the hall in her dressing gown with her hand out.

"Come on wee love, this flat doesn't heat itself. That food you eat isn't free either. Hand it over." She said to me in her big fluffy green gown.

I held out my hand with the pound note and the three shillings sitting on top of it. The wee bitch took the pound note and left me with the shillings. I was raging! I had to work two late nights to buy one LP, which cost six shillings.

"Martha, you have to put money away for a rainy day. What reason would you have to spend money other than dirty old fags, sweets, and the records? The Credit Union is the best place for it" Mammy and her wisdom. That became the routine, working two nights a week. I gave Mammy the pound note and kept the tips to myself on a Friday and Saturday night.

The Credit Union had only been established eight years when my account was opened. It helped hundreds of local families have fair and reasonable access to affordable loans. Mammy and Daddy were always big savers, I was always a big spender. The Credit Union hated seeing me coming over the years. I had about forty fridges break down, twenty cars stolen, and seven Grannies that died in England.

***

The second First Aid lecture couldn't come quick enough. Wee Caroline, who decided not to backcomb her hair or look like David Bowie this time, said to me, "I hope you have been studying your bones now!"

"Aye, I have ya mouth ye, and if you question me again, you will get a slap in the Inferior Maxilla!"

"Wise up Martha; you're as weak as water!" But she was impressed, she forgot that I signed her up and not vice-versa! Everyone was greeted with smiles, and we all got stuck into lecture two's theme, the different body systems, the respiratory system, the digestive system, the nervous system, and bones and joints prone to injuries like the collar bone and ankle.

The demonstrator had a linen first aid bag with a red cross on it. We were shown all the contents we would have with us, triangular bandages, wrap bandages, sterilised pads, scissors, tweezers, antiseptic cream, a water bottle, cotton wool, and smelling salts.

"This is everything one could possibly need in their First-Aid kit bag," the lecturing doctor bellowed around the lecture room in Ozanam House.

I immediately sniggered and whispered to Caroline, "and you'll have to put spare knickers in yours." She elbowed me in the rib.

We did some practical stuff in the second lecture, I had to put a splint and sling on Caroline, and she tied a bandage around my head so tightly that I thought I would faint! We were only fifteen; of course, there would be some messing about. The demonstrator and the doctor sternly looked toward us when wee Caroline and I would giggle to ourselves.

The third lecture was an absolute scream! It was all about pressure points on the body, which are used to squeeze an artery against a bone to stop severe bleeding. The three most common are between the shoulder and elbow – brachial artery, the groin area – femoral artery, and behind the knee – popliteal artery.

In the Irish Kitchen, or sitting on the thrupenny bits outside the flats, I would squeeze behind Caroline's knee, and she would do the same back to me. We were terrible. Wee Caroline's long bony fingers, perfect for playing the piano, used to nearly nip the arteries inside my arms!

She got me a belter one night while carrying a pint tray. She came out of nowhere, like a silent ninja, and nipped me behind the arm. I dropped the tray and ended up wearing about nine pints of stout! Mammy marched me to Woolworths the following day to buy a new scarf, dress, and ribbons.

I had to pay for it myself; the only way I would get wee Caroline's pound and tips to replace my uniform would be if I grabbed it out of her cold dead hand. She had a head like an elephant, “mind, you wrecked my good school shoes when you pushed me into cow shite!” she smugly said to me.

“Seriously?!” I said, “gone get over yourself, wee girl!”

At night, I was still studying away at the First Aid book. It all comes rushing back whenever I read it—sitting on my eiderdown in the flats, at night by lamplight, and writing down the bones, arteries, and joints.

On the Friday morning before my fourth First Aid lecture, I saw people putting posters up all over the place, on the stairwells and the balcony walls of the flats – DERRY HOUSING ACTION COMMITTEE. Big yellow posters with bold red slogans – ONE MAN ONE VOTE, END GERRYMANDERING, POINTS SYSTEM FOR HOUSING – NOW!

Wee Caroline and I had to cross the Guildhall Square to get to the Irish Kitchen that Friday afternoon, and there were about four or five hundred sitting on the ground outside the Guildhall. A mass sit-down protest and we sat there for about half an hour. Not because we deeply cared about Civil Rights, more so to see what was happening.

At the start, all we did was eavesdrop; the protestors wanted an end to the Corporation. I remember them being cheeky to Mammy one time whenever she wanted to move after Daddy died. I had forgotten about that time until I sat down outside the Guildhall that afternoon. I told a fella sitting beside me what the Corporation said to Mammy, “it isn’t our fault your husband killed himself”.

There was a chorus of tuts from the people sitting around me,

“Aye, they’re bastards hi!” a couple of them said toward me, and all I did was nod and agree. One of them asked me if Francis Bradley was my father; when I said yes, he told me that he remembered him well and said he was the world's biggest gentleman. He told me that he worked over at the railway station and knew him,

"The foreman used to send the wee boys up the train smoke-stacks to clean them; any time your father was there, he told them not to worry, and he would do it himself. Said he wouldn't have his own children up the train chimney so wouldn't have somebody else's up there."

My lip wobbled, but I held in the tears. Wee Caroline hugged me, and the man put his hand on my knee.

My Daddy was gone before I was ten, and some people had more memories of him than I did. I was learning more about Daddy from other people who knew him much longer than I did. That is the way it goes when parents die young. I didn't think about Daddy often, but that night in the Irish Kitchen, I went into the ladies, locked the door, and cried my heart out.

Seven

The Irish Kitchen

Monday evening came again, and the nights were getting darker. Monday night was Malta night, as I called it, and I sat on the balcony to have a cup of tea before I went down for wee Caroline.

In the car park, Caroline's brothers and Hugh were playing football. They had their jumpers down for goalposts, and now and again, the garage doors in the car park would boom after the football struck them. There were two car parks by the flats, the central courtyard at the rear and one at the side near Fahan Street which was a bit more secluded.

The main carpark was empty because only about three or four people had cars, and those that did parked in the wee cark at the side of Fahan Street because they knew that a football would bang their cars if they used the main carpark. Hugh and the boys knocked at the flats where the car owners lived and asked them ever so politely to move their car as it was getting in the way of their football match. The best about it is, people moved their cars!

Hugh was far better than the rest of them, a brilliant footballer. It wasn't that wee Caroline's brothers were donkeys, but I learned later that Hugh had football in his genes. Harry Gilmour,

Hugh's father, was a prolific goal scorer for Derry City pre-second world war.

I was genuinely interested in the game and always enjoyed watching football on TV. I would have loved to have tried it, but there weren't any girl's teams at that time. My Joanne is a brilliant footballer, and I encouraged her to join a girls' team when she was young. She kept it up and coaches a girls' team on a Saturday morning whenever her husband doesn't make her milk cows. I can remember Hugh and the boys battering the garage doors with an old heavy ball but can't remember the wee team Joanne coaches.

***

Wee Caroline bought herself a Wurlitzer keyboard in Henderson's Music Store with her wages, and she could be heard all over the flats. There was a young fella that played the clarinet in block one, Goodman, I think his name was, and you could hear him from Mars. The flats had quite a musical heritage; there was a wee girl called Rosemary, who became known for being able to sing a good tune.

I could hear that keyboard whilst drinking my cup of tea and made my way down to the awful racket she was producing. I popped my head in the door and shouted, "First Aid! Help! My ears are bleeding."

"Shut up you Martha!" she shouted out. Her Mammy was at her wits end with the keyboard. She only just bought it, and there had already been complaints from neighbours. Then again, you could hear custard rustling next door in the flats, so a Wurlitzer keyboard was as loud as Liberace in your front room.

Mrs McLaughlin said, "you know she wanted to buy a piano Martha? Only reason she didn't was that they couldn't get a piano to fit inside the lift, nor would they carry it up the stairs."

"Sure, it might be able to fit down the rubbish chute if you get fed up with it."

"Now you're talkin!"

The racket stopped, and off we went to Ozanam House. We were halfway through the eight weeks First Aid training lecture series and were told that our exam would be on the 9th of January 1969. By this stage, we all knew one another by name, and we were gathered around the top table in the lecture room to see a resuscitation dummy lying on its back on the table.

It was a bit creepy. It was like a bald man and was just the torso — no arms or legs on it. The practical activity for the session was artificial respiration. A few cadets were there to demonstrate how they performed artificial respiration, holding the nose and taking deep breaths into the dummy until the chest inflated.

The doctor asked the group, "would anybody like to come forward?" Then as if in revenge for all the evil I caused her, wee Caroline pushed me forward. I was shocked! I turned around to her, and her smug face was one I would never tire of slapping.

I was out in front of everybody, all eyeballs on Martha. "Excellent, we have a volunteer," the doctor said. I froze in front of him and the two smartly dressed cadets standing before me. I didn't know what to do. I was mortified! I was looking out into the group; they all had relieved faces that it wasn't them in my position.

"Now, what is your name?"

"M-M-Martha," I said timidly.

"Now, Martha, what I would like you to do, is pinch the nose there."

So, I pinched the nose of the dummy, hoping and praying this wasn't going where I thought it was going. There were some discreet sniggers among the group; I heard the faint whispers and chit-chat.

When I pinched the nose, he said, "now Martha, take a deep breath in and breathe into the dummy in a controlled manner."

I panicked, and when I panic, Mouthy Martha comes out. "What? Put the lips on him. Is he going to buy me a drink first?" The room descended into laughter from everyone, bar the doctor and the cadets.

"Now, Martha, this is life or death. I understand it may be slightly odd at first, but this may save somebody's life one day." The doctor brought the room back into focus, and made me feel slightly guilty for being a smart arse.

I eventually carried out the task, and it was grand when it was over and done. It was a new skill I learned, and I enjoyed the experience. On the way home that night, I stormed ahead of Caroline. I left her in my dust and ran up the steps without saying bye to her.

***

The Derry Citizens Action Committee (DCAA) posters and NICRA were everywhere now! You couldn't turn your head without seeing them. Everyone was talking about them, and the organisers were around the flats; Eamon Melaugh, Fionnbarra Ó Dochartaigh, and JJ O'Hara were very visible.

As far as heroes to come from our city, one can't look far beyond John Hume. He had been elected in 1969 as an independent nationalist, and I met him for the first time as a teenager in the flats. He would knock on the doors and listen to people's thoughts on current events. What struck me was how he genuinely cared about how we were all feeling. The caring nature of John Hume will never be replaced in our city.

Eamon McCann is a fantastic speaker and would have come with a bullhorn and spoke about Civil Rights at the bottom of the flats. He was a leader, a revolutionary, and dare I say about one hundred years ahead of his time, and still is. Everyone loved listening to him; a sign of authentic leadership is caring about something and sharing why others should care about it, too, like Mr Day did in our first First Aid lecture.

"Even if they make our gatherings illegal, we will still gather and assemble," McCann bellowed through the bullhorn. People were shouting their approval from the living room windows of the flats. "This place is a vertical ghetto," he continued, "designed to oppress the working class of this area." I was captivated; everyone was. I think this was the first seed of discontentment sown before the residents of the Rossville Flats.

As sure as shite on a mountain, protests and large public gatherings were illegalised that November. It was near the end of our first aid lecture series, and wee Caroline and I were sticking it out and making new friends. The exam nerves were starting to set in, and I didn't want to fail. I studied more for my Order of Malta exam than my paramedic exam in 1982.

I even got my Mammy to ask me questions; God love her, she couldn't read or write very well, and I couldn't bring myself to cackle at her when she couldn't read the Latin names for bones and muscles. It must have taken her about ten tries to say haemorrhage. "Hee-more-hage".

The last four lectures were very practical based and dealt with fractures, burns, scalds, dislocations, sprains, shock, and, interestingly, foreign bodies. Of course, this generated some wee giggles from Caroline and me. In grown-up, mature terms, this is removing pieces of glass from the skin or dust from the eyes.

Caroline and I were separated for the practical tasks that required us to split into pairs because we were too immature to be together. It was for the best because I was paired with other people who took it very seriously. Even then, I felt that if something happened to me that I would be happy to be treated by them. I felt very comfortable around the others, and it was lovely.

***

The lectures were all over in a flash, and it was time to prepare for the exam. December of 1968 was upon us, and wee Caroline and I took on more shifts in the Irish Kitchen leading up to Christmas. The three men and the fiddle played Christmas carols, and the atmosphere was incredible. To me, that was real Christmas music. Not the commercialised shite that came later. I love Christmas, and every year I think of that time. The swinging sixties in Derry were unbelievable until 1969. We fell at the last hurdle.

It was busy, packed almost every night. Some emigrated to America in the past decades but would return home for Christmas. We wore green dresses, played Irish music, and it was the most Irish venue in all of Ireland.

I made a fortune in tips and felt no issue giving Mammy the pound note. We worked at least five nights a week in the lead-up to Christmas. Sometimes I came home with another pound in tips due to the American tipping culture. That month, I treated myself to a pile of records and got Mammy and Derek brilliant Christmas presents. I got Mammy a coat in Austin's that cost me two nights' tips and Derek a sharp pair of brogues. I even got new clothes for myself, and I was one of the wealthiest fifteen-year-olds in Derry at that time.

We stayed on to close the night before Christmas Eve, and as a thank you, the bar was passing around drinks for the staff after the patrons left. We had a lock-in!

Wee Caroline whispered to me, "Martha, should we? If we don't take the drink, we might give ourselves away."

"We are going to have to wee love, oh dear! Do we say we are pioneers instead?"

"No chance, we are doing it, Martha."

Mammy didn't drink; Daddy drank recreationally but never inside the house. Derek was going to dances at this stage, at seventeen, but didn't abuse Mammy's trust in letting him go out. He was always home before me.

The barmen poured their own pints, and I was handed a gin and tonic. This was the first time I held an alcoholic drink in my hand for myself. I didn't even know what to do, the men downed the pints, but the girls were sipping their drinks so elegantly. We stood slightly away from the benches and booths where all the staff were, but we edged closer to them.

"Sip it, Caroline, don't be necking it." I said to her. She took a sip and did her best to put on a straight face. I knew she hated it, but she had to grin and bear it, not to blow our cover. I put the glass to my head and had a sip. Even after one sip, the most deplorable feeling came over me. I felt invincible.

I mostly stuck to wee Caroline, but after two downed gin and tonics, I talked to the rest of the staff like I had known them for years. When the trays of whiskeys came down, the first hand on the tray was mine. I took to drink like a duck to water, wee Caroline, not so much. She hated the taste of it.

A record player appeared as the three men, and the fiddle went home long ago. When "The Locomotion" came on, I was straight up onto the dancefloor alone. I remember everyone cheering, "go on, Martha!" What I couldn't do in singing, I made up in dancing. I was swinging my hips, really giving it all I had.

I thought, If my Mammy saw me, she would batter me, but Daddy can see me. When this thought crept into my head, it was just as the song finished, and I went straight back in for the magic elixir that made me unstoppable.

Wee Caroline didn't look happy; she kept pushing me away when I tried to go near her. I kept urging her to join the fun, but she looked at me with disgust. I didn't want to stop, but wee Caroline was nudging me to go home. "Martha, come on! We have to go home now."

"Will…hic…you…wise..hic…up…wee girl." But when wee Caroline went to leave without me, I stood up that quickly that the room started to spin. I was able to save face; I remember saying to everyone on the benches, "I've had too much fun; time to go home, see you all next week, and have a lovely Christmas."

Everyone said their farewells, and I could barely walk. On the way home, I pressed my hands onto every concrete or brick surface. I was roaring across the Guildhall Square, "WOW WOW, NOW THAT YOU CAN DO IT, LETS MAKE A CHAIN NOW, COME ON BABY DO THE LOCOMOTION – A CHUGGA CHUGGA MOTION LIKE A RAILROAD TRAIN NOW!"

Wee Caroline was roaring at me to shush! But when I said railroad train, I started hyperventilating because I knew Daddy was watching me somewhere. To make matters worse, two RUC men on the beat came over to us.

"Bit too much to drink, have we girls?" the rosy-cheeked cop said. Before I could get a word in, Caroline grabbed me and said, "aye, it was our Christmas party at work, and we are just going home now. Goodnight!" We were wearing our Irish Kitchen uniforms, so it didn't raise any suspicion from the policemen who tipped their hats and walked away.

I was dragged along William Street, down Chamberlain Street, and staggered across the flats' carpark. No doubt if I was alone, I wouldn't have made it. Wee Caroline was my guide home. I could barely stand.

I kept tripping up the stairwell of the flats, and wee Caroline had to scoop me off the ground several times. Caroline was telling me to light a cigarette so it would take the smell of drink away from me.

Mammy always left the door open when I was on a late-night shift, so coming in when Mammy was sleeping wasn't unusual. My drunken stupor was unusual, but wee Caroline guided me through my bedroom door frame and lowered me onto the bed to avoid disturbing Mammy and Derek. She opened the window, gave me a wee kiss on the head, and went home.

When my eyeballs scraped open on Christmas Eve morning, I felt like I was kicked in the head by a horse. But I didn't care. The night before, I was Martha Bradley, Queen of The Universe.

Mammy knocked on the door and peeked in, "do you want your breakfast in bed, wee love? You have worked that hard, and you are tired." I nodded to say yes; the wee angel thought I was tired and nothing else. I barely touched the porridge beside my First Aid books on my bedside table.

The night before, I was legless, absolutely disgusting for a fifteen-year-old wee girl. The 23rd of December 1968 was the night the slippery slope was stepped upon.

Eight

Free Derry

The 4th of January 1969 was another date that etched itself into history. A march was planned from Belfast to Derry and organised by People's Democracy. It was to take place from New Year's Day until the 4th of January. This was another group that Eamon McCann was prominent in and included a young Bernadette Devlin.

Mammy wasn't very political but was expressing her disgust at the fact that our police, the Royal Ulster Constabulary (RUC), stood idly by while the peaceful marchers were pelted with bricks and bats with nails hammered through them at Burntollet Bridge, about five miles outside Derry. It had made the news, and even on our television, the marchers were called "Catholic agitators".

The following nights, the RUC upped their presence around the periphery of the Bogside and near the Rossville Flats. This was when I witnessed my first riot. The first night, I stayed indoors, and Mammy didn't let us out of the flat.

The second night, I ventured down to the ground. I stayed well back, from the reasonably safe distance at the thrupenny bits. I sat on the wall, dangling my feet and looking toward the junction of William Street and Rossville Street, watching the bricks and bottles fly toward the RUC. I couldn't believe it!

Across the road from the high flats were other blocks of maisonettes being built, complete with pedestrian ramp walkways on the sides of them. I peered over and saw a clump of first aiders sitting within the railings of the rampway, about one hundred metres from where the riot was taking place. They had the linen kit bags with them, and I wondered if this was what I would end up doing.

They weren't called into action in the hour I was there, but I was called upstairs to the flat whenever Mammy opened the sitting room window that faced the direction where I was sitting and called me back inside. All the flats had tilt-turn windows, and she could open the window and look right down to see me.

The wave of disillusionment among Nationalist communities in Derry was simmering at a critical level. Derek couldn't get a job, we lived in high flats, housing lists were still ridiculously long, and many weren't allowed to vote. Votes weren't for everyone back then; it went by how many properties one owned. Only a person paying the rates could vote. I can't remember; they made it up as they went along.

In the lead-up to the First Aid exam on the 9th of January 1969, we went down to Quinn's chemist at the bottom of the flats to see if they would sell wee Caroline and I bandages and First Aid stuff to practice bandaging each other up. Luckily, we got loads of stuff; bandages, eye drops, ointment, sterilised pads, etc.

In hindsight, the riots and public disorder increase prompted them to stock more first aid supplies. I noticed something for the first time that week. While standing under the canopy of the row of shops, I saw a significant work of graffiti for the first time, "YOU ARE NOW ENTERING FREE DERRY", painted on the gable wall of a house facing block two of the flats.

This was the beginning of the Free Derry period; that gable wall is still known as Free Derry Corner and is a globally recognised tourist attraction. I could see it from my living room in the flats, and photographers photographed it from the moment it went up. That was our wall. Yes, the Great Wall of China and Hadrian's Wall might have more splendour, but our wall has more culture.

On the morning of the 9th of January, a Thursday, my nerves were wrecked. Mammy told me she would light her wee candle, which made all the difference. Lighting a candle for someone doing an exam is much more comforting than going and doing the exam for them — just another Derry custom.

Mammy lit her candle when I started something new or had a hard time. Mammy had the candles lit on the two days I gave birth and must have burned about five hundred candles when I was going through my divorce.

We walked up to Ozanam House in the rain. It was bucketing down, and we got soaked. Wee Caroline was slightly distant from me since the incident in which she had to carry me home,

"Right Martha, no being a smart Alec in here. I don't want to pass this test on my own; you have to pass it too!"

"I will wee love, don't worry, I won't let you down."

Upstairs in the lecture hall were seats and benches. All of them had some distance between them so we couldn't cheat. I didn't need to cheat anyway; I knew the first aid book from cover to cover. The test was an hour and was focused on anatomy, scenarios, and selecting the appropriate treatment option.

The questions were things like, "how would you become aware that someone is experiencing an internal haemorrhage?" Dead easy! The skin is cold, clammy, covered with cold sweat, and shallow breathing. And "how would you control arterial bleeding using a tourniquet?" Yet again, it flowed onto the page.

A tourniquet is only used when other methods have failed to control the bleeding and can only be used for pressure against the humerus and the femur.

I think I finished the exam in twenty-five minutes, with thirty-five minutes to spare. I got into the zone for the practical aspects afterwards. There was smoke coming out of wee Caroline's ears. She was stuck! She didn't look at me once, and I had to stop myself from getting off my stiff wooden chair and bench to help her.

The larger room downstairs was where the practical element was. I was called forward and asked to perform artificial respiration on the dummy lying on the floor on a white sheet. Without wondering if the dummy would buy me a drink first, I pinched the snout, planted the lips on him, and watched the chest inflate. Boom!

The second task had a cadet sitting on a chair, clutching her left arm with her right. She was wearing a big thick brown coat over her cadet uniform, and I immediately thought, remember to remove the coat with care beginning with the sound and uninjured side first. The role-play was for a fracture of the shaft of the humerus.

I had learned to bandage a moving target, Caroline, so a trained cadet sitting still would be an absolute walk in the park.

I removed the coat, secured the splint with bandages along the forearm to immobilise the fracture, and made a sling that looped around the head and tied to the wrist. When I was finished, the wee girl on the seat gave me a subtle thumbs up, and I was delighted. I felt fantastic, and Caroline breezed through her practical elements too.

We knew we had passed, but when the post came a couple of weeks later with the Maltese Cross and Order of Malta emblem on the envelope, I screamed the flat down. My first-aid certificate and an Order of Malta Identity card were inside it.

My identity card, which I still have, is like a miniature passport. It says, "Sovereign Military Order of St. John of Jerusalem and of Malta – Irish Association – Order of Malta Ambulance Corps". The identity card number is #4623. I ran down the stairwell toward the horrific racket of Wee Caroline's Wurlitzer keyboard, and she had received hers too. I brought mine with me, and we were so delighted.

There was an order form inside the welcome pack so that we could order our uniforms. Our Mammies let us keep our money and treated us to the First Aid Uniforms, one grey dress uniform, three white first aid coats, and kitbags. The reason for buying three first aid coats was one for the wash, one on us, and a spare in case we destroyed one. A Mother's instinct, eh?

The grey dress uniforms were a long grey skirt, a blazer, undershirt, red tie, and grey cap. This was the uniform worn at events, if the papers ever photographed us, and for mass and ceremonies. The white coats were introduced for the riot duties because the grey uniforms were more expensive and impractical for riot use.

When my uniforms eventually arrived, I smelled the newness of them. I loved the long white first aid coats, with separate red heart-shaped patches and a white Maltese Cross. Mammy had to sew the patch onto each coat's left breast pocket and put a label on the inside of the collar – "M Bradley 73 Mura Place".

I still have one of those very coats. I'm a big softie, and I keep things; there, I said it! It is my most prized possession, and I want to be buried with it.

A full-length mirror was in Mammy's room, and I posed in front of the mirror with my crisp white coat on. The dining room was Mammy's room, and it could never be heated because the gas heater in her room had stopped working. I have no idea how she slept in there. I noticed how draughty the flat was in that room. Even with my thick first aid coat on, I felt it colder in there than I did outside.

Being relatively young, we weren't sent to the occasional riots. Caroline and I had just started, and our first official first aid duty was at a Derry and District (D and D) football match between Wellington Rovers and Foyle Harps. It was a Saturday morning in late January or early February.

It was standard for the Knights of Malta to do first aid cover at D and D matches at that time. There were five of us there; me, Hugh Deehan, Attracta, Caroline, and Mr Day himself. The game was at the Daisyfield football pitch, along the Foyle River.

We stationed ourselves on the sidelines, opposite where the two team managers and substitutes were standing. The Foyle Harps team were warming up by jogging up and down the touch-line. They had lovely crisp black and green rigs, occasionally stopping to drink water from water bottles. Wellington Rovers just stood about smoking their fags, waiting for the referee to come.

Wellington Rovers weren't exactly known for their sporting integrity. They were cheating wee bastards. It was where I lived as a child, and I quietly supported them. This match went down in Derry folklore because of twins Paddy and Sean Murray. They lived in Wellington Street and were old friends of Derek when we lived there.

Paddy Murray, God rest him, had the world at his feet. He could thread a pass through a needle's eye and blast a shot into the top corner from thirty yards. All the girls in the town fancied him, and all the wee boys wanted to be him.

On the other hand, Sean couldn't hit a barn door with a banjo. Absolute donkey! Of course, Sean was registered as a Wellington

Rovers player, and when they were losing consistently week after week, they came up with the least cunning plan in the history of deceit. They would persuade Paddy to play the match instead of Sean.

The match got underway, and Foyle Harps scored after about thirty seconds. I remember putting my head in my hands, and first aiders raised eyebrows at me. "Wellington Rovers are my team! That's where I used to live!"

I could hear the shouts of Wellington Rovers, "man on, Paddy! Ah! I mean Sean!"

Jesus, it was a farce. Foyle Harps grew more and more suspicious as the game went on. Sean Murray, worse than having two left feet, was suddenly gliding between the Harps players. Carefully placing his passes and not knowing the names of his teammates. The Harps boys all knew what was going on.

The Harps players were trying to take Paddy out, but he jumped over every tackle, stayed on his feet, and a hurricane couldn't knock him down. They don't make footballers like that anymore. I used to go to my Sean-Paul's football matches because their Daddy was always "away on business", and I remember the manager shouting to Sean Paul to "go down" whenever an opposing player came within five yards of him.

Even with a class act on their side, it wasn't enough to stop Wellington Rovers from getting stuffed 7-0 that day. Very uneventful, with no injuries, but we stayed in the background just in case. When I went home and told Mammy, she had a good laugh at it. That was an occasional occurrence for me, going to football matches and some community events.

It was all very innocent in the beginning. We had a duty rota for mass, and we would stand at the back of the chapels and provide elderly people with a drink of water if they felt ill. Most of the time, it was uneventful, but we got to wear fancy uniforms.

Standing in the back of the chapels, I could never in a million years have imagined how quickly our roles would change from being somewhat innocent to be in life-threatening situations.

First aid competitions and meet-ups were reasonably common, and everybody looked forward to them. I could never go to any of them because they were held at the weekends. I worked in a pub, and I didn't want to risk losing my job. The unit often returned with trophies and medals, and travelled around Ireland to meet the other units.

We went to a fair up in Longtower, where there were Irish Dancers and singers, and Mr Day gave first aid demonstrations to interested onlookers. People were genuinely very interested in first aid, which was quite an evolving movement back then. Wee Caroline told me that day that she was thinking of becoming a nurse when she turned eighteen.

I very much enjoyed it too, and never considered a job in any form of healthcare until I joined the Order of Malta. Many of them went on to become nurses in later years, Attracta became a nurse, as did Robert Cadman, and Hugh Deehan and I became paramedics.

The rioting was increasing in the streets but was still far from a daily occurrence. I was only fifteen, so as a first aider, I wouldn't have been sent to the front of the riots. The men and boys were mostly sent to be present. The logic was that they could carry people away more easily on stretchers and bring the Malta ambulance. Riots were relatively small then, a couple of stone and bottle throwers.

I remember venturing down to one of the riots in my white coat; there were two first aid boys in the ambulance in the waste ground of what would become the Glenfada Park carpark, directly across the road from block one of the Rossville Flats.

When I approached, one of them opened the ambulance's back door and let me sit in.

It was an old white Bedford van that was converted into an ambulance. The side had “Order of Malta Ambulance Corps – Derry Units” painted in red on the side and across the two rear doors. Inside was a bed that could be pulled out on rails and a first aid kit sitting on it. The two boys were in officer-type uniforms, and I was wearing my white coat, with my kitbag over my shoulder.

I remember the boys yawning; they were bored. We exchanged chit-chat, and I told them that I saw the ambulance and wanted to come over to see if I could do anything. They had been sitting there for two hours, but about five minutes after I got into the ambulance, a wee boy came around the corner of Glenfada and looked toward the ambulance. There appeared to be a laceration over his right eye. He wore a nice, checked Ben Sherman shirt, and had a white hankie over his face. The way he carried himself was very familiar, and as I looked toward him, one of the boys in the ambulance turned to me and said, “go ahead!”

Excited at my first slice of the action, I lept from the ambulance and went toward him. I had my bag over my shoulder and rifled through my kit bag for a sterilised pad when I was on my way over. It was just a cut on his face, he was still on his feet and could come over himself.

I stood before him, opened the pad, and put antiseptic ointment on it. The blood had trickled from just above his left eyebrow down the side of his face, then I looked in the big familiar brown eyes.

“What’s the craic King Brian?” he said to me. Being the first aider doesn’t bring many opportunities for a giggle, but this did.

"Doing a wee bit better than you! Freeing the nation, are we?" I quipped back to Hugh.

"Awk, sure, it's a bit of craic; they have armour on them anyway! Sure, what else would we be doing?" That was Hugh's attitude, it was all a bit of innocent fun with his mates, and the only person that got hurt that day was himself!

I looked right into his eyes when I wiped the blood away from the top of his eyebrow. Big brown eyes. It wasn't a deep cut, but the area above the eyebrow can bleed profusely and look worse than it is.

"What happened?" I asked him.

He looked down at his shoes, "I got a new pair of shoes, a wee bit big on me, but sure I will grow into them. I turned to run when I thought the RUC were coming forward and slipped. Down I went, a sack of spuds just!"

He didn't need a stitch, and he was lucky! I looked toward the boys sitting in the ambulance, and they gave me a thumbs up. My first riot injury was successfully treated! I was all chuffed.

Before departing, Hugh lifted the Peter pointer finger of his right hand and put it in front of his white handkerchief-clad face in a shh gesture, then off he went. We all know in Derry that this is the unspoken symbol of "say nothing until you see Claude". Claude Wilton, a protestant, was a solicitor who represented Nationalist cases then. "Claude, Claude the Fenian prod".

People need to know that the Civil Rights association was not exclusively a Catholic movement. Claude Wilton and Ivan Cooper were two leaders of the Derry Civil rights movement during this period and weren't Catholics.

I peeked out from behind the gable wall of Glenfada and looked left down Rossville Street. I was able to count nine RUC officers and fifteen wee boys. There was a makeshift barricade of rubble, old crates, tyres and any other brock the wee boys could get their hands on. I kept an eye on Hugh to make sure he was alright.

Suddenly, the young fellas turned away from the RUC and started walking down Rossville Street.

"Boys, I think they are giving up," I shouted back to the ambulance. I walked back toward the ambulance; the youths were walking toward the opposite flats, taking their white hankies off their faces.

The two first aiders chuckled, "naw, they are going in for their tea. It is just going on five o'clock, and we are going for our tea too, cheerio!"

I walked across the road, and the ambulance horn tooted at me as it turned right out of Glenfada Park and disappeared behind Free Derry Corner.

Nine

Rossville Street

Wee Caroline's life changed forever in March of 1969, and Neil Diamond changed it. Suddenly, everybody sang "Sweet Caroline" to her, and she hated it! Me being me, I took every opportunity to roar it in her face and blast it out of my record player when she came into my flat.

Anybody with a name like Caroline, Mandy, or Jude, is condemned to a life of everyone singing to them and thinking they are hilarious! I always thought I was hilarious, singing at wee Caroline, and she was seething. Everybody sang it to her; when she appeared on the balcony when the young fellas were playing football in the car park, they would break into the chorus of Sweet Caroline. She hated it; I loved it. My neighbour Mandy comes in for a cup of tea and gossip now and then, and I still sing "Mandy" to her. I've done it every time she comes in for the past twenty years.

***

The thrupenny bits were still very much a meeting point for all of us in the flats, and wee Caroline and I still met down there to watch the world go by. It was more interesting, like a cinematic epic unfolding before us. There would be stone-throwers, RUC officers edging closer to Rossville Street toward the flats, and it was all a bit of craic and drama for us.

At the shops, a wee boy about nine or ten years of age ran up to us and said, "are you first aid girls?"

"Naw, we wear these white coats for the craic," I told him, "What's wrong?"

"Come with me quick!" he shrieked back at us.

"Right, okay," Caroline said back, and we looked at each other as he ran up the stairwell behind him. We ran up to the Garvan Place balcony at the rear of the flats on block one and were taken to the rubbish chute. Each balcony on the three flat blocks had an outdoor sheltered chute, which was all the flats' waste disposal method. There were large containers at the bottom that were emptied every Thursday.

Wee Caroline asked what was wrong, and when we walked inside, we saw nothing. I intervened,

"Here, mucker, what have you taken us up here for?" I barked at him.

"M-m-my friend is stuck in there?" he whimpered to us.

"Are you joking?" wee Caroline said and tried to control her sniggering.

I opened the lid of the chute and could hear whimpering inside the chute.

The chute flap was raised, and I held it in my right hand and shouted down "hello!" and then a ghostly echoey voice came back up the chute,

"Hellllоооо."

I looked back at the wee boy and Caroline, "is this a joke?"

"Naw, it's not, the big boys dared him to go down the chute, and now he's stuck!" When the wee boy started laughing nervously, I demanded Caroline go to the bottom of the chute and see if there was a wee boy down there. This had to be some sort of prank.

The youth stayed with me, and after a few minutes, I shouted down the chute, "Caroline, are you down there?"

"Aye, Martha, there's no wee boy down here."

"Gone please help me! I'm stuck. Please!" the sniffling voice echoed through the chute.

For fuck's sake! I'm standing at the top, Caroline at the bottom, and the wee boy in the middle. I turned to the wee boy beside me,

"Why didn't you phone the fire brigade, an ambulance, or even his Mammy?"

"Sure, the police and everyone else are scared to come here in case they get pelted with bricks and stones. I'm no tout either; if I go up to his flat and tell his Mammy and Daddy, they will batter him!"

"Fair point. Caroline, what will we do?"

"I don't know Martha, but don't worry wee boy we will get you out." I could hear the wee boy too, and he started to cry. I shouted my reassurances down the chute and told him I would go and get help from a neighbour.

"Can you do me a favour miss?" he whimpered up to me?

"Yes, wee love," I said.

"Gone go up to Mura Place above because the neighbours here will tell my Mammy."

So I went up the steps to Mura Place and banged on the first door I could see at the top of the stairs. A lady answered the door, and she looked very bewildered when I told her a wee boy was stuck in the chute and we needed to get him out.

"Awk, dear! Sure, if you throw soapy water down, he might be able to wriggle free," she enthusiastically said to me. I had no better ideas, and she gave me two buckets of soapy water in heavy metal buckets.

I got back down to the chute and shouted down, "here, mister, we're throwing soapy water down; close your eyes!"

The two buckets were tipped down the chute, "ah! That water is scalding, hi!"

"Right, start wriggling now and see if you can move," I shouted to him.

"I'm still stuck!"

Caroline had a bright idea, "Martha, would oil or lard be better to grease the sides of the chute? I could go into the chip shop and see if Mr Harley will give us a bit of lard to throw down."

"Aye, gone ahead, love, sure this boy won't be going anywhere anytime soon."

Two ladies from the chip shop came up to where the wee boy and I were at the top of the chute, with melted lard and the extendable hooks with which the chip shop shutters were closed.

"Right, love, we have a couple of buckets of lard coming down. Wriggle when it hits you."

I said to the wee boy beside me, "make sure you give your mucker a change of clothes and let him wash in your flat. I don't want to have to give him more help later when he turns up to his Mammy's door covered in lard and soapy water." The wee boy nodded right away; that was when I figured it out. The wee bastard had dared his mucker to go down the chute.

After the lard glugged out of the bucket and down the chute, he shouted that he could move a wee bit. I lifted the extendable pole and told him to try and pull himself up a bit whilst grabbing the pole. He heaved himself inside the chute, and he shouted up,

"Yes! I'm free. Thank you, miss." He hurtled down the chute and knocked wee Caroline flying at the bottom! He landed on top of her—the two of them lying in a heap inside the skip. I forgot to tell her to watch out! Whoops.

***

Barricades were becoming more widespread, and outside block one of the flats, the makings of the infamous rubble barricade across Rossville Street were starting to appear. It didn't block the road entirely, but there was a gap in the middle to allow civilian traffic to come through. There were two makeshift barricades, so traffic had to go through the barricades in a zig-zag fashion.

The barricades were made of broken prams, rubbish, rubble from the building site opposite the flats where Glenfada Park would eventually stand, and pretty much anything people could get their hands on.

I don't know why, but I always counted the rioters at the barricades. The first was fifteen wee boys; as the weeks passed, it crept into the twenties. Same with the RUC on the other side of the barricades. As the riots started to increase, more first aiders were present.

Wee Caroline joined me down in the Glenfada carpark where the ambulance was, and the first aid cover at the riots had doubled in a few weeks; there would have been six of us there routinely. Hugh Deehan was the regular ambulance driver, Attracta was a nursing student and handy to have around, and Marie, Eiblin and Antoinette started coming too, as did everybody, including Leo Day.

The riots were starting to get out of control for the RUC, and the B-specials were brought in to bolster the ranks. The B-specials were an auxiliary reserve within the RUC, and they didn't think or talk; they just swung their batons.

Sometimes the riots were quiet, and not on at all on a Sunday. The first bad injury I saw was a young fella being dragged to us on either arm by two of his rioter friends.

They shouted, "the fucking B-men smacked him with a baton!" I didn't look at him closely as Antoinette and Attracta ran over first. "Looks very much like a concussion and maybe a fractured eye socket," I think Antoinette shouted over.

One of the rioters grabbed me by the arm and said, "they just smacked him, and we grabbed him before they could scoop him, hit him right on the temple. Attempted murder, that is!"

I was slightly shaken; sure, the police are supposed to protect us, I thought. Hugh Deehan took the wee boy in the ambulance, and away he went. I remember feeling quite exposed in the white coat in the middle of the street as the ambulance was our shelter.

The riot ended, and I went home. I remember Mammy asking me if I was okay, and I was shaking slightly while eating my tea. The notion came into my head; I felt vulnerable out there; I need to feel invincible again. Me only fifteen, soon to be sixteen.

***

Wee Caroline and I kept up our jobs in the Irish Kitchen, and at times we had to cross through riots to get across the Guildhall Square, along Foyle Street, and down to the Melville at the foot of Orchard Street. That night, I felt my hands shake when I was carrying the trays of pints.

Tourists and punters were very kind in the Irish Kitchen; when they would pay for their drinks, they would say, "and get one for yourself, love". Some of the girls would have a drink at the end of the bar; I sat with them too.

The Ferry girls, Bridie, Betty, and Maeve, worked with us. Betty was the eldest and did the tills because she worked in Woolworths, and Maeve did the coats. Most nights, they would go on to the middle of the dancefloor and do an Irish dancing performance. The punters loved it, and so did I.

Caroline didn't touch a drop and said to me, "two is the limit, Martha". Her eagle eyes were on me, and I knew it. Caroline wasn't a fan of the drink; she would maybe have had one on a rare occasion at that stage. She developed a brilliant strategy; she would thank the punters who bought her a drink, have lemonade with a dash of lime and keep the rest.

The shaking eased as soon as I downed the first G and T. After the second, it stopped altogether. Caroline's two sisters, Helen and May, had started in there and Helen worked the room with the trays of pints like me. Wee May came with us one night to see if we could get her a job, and the pub landlord told her to go away because she was only a child. We told him she couldn't because she wasn't allowed to walk home on her own. Working in a pub full of drunk men was fine but walking home alone was off limits. God Love her, she got the job, but she stood on a crate because the bar was so high.

I didn't want a repeat of the last time Wee Caroline had to drag me home, so I stuck to the two-drink limit. To be honest, I don't believe the staff suspected for one second that I wasn't eighteen.

Mammy was none the wiser whenever I went home. I liked reading my first aid books at night, but the electrical sockets in my room stopped working. Mammy got the caretaker of the flats to come up and see if he could fix it, but he couldn't. The light in my room and Daddy's room stopped working for whatever reason. The Rossville flats were like a charming man. Lovely for the first two years, then the cracks begin to appear.

***

In April that year, things got really bad. The RUC and the B-Men stormed into the house of Sammy Devenney and severely beat him with their batons. I was utterly horrified. I saw an interview with his daughter and son on the television, and she described how the RUC went into the house and battered everybody in sight, including the children.

There is a poignant part of this interview where she rolled up her skirt slightly to show the bruising on her legs. They weren't superficial bruises; they were deep and boldly coloured. Even on a black and white television, I could see that she had been hit an awful smack in the legs. I wept when I saw the bruises on that girl's legs and the wee boy's back.

The people were up in arms, and the rioting became more frequent again. In the flats, we could see and hear everything. Sleeping at night or even taking a nap during the day was becoming impossible.

The noise was something I hadn't noticed when everyone was happy. I didn't mind the joy around the flats when we moved in; the noise when the rumbling resentment started to grow, I did mind. It was getting tense; domestic arguments were picking up inside the flats. Almost daily, I could hear in the flats around me,

"Where the fuck were you?"

"I found a white handkerchief in your coat pocket when I washed it."

"You better not be out throwing stones!"

"I will skelp your arse if I hear you are down at that barricade!" Etc.

The demonstrations and marches were still banned, and I overheard people wondering if the Apprentice Boys' parade would still be allowed to go ahead in August. I thought this myself too. Indeed if one section of public demonstrations were banned, the other would be prohibited too. Perfectly logical in my mind.

The rioting swelled through July, and counting the number of rioters became impossible. The RUC were mercilessly pelted, and there were swarms of first aiders. It was becoming more common to see members of the unit stretcher people off the street to the ambulance or even people's houses before the first aid posts were established.

Even though the RUC were the enemies of many of my neighbours, I was an indoctrinated First Aider and often flinched when bricks hit them. I didn't want anybody to get hurt. When sitting in the corner of block one of the flats, facing down William Street in a heavy riot, an RUC officer was smacked on the head with a brick. When he jarred and fell on his back, I could see the trickle of blood going out onto the road and Caroline, and I ran out. We could hear the cheers of the rioters, and when we ran out, there weren't as many bricks flying our way. I had a sterilised pad in my hand and gave it to one of the other officers, who nodded and said, "thank you, we will take him from here," and carried him offsides.

"Martha, them rioters know us; what if we get abused for helping the police?"

"Jesus, I never thought of that!" I trembled.

It was just my instinct, we swore an oath to serve everybody, and I was sticking to it. In my head, that was somebody's brother or son. I wasn't reared with any sectarian sentiment whatsoever. Sure, Protestants carried my Daddy's coffin before he was buried.

We were afraid to walk back down Rossville Street; what if we got pelted? We had run out and helped a policeman in plain view of everybody at the barricade. I walked past, and I saw the big brown eyes above Hugh's concealed face. Once again, making his shh gesture. I was dying to go over and tell him to be careful, but I just wanted to get back home.

Not a single word was said to us. Nothing. There was an understanding among them; the first aiders had to help and serve everybody. The rioters knew that it would have been extremely frowned upon if they pelted Order of Malta Volunteers. Did we get some dirty looks? Of course, we did, but nobody called us anything or criticised us.

That was the power of the white coat.

The adrenaline was flowing, and I was shaking again. I must have chain-smoked a full packet of cigarettes and remember thinking it was a shame that it would be a few days until I was back at work again. At fifteen, I wouldn't have been given Valium or been able to buy a drink for myself, so I had to make do with the hot chocolate Mammy made me.

She was so proud of me. When I came in from a night on the riot lines, she made me a hot chocolate with hot milk instead of hot water. It was a mighty treat; it tasted lovely but didn't take the edge off too much.

***

There was a massive outpouring of grief when word began to circulate that Sammy Devenney had passed away in July 1969. I remembered the wee girl from the television, and I knew first-hand that losing your Daddy is like a dagger through the heart. I didn't often go into Daddy's room, but I did the day I heard Mr Devenney died.

I sat cross-legged in the cold room and said aloud, "Daddy, I'm scared things will get worse." The leather suitcase I have now sat in that room, and I looked over at it. I didn't want to open it. Mammy had put his clothes in the wardrobe, and I started smelling them for some reason. I tried to get Daddy's smell, but by that stage, it was gone.

Derek came into the room and sat with me. "I miss him too sometimes, Martha, I was thinking about Daddy too since I heard." Derek was always immaculately groomed and had the best style of any man in this town. He broke many women's hearts when it became widely known that he batted for the other team.

We hugged each other in the room, and I felt reassured. As people, Derek and I are a million miles apart, but he was always there for me. Derek was eighteen the month before and had met "a wee friend," as Mammy called him. Of course, this was Derek's partner Liam.

Mammy is incredibly religious. Although, she never disapproved of Liam in the slightest. "As long as he is happy, and Liam looks after him like your Daddy looked after me," she used to say.

Of course, Derek lied his arse off and insisted it was his "friend", but I used to tease him about it. I am allowed to; I'm his sister!

They didn't get any homophobic abuse from anyone else either. One night in town, after the pubs closed, somebody called them names and started throwing bottles at them. Unbeknownst to the hooligan, Liam was a boxer and broke the boy's jaw. That was the end of any homophobic abuse toward them.

The funeral of Sammy Devenney was a massive affair. Thousands turned out, and the city was united in grief: a horrific murder, no other word for it. I couldn't look at it. I stayed in my room because it made me think of Daddy too much. My heart ached for them; it was horrendous. Indeed, I assumed that the Apprentice Boys march in a few weeks would be cancelled after this turnout.

TEN

KANDY KORNER

Guess what? The fucking march wasn't cancelled. It was unbelievable. We all knew things would change when we were told the march was going ahead. The unit's leadership needed to devise a strategy to cope with what was coming as best they could.

Leo Day partnered with the Derry Red Cross in the summer of 1969. The Order of Malta is the Irish Association of The Order of Malta, The Irish Red Cross was headquartered just a handful of miles away at Fowler Hall in Fahan, and the Derry Red Cross was British Red Cross. Despite this, there was collaboration, and all entities were politically neutral.

The Red Cross in Derry was under the leadership of Mrs Aileen McCorkell. You may have read her name as 'Eh-leen' but quickly stated that her name was pronounced 'Eileen'. Her husband was Colonel Michael McCorkell of the Territorial Army, who came from the old Derry shipping family. We all called her Mrs McCorkell; now and again, she said, "you may refer to me as Aileen, as my mother-in-law is Mrs McCorkell." We still called her Mrs McCorkell, and she was very interesting.

She was born in India, where her father served as an Army Doctor. In 1924, she returned to the family home in Co Louth and later was sent to boarding school in England. After a time in Paris, she came home, and when war broke out, she joined the Womens' Auxiliary Air Force (WAAF). She moved to Derry after her marriage in 1950. Her accent was quite hard to place, and she never had to shout at anybody. She was the same as Leo Day in that they were reasonably soft-spoken, yet we could still hear them in the middle of a riot.

Mrs McCorkell was instrumental in establishing Glenbrook Day Centre in Derry and was always driven to serve the sick and disabled in our communities. She started the meals on wheels service locally, which was the first of its kind here. She was a key person of influence in her own right and used this influence to make Derry a better place. I always told my children to leave the world in a better state than what they found it. Mrs McCorkell dedicated her life to that.

One time, I went to Mrs McCorkell's home. She lived in a big stately home in Ballyarnett on the outskirts of Derry with Colonel McCorkell and her children. She kept horses and hosted Show-jumping events. Her home was stately and stunning, and I was in awe of it. They had rooms I didn't even know existed, like a drawing room and a salon. To me, a drawing-room was where crayons were kept, and a salon was where Mammy and I got our hair done.

We petted the horses and ate the best cake in the world. Mrs McCorkell's housekeeper was an incredible cook and baker. When the wee cakes came out, I dived into them. I made a promise not to leave that house with a single cake. I had one in each hand, two in my kitbag, and one in my mouth as I left. That house would go on to facilitate secret talks between the IRA and the British Government in the summer of 1972.

***

We had a nice meal in the City Hotel on Foyle Street for my birthday, and I noticed many journalists there. Big cameras were on the table and were there to document and witness the faecal matter hitting the fan. I barely touched my steak and Guinness pie.

"You alright wee love?" Mammy asked me, and she held my hand on the table.

"Bad things are coming, aren't they?" I said to her.

"Yes, they are. We will get through it, wee love. Your Daddy can see us, and he will look after us."

I didn't take any consolation in this whatsoever. The RUC beats were increasing around the city centre, and it was clear that preparations were underway. The Twelfth that year was on a Tuesday, so at least we could go to our jobs in the Irish Kitchen the weekend prior.

On Friday, it was quiet, and I was desperate for a punter to say, "and a drink for yourself love". Nobody did, and I barely slept on Friday night. I tossed and turned all night, and my nerves were nipping. It was so tense I could have screamed. I was wide awake, and I remember feeling so frustrated.

The Saturday night was busy, and a bunch of journalists had ventured over from the City Hotel. Some of them I recognised from my meal there two nights earlier, and they were all swapping stories.

Nobody else seemed to be worried; I was the only one. Wee Caroline was gliding around the bar, Helen was the same, May stood on her crate, the Ferry girls did their Irish dancing, the punters were laughing, and I was shaking like a shitting greyhound.

I didn't care; I had more than the two-drink limit that night. I was disgusted at how the other girls I was having a drink with were so carefree, and there I was, drinking and overthinking. I had a gin and tonic or two, but then I asked for a large straight gin. One gulp and gone.

We didn't stay for a late night that night, so wee Caroline and I got our ten shillings and walked home.

"Martha, you need to be careful, you can't be drinking like that at work," Caroline said.

"Awk wise up, I will be grand. Sure, they give wains whiskey for a toothache, and it's good for the nerves. You're lucky; sure, you can disappear down to Newton to your Granny!" I barked back at her. I felt the drink, but mastered the art of walking in a straight line when I was half-cut.

The RUC passed us, but the tension was removed for me. It was like the events of the past six months had disappeared entirely in my mind. I went home that night, bid goodnight to Mammy, and slept like a lamb.

***

When I woke up, the tension was back again. At mass, Father Daly called for calm and restraint for Tuesday. I remember sitting there on the wooden pew in St. Eugene's Cathedral thinking, that won't happen, not in a month of Presbyterian Sabbaths. I sighed out loud, and Mammy did her disapproving frown at me. I folded my arms and looked away from her.

As Mammy and I sat having our lunch on the Monday afternoon of the 11th of August, our phone rang. Mammy left the kitchen to get to the phone in the sitting room, and all I heard her saying was "yes Dr MacDermott, that's quite alright, I will tell her now, cheerio." Mammy came in and told me that there was a special meeting called to discuss first aid cover for the following day, and that I should go down and tell Caroline and anyone else nearby.

Not all the unit members had a telephone at home, and it was then that Mammy told me that she had given her permission for me to be on duty the following day. For everyone under the age of eighteen, we had to have our parent's consent to go on first aid duty the following day. When I went down for wee Caroline, we got ready for the meeting and Mrs McLaughlin called Dr MacDermott from our telephone to give her consent also, but if the disturbances were to stretch into additional days that Caroline wouldn't be there.

Wee Caroline was lucky; she had an escape pod, "Martha, Mammy and Daddy said we are getting out of there if it all kicks off. My Granny lives in Newtoncunningham and the first sign of bother we're away!" It wasn't surprising; a couple of her siblings were relatively young. Although I was a bit miffed, I understood and didn't pick a fight with her as we walked toward Ozanam House that evening to go to the briefing.

Men were walking around with white armbands on their arms as we walked across Joseph Place to climb the steps up to Fahan Street and over to our meeting. They waved to us, and we waved back. One man summoned us over, an older man.

"Girls, how many first aid posts are going up?" he asked.

"I'm not sure, two maybe," Caroline replied to him. We didn't know for certain how many there were going to be, but there were some whispers here and there in the previous days.

"Just two?" the older man's eyebrows climbing up his forehead, "I think we might need more than two. There is going to be murder on Tuesday. There was a last-ditch effort to cancel the Apprentice Boys' march, and it failed."

The white armband men were the Derry Citizens Defense Association (DCDA). Almost like police or stewards for the Bogside. The people of the Bogside started to refuse the RUC as their police force, which was understandable given that they had battered a man to death. I didn't notice the DCDA before then because they had only formed a couple of weeks prior, but his concern that only two first aid posts were being set up was of grave concern to me. It confirmed my worst fears.

The meeting was called to order when we were all present, and we were told that three first aid posts would be established. Kandy Korner, a sweet shop at the top of Westland Street would be the main post. A picture framing shop is there now, just beside the New Road on the way up to Creggan. The second post would be West End Hall near the foot of Westland Street, and a third would be established near Bishop Street, near the route of The Apprentice Boy's Parade, and a potential flashpoint for violence.

The girls and ladies would be mainly inside the first-aid posts; the gents would be distributed among the first aid posts at West End Hall and Kandy Korner, with stretchers to carry people off the street and for everyone to remain in cover as much as possible when out on the street. Kandy Korner would act as the main headquarters, and we could have telephone contact between the other two posts. The ambulance would have to be stationed in a central position to access the walls or the bottom of Waterloo Street, so it was decided it would sit near Fahan Street so Hugh Deehan or Jim McDaid could either drive it down the hill of Waterloo Street or swing it round to go back into the Bogside behind.

Dr MacDermott clearly explained what was expected of us during any trouble, stressing that all injured were to get the same treatment regardless of who they were, what they were, or how they received the injuries. Dr Cosgrove talked about the type of injuries to be expected, dealing with burns, haemorrhages, unconsciousness, and treatment.

There was a sense of tension in the room, I looked around the unit, and there was a sense of fear on their faces. We were mostly children! Most of us were under eighteen, and my sixteenth birthday had just passed, five days before the Apprentice Boys' march. Although, it was pretty exciting at the same time. I was too immature to understand the gravity of what would occur the following day. Our final instruction was to report to Kandy Korner at ten the next morning to get our final postings and fill up our kit bags.

***

When we returned to block two, I bid wee Caroline goodnight and went upstairs. When I reached my balcony, I decided to keep walking around because I wanted to walk off the nervous energy. I crossed the walkway into block one and heard a commotion from the top of the flats. It wasn't a fearful commotion but an excited commotion. I heard a voice say, "this is going to be a cracker! Gone look at this; everyone will love this."

What on Earth would anybody be excited about with it being the Twelfth the next day? Nosy Martha wanted to know what was going on.

It was just after nine at night, and of course, the lift was out of order, so I walked up the steps at the side of block one. I got to the very top, and boys were running wires out of a flat on that row. At the side of the lift shaft, another door was open. So, I went through, up the enclosed stone steps and opened the door at the top. I was on the roof of block one, and a big blast of cold air hit me. I had never been on the roof of the flats, and the caretaker recently warned every household that no children were allowed up onto the roof. I am the type of person who, if somebody says I can't do something, makes me want to do it more.

The roof of the Rossville Flats is now as mythical as Atlantis or Heaven itself, but it was just an aerial and flat ground. The view was nice, but one would get the same view from standing on the Derry Walls. It was freezing, and curiously, there were no railings at the top. If you got too close to the edge and lost your footing, you would splat onto Rossville Street.

What was different this time was that a boy was messing around with one of the aerials. I was dying to know what was so exciting. I don't think he noticed me coming onto the roof as he didn't look in my direction when I arrived. He was wearing a beanie hat and a black denim jacket.

"Hi!"

When the boy looked around, he was spooked! He let out a bit of a gasp.

"What are ye doing?" I asked him as I lit a cigarette.

"We got an old radio box from Belfast and want to set up a radio station to let everybody know what's going on. We want it set up on time for the parade tomorrow. We tried running the wire out the sitting room window of the flat below, but it broke."

I don't remember asking his name, and if I did, I either didn't take it in at the time, or I can't remember it now. He was trying to adjust this other aerial for the radio, and I warned him not to be messing up the television because Mammy would go mad.

"Don't worry, this is just a radio transmitter; it won't steal the television waves!" he chuckled at me. I was still wearing my white Malta coat, so that probably put him at ease. If I had been in my civvies, he probably would have shat himself.

"That's class!" I got all excited, "are you going to play music and all? See if you are, can you please play Sweet Caroline for my friend Caroline, she is in 27 Garvan Place in block two, she absolutely loves that song, so she does, and she fancies Neil Diamond."

"Not sure we will be able to play music now!" But he laughed again. "We were set up in Wellington Street, and we moved it here, a bit safer in case the house got raided and the radio taken." He seemed to know who I was, and the Wellington Street connection was made. His name has left me entirely; with each passing day, little details leave my mind, and it scares me.

Even witnessing the very beginning of Radio Free Derry that night, I didn't ask if I could be a guest. I had to find a way to have a go at wee Caroline.

I'm a wee witch!

Part Three

"No Fears!
No Tears!
You pay the piper
You call the tune."

Eamon Friel

ELEVEN

BATTLE OF THE BOGSIDE

The Twelfth finally came, and Martha's shakes were back. Mammy made a fry that morning, and I think I had a mouthful of beans and half a slice of toast. I could barely eat a bite, and before I left for Kandy Korner, I sat in Daddy's room for a while. I didn't have to say or do anything; I just felt him and knew he was near me. Mammy gave me a big hug before I left, and as I walked up Westland Street with wee Caroline, I realised that Mammy didn't hug me very often.

Some of us were unfolding camp beds inside, and a sign was put outside – FIRST AID POST – in big green letters with a red cross drawing. It was a very basic post, there was no running water inside it, and we would have to rely on nearby houses for running water and toilet facilities. There was a large treatment room with four beds, a nurse's station, and another storeroom with a pile of first aid supplies.

After doing our bit in Kandy Korner, the nurse in charge of the post, Ursula McDaid, sent wee Caroline and me down to West End Hall to see if we could do anything. When we got down there, we agreed that we would be attached to this post but go up to Kandy Korner to relieve other volunteers if needed. Both posts had a storeroom where we were told to retreat and restock supplies if required. "Jesus, what are you all expecting here?" I said; they all stared back at me without uttering a word. I was sent back to the storeroom to fill the kit bags with bandages and other supplies. They were kept as spares if we lost our bags or whatever was in our bags ran out.

What caught me was the desire to be prepared and serve the injured. I was terrified and would have given anything to be as courageous as them. Their determination helped me immensely. For years since, the volunteers from that time would tell me that they didn't smell fear off me whatsoever, and they didn't. It was because of them. My unit made me feel safe. I can't imagine going through what I did without them at my side.

Wee Caroline isn't one to get scared, but she showed me a holy medal that her Mammy gave her to keep in her pocket. She wasn't herself one bit. Some of the more experienced volunteers decided to go down to Waterloo Street, in the event we were needed on the street, and wee Caroline and I agreed to go with them. We paced over to the foot of Waterloo Street and stood around. We could hear the thumps and bangs of the Orange drums in the distance and the screech of their flutes. The first aiders stood in a clump, some of us in white coats and the boys in grey uniforms. Marie was there and told us to stay in one of the side laneways along William Street, and to flee back to West End Hall if the situation got out of hand. Marie ensured my kitbag had everything I needed before she disappeared into the crowd.

I had my back against the wall and crouched down; I rested my elbows on my knees and barely looked in the direction of wee Caroline. There was an eery atmosphere, and the crowds began to gather at the bottom of William Street. These were the Bogside residents, making sure that the Orange march didn't venture too close to the periphery of the Bogside itself.

"Look, there are the Red Cross girls!" one of the crowd shouted as he walked past us. People called us the Red Cross, even though we technically weren't. It was starting to become a custom among the rioters to take a note and circulate where we were standing at any one time. We were well covered and in a good place if someone was carried into us.

One of my nervous movements was constantly adjusting my linen kitbag over my shoulder. I did it constantly and was pacing up and down in the laneway. The drums and flutes got louder as they approached Waterloo place. I was terrified, all these men marching and banging their drums. The tension was unbearable, and the RUC started swarming in front of the Bogsiders to push them back from the metal crowd control barriers.

It wasn't working. The roars of the disenfranchised nationalist crowd were drowning out the collage of banging drums, flutes, and the police whistles as the Apprentice Boys passed through Waterloo Place. The foundations of all the buildings started to shake when the first hail of rocks flew and crashed onto and around the RUC.

The RUC had piddly little helmets on and shields as large as a dustbin lid and no more. Wee Caroline and I were well out of the way but could see the riot progressing out the gap of the alleyway in which we were standing.

It was well over an hour, the police were getting pelted, and petrol bombs started to be thrown. When I saw the lightning flash of the shattering petrol bombs, I looked inside my bag to see if I had an ointment to treat burns. Three miniature tubes were packed; that was it.

"Alright, lads, move forward!" one of the RUC leaders shouted, and they pressed forward to baton charge the rioters.

"Come on, Martha, we need to move from here."

Just as I peeked my head around the corner of the lane, a brick shattered just above my head, and I screamed! Far too close for comfort. If I were a leggy six-footer, I would have been sparked out.

The RUC had done their baton charge to the left of us, and we stayed in the laneway longer. The RUC were now on William Street, throwing the stones back at the rioters! We were stuck right between the RUC and the rioters at this stage. I peeked out again and saw what looked to be a television camera interviewing a news anchor to my left behind the RUC lines.

I was dismayed; the police, the keepers of law and order within communities, had lowered themselves to throwing the stones back at them. Caroline and I just stared, it was probably one of the most surreal things happening in the world, and there we were watching it.

"Jesus love, we're trapped! Look! The RUC are starting to charge forward," I shrieked behind me to wee Caroline.

"Go Martha, go now! Quick, we need to get back to West End Hall," wee Caroline shoved me out to the middle of the riot, and we sprinted down the right-hand footpath of William Street. We ran out toward the rioters, not because we were taking their side, we were impartial. But it was closer to where we lived, just in case we got too frightened and decided to go home.

Luckily, wee Caroline and I were like nimble lemmings with our white coats and kit bags, leaving cover. The bricks and petrol bombs flew over our heads, and the returned bricks cracked around our feet. We made a sharp right while we were running and crouched down and stayed in cover until the roar of the armoured police vehicles shot up William Street toward Rossville Street.

When the police charged up William Street, one of the rioters bellowed out,

"Stand your fucking ground boys! They don't have jails big enough for all of us!"

The crowd erupted, and the rebellion was underway. The rioting crowd swelled, and pelted, swelled, and pelted. The police had no armour other than their shields. The RUC vehicle hurtled past us and screeched to the left to go down toward the flats.

"Jesus Caroline, they will burn our homes down, let's go through Chamberlain Street; come on!"

We took off sprinting again, and we stopped dead in Chamberlain Street when two wee lads had been struck with the bricks. One of them was about twelve and crying his eyes out; I went into softie Martha mode and was able to tell him he didn't have a concussion. He was just in shock, bleeding, and needed home to his Mammy.

Wee Caroline's casualty was a bit more severe; the brick had hit this boy's face and knocked some of his teeth through his tongue. He couldn't even talk, and wee Caroline was shouting, "he has to get to Casualty, nothing else will do!" two boys in our unit came out of nowhere and took him away toward the ambulance; I can't remember who though.

At the end of Chamberlain Street was the carpark to the rear of the Rossville Flats. We ran through, and as we peeked through the gaps in the houses, out onto Rossville Street itself, anarchy had descended upon us. Hundreds of men and women of all ages had taken to the streets to banish the RUC from the Bogside.

I had a full view of the violence from my position in the Rossville Flats car park. From across the street, two other white coats were running down the street with the stretcher, and I could swear a brick hit one of them on the shoulder. They didn't stop; they just kept going.

I moved to the side of block one and took cover beside the stairwell. Wee Caroline and I had become separated, and I assume she ran off to help someone. It was like watching the apocalypse; watching your worst fears unfold in front of you is horrific. What made it worse for me was the delight from some of the crowd.

The rebellion had come, but I learned on the first day of what became known as the Battle of The Bogside that those who love and talk about revolution and resistance don't have to pick up the pieces themselves. I was part of the team that did. We had swarmed the place, ducking in and out of cover to drag wee boys to cover to treat them. I was running up and down to West End Hall with some of the injured wee boys needing sutures, especially ones who kept bleeding through the bandages I was putting on.

Behind the RUC were the Protestant rioters who were bolstering them. After the police jeeps had smashed through the barricade and landed on Rossville Street, we could see them smashing windows and hurling bricks at nearby houses. It was a deeply confusing sight for me. "Why are the police allowing the Protestant rioters to break windows and throw bricks toward us? How can a civilised police force allow this to happen?

***

Then the rain came on. Not the lovely rain that is the water of life and helps the plants to grow. The searing hot rain exploded when it hit the ground and wisped flames all around. It started as a trickle and graduated to full-blown showers of burning rain, as youths began to hurl petrol bombs at the RUC from the roof of the flats.

Without thinking, I ran up the stairwell, and nobody stopped me because I was a first aider. The stairwell to the top of the flats was well guarded, but I was quickly recognised because I lived there. There were about fifty people up there and some crates of petrol bombs and rocks to throw down. I knew many faces, some others I didn't, but some of the wee boys had burned themselves with the petrol bombs. The wicks were too long and burning their hands and necks, so I was handy to have about the place. Although ironic to say, I felt safe up there because I knew I wouldn't be hit by a petrol bomb or split open by a stone.

Before long, a group of young men came up the stairwell with a Tricolour and an American Flag! One of the men up there, who I think was one of the Young Socialists, echoed my thoughts exactly when he asked, "why the fuck have you got the Stars and Stripes up here for?"

A well-spoken young man replied, "the television cameras are everywhere; if the RUC and Paisleyites are seen as attacking the flag of America, it will be a great result for us in terms of propaganda value."

I'm no military strategist or PR expert, but in my head, I thought this was a fantastic idea. Although the Young Socialists weren't too keen, they didn't want to defend the Bogside under the flag of an imperialist nation that was killing in Vietnam. So, the American Flag was taken down as quickly as it went up. After a while, I went back down to Rossville Street.

I stayed in cover at the rear of block one just inside the flats carpark, and Bernadette Devlin was telling the people how to strengthen the barricade to prevent the RUC from being able to bulldoze through it and on towards the flats. Bernadette was our MP and only twenty-one or twenty-two at the time.

One of the more serious injuries was Johnny White who was standing near the stairwell of block one when an unlit petrol bomb fell off the roof and landed on his head. It split his face wide open, and he was ushered away to be treated. Johnny was a regular sight around the flats and the entire area at the time. He gave talks and hosted meetings about Socialist Republicanism and was one of the founder members of the Derry Citizens Defence Committee.

As the boys were coming round the corner, I was cutting off bandages, and wrapping them around their bleeding heads. The RUC were still throwing the bricks back toward them, like a game of tennis. I stepped out of cover and saw some more of the Knights of Malta dragging people into cover or carrying injured people on stretchers. I couldn't watch, as I couldn't cope if a brick had hit one of them.

The dusk started to descend and a lovely lady, who was one of my neighbours, came down to where I was standing and gave me a cup of tea and a ham sandwich. I gulped both, and to this day, it was the nicest cup of tea I ever had. I made sure to say,

"Can you go to 73 Mura Place, please, and tell my Mammy that I am okay, Martha is okay."

"Aye, not to worry, I will go up right away. You be careful now."

Just as I handed the piece dish and cup back to her, a casualty was brought round to me. He wasn't wearing a mask over his face and seemed like quite a well-to-do chap. He was groaning, clutching his right arm with the left, and his face was contorted in pain.

"Hi love, this boy fell off the canopy above the shops," his comrade told me before running off to the riot.

Textbook fractured collarbone. So out came the triangular bandage, and some music started to play from the flats, "Somebody to Love" by Jefferson Starship, or Jefferson Airplane, or whatever they are called this week.

There's me singing, "Wouldn't you love somebody to love? You better find somebody to love." The man I was putting a sling on didn't know where to look! Multitasking Martha, being able to sing, swing the hips, and sling up a broken collarbone at the same time.

"There ye are now! That's you out of commission now" I smirked at him when he stood up.

"Aye, right! God gave us two arms for a reason hi. That's the gammy arm that's away; I still have the good left," he said smugly before picking up a brick beside our feet, and off he went again.

Various people were coming and going, and my supplies were running low. I must have gone through three rolls of bandages in a few hours. The ambulance was going intermittently, and wee Caroline came back to join me. She had been up and down to Kandy Korner, and was telling me of some serious injuries, and that none of them wanted to go to Altnagelvin Hospital, no matter how persuasive they tried to be. More doctors and nurses were going to the posts, which were jam-packed by the evening.

I got more supplies, and steadily these were running out too. The ferocity of the riots meant that blood injuries were happening every few minutes, and when more petrol bombs were made, there were more burns. The tubes of ointment were small, and one tub of burn ointment would only serve one or two people. The treatment given at the first aid posts went beyond the limits of first aid, and although I was supposed to stay inside a first aid post, I was mostly outside helping to bring people to the post with a group of other volunteers.

We went in pairs to restock our kit bags at West End Hall and bring another spare so we wouldn't have to keep running back. On the beds in the first-aid post, there were four lying in the beds and another four lying on the floor beside them. It stunk of petrol in there, and when I came out of the safe spot of the first-aid post, I saw a group of women sitting on the ground in Meenan Square, adjacent to the pop-up first aid centre.

Crates with bottles, giant bags of flour and sugar, jars of petrol, and long lengths of fabric for the wicks. An outdoor petrol bomb factory, with different small groups doing their tasks. Some measuring flour, others poured petrol into the bottles, and others stacked the made petrol bombs near the corner for the men to lift and take to the front line.

The power women of the Bogside worked in shirt factories and had extensive knowledge of assembly-line production. From making shirts, curtains, knickers, and now petrol bombs. I was mesmerised by it; they were a joy to watch even though I couldn't help but wince because the thought of anybody getting hurt troubled me.

The whole community were involved. Older people brought out meals, tea, biscuits, and cakes, and everyone had their role. Even if it was as minor as letting one of the rioters go in for a lie down for ten minutes on their sofa, everyone played their part.

I was only sixteen, and the Corporals and Sergeants in the Order of Malta would stay out to cover the rioting at night. Wee Caroline, I, and a couple of the younger volunteers were ordered to come back in the morning at seven to relieve the night crew of first aiders.

Darkness brings a new dimension to rioting, the streetlights were smashed, and I'm not sure if I would have been confident or experienced enough to put bandages on or treat people in the dark. The adrenaline high was immense; wee Caroline and I reached the alcove between blocks one and two of the flats,

"This is complete madness; what the hell is going on? What if they burn our houses down, Martha?"

I walked onto the footpath along Rossville Street and looked down the street toward the tiring RUC. I knew they were all the same cops there all day.

"Sure, the RUC can withdraw, they can pull out, we can't, we live here. There are more rioters than there are police. Sure, it will die down; it will all be over in the morning..."

Twelve

Day Two

Block one was to my left as I stood on my balcony, and the orange flickers flew off the roof. The little fiery dots would hurtle downward and collide with the ground, sending plumes of flames around the impact. It was impossible to count how many were on the roof, but I could see about twenty on the morning of the second day of the riots.

Nobody believes me when I say this, but I slept soundly on the first night of the Battle of The Bogside. I was rushed off my feet the day before, slinging, bandaging, gauzing, comforting, reassuring, restocking, and running up and down Rossville Street to West End Hall.

I jumped out of bed at six in the morning, took my freshly washed white coat from the airing cupboard, threw it on me, brushed my teeth, a swig of tea, and a wee kiss from Mammy; happy days. Mammy had slept like a lamb, too, after pacing around the flat all day worrying about me.

Some volunteers stayed in the first aid posts and on the streets until four o clock in the morning and went home for a few hours of sleep before going to their day jobs. Just past six in the morning, I hurtled down the stairwell to fetch wee Caroline to relieve the first aiders who kept the first aid post running through the first night of the riots. Mr and Mrs McLaughlin were at the front door, telling everyone to get out with their things.

Wee Caroline came outside, "we are away to my Granny's in Newton; it is too mad here. Mammy wants the boys to stay out of trouble, and me too! Gone, please don't be angry with me."

"Don't be worrying, wee love; if I had a spare Granny down south somewhere, we would be away too!" I won't lie; I felt jealous.

"Here, Martha, wear this so your big scraggly mop doesn't block your eyes when you are helping somebody," and she handed me a white hairband. One that I still have.

I said to her, "so you want me to go out into the riots dressed up as Billie Jean King, do ye aye?"

She was getting to escape the madness to the peace and quiet. I wouldn't have that luxury. We exchanged hugs and comical kisses on the cheek where we would say, "Mwah! Mwah" on each cheek. We bid our farewells, and down the steps I went.

There were more on the streets than yesterday, more rioters, and not enough RUC on the other side. Back then, the Bogside was like a vast construction site, with bricks lying everywhere. There wasn't a requirement to bring in quarry loads of bricks and rocks to throw at the RUC. Everything was just there!

I was fucking terrified. I would have to scuttle over to the West End Hall from the bottom of block two of the flats. To my right, past the end of the row of shops toward Rossville Street, hundreds of people had gathered; they were shouting up to the roof of block one and bringing crates of petrol bombs up the stairwell.

There was a radio documentary being made about the Battle of The Bogside a few years ago to mark the fortieth anniversary in 2009, and I didn't take part, but what was interesting was an observation of one of the rioters being interviewed. One of my strange habits is singing when I feel incredibly nervous.

"One of the first aiders was wearing a distinctive white hair-band, walked toward the first aid station at the bottom of Westland Street alone and sang, "sunshine, lollipops, and rainbows, everything that's wonderful is how I feel when we're together!"

I loved that song and sang it all the time. It was me who the interviewee was talking about! There is some science to singing and overcoming anxiety. My Frankie had an awful stammer as a child, and I used to take him to speech therapy. A big part of it was singing his words, which helped him overcome it.

Around midday, my eyes started welling up and stinging when I was inside the first aid post. I was helping someone who had burned his forearm trying to throw a badly made petrol bomb. It must be all the petrol fumes, dust, and whatever else. I took a spare piece of bandage out of my kit bag and held it to my eyes. It wasn't helping at all, and I got paranoid that the rest of the first aiders would think I was weak because I was crying. I wasn't alone; the hall descended into coughing fits, people rubbing their eyes, and the mortal screams of everyone inside and on the street were deafening. We didn't know what to do, and we decided to evacuate the West End Hall post and take everyone up to Kandy Korner after the Bogside became enveloped in the CS Gas cloud.

Shortly after I got to Kandy Korner, Dr MacDermott was constantly on the phone with the hospitals trying to get advice, resuscitation apparatus, and masks for those most seriously affected by the gas, particularly older or vulnerable people with breathing problems. The Hospital Authority were as good as a chocolate fireguard and told Dr MacDermott they were unable to help. However, we got some exciting visitors, one being an American journalist with some experience of gas warfare in

Vietnam. He suggested a Gas Treatment Post to be set up on Elmwood Road to relieve pressure on Kandy Korner after West End Hall was evacuated. Before I arrived, Mrs McCorkell had come to provide us with food and blankets, and went with our Sergeant Jim McDaid to evacuate some families from Linenhall Street. Disturbances were becoming rife in Rosemount, so another post was set up on Artisan Street. Although, after a few hours of being stuck in the middle of a riot zone, it was abandoned later in the day.

Three French girls and a Belgian girl also came in to visit us. They started to show us how to cope with the CS gas by making makeshift gas masks using sanitary towels and Bicarbonate of Soda. They told us they were involved in the Paris student riots throughout May of 1968 and were more helpful to us than our own local healthcare network. Some of us went off on a bizarre mission to buy every sanitary towel, Paddi Pad, and box of Bicarbonate of Soda that we could get our hands on. These gas masks were highly effective and gave us some much-needed relief. The demand was so high that Mr Day created an assembly line of his children to assist in manufacturing them.

What was worse was that CS tear gas hadn't been used before. It was never mentioned in our training, and there were rumours that the gas was poisonous. It was perfectly logical to feel that it was. Even the doctors, mainly Dr McClean and Dr MacDermott, were unsure how to treat people suffering from inhaled gas. The CS gas was fired from a big gun, and people were coming to the first aid post who had been hit in the face with the gas canisters. We didn't know what to do, as this was a completely new injury.

The first aid post was jam-packed and full of people. A couple of nurses, and student nurses, were putting stitches on people's heads. Fear was setting in among us that we would run out of supplies; luckily, some local pharmacies and shops donated first aid supplies to us as they were no good behind boarded-up shops. By the late afternoon of the second day, the doctors and nurses were suturing people with household needles and thread.

We were all quite shocked; one thing I can't stress enough is that we were mostly children. Most of the Knights of Malta of this period were between sixteen and twenty. It wouldn't have been the done thing to send first aiders under the age of eighteen into the middle of a riot zone, but what choice did we have? All the cover that was needed had to be provided. We all had to do our bit, and we did.

Looking back on that era, what makes me so proud of the Knights of Malta, was the quiet and determined attitude to help. We had sworn and devoted ourselves to helping all the sick and injured that needed us. Nobody did it for accolades or praise because people needed to do it. Marie had tried to teach Daddy sign language, and if I could make someone feel the way she made me feel, it was all worthwhile in my eyes.

One of the Lieutenants or Sergeants asked me to take a bunch of these gasmasks down to the high flats because word had come up that the RUC were firing CS canisters onto the roof. I filled up my kitbag, took the masks, and off I went. Caroline wasn't with me, so my wee shaky hands started going again. The devil was whispering in my ear as I walked back toward the high flats and into the riot zone, telling me that I would be back at work in the Irish Kitchen soon. The sweetest words were echoing in my ears, "and one for yourself, love".

"Boys, let her up the stairwell to the roof!" A group of men guarding the stairwell entrance stood aside, one saying, "what about ye, Martha?" A neighbour I didn't recognise with a handkerchief over his face.

"The bastards are firing gas up at the boys on the roof. Can you go up and see to them?" Just as I said that, more crates of petrol bombs arrived and were being ferried up the stairwell. I stood with my box of gas masks, and some of the men at the stairwell took some masks for the boys on the barricades. I voiced my concern that if someone became gravely injured, or overcome by the gas, I wouldn't be able to do much.

He roared back at me, "Don't worry, missus, all you do is shout down the stairwell, and we can carry anybody down that needs to be carried down. There's more Knights of Malta floating about with stretchers, and we can go and get them."

I entered the stairwell and climbed eighteen flights of stairs to get up to the door that had the nineteenth bonus stairwell onto the roof. The stairwell was full of people going up and down, and it took me about twenty minutes to get to the top. The boys on the roof had made quite an intricate communication system of shouting messages down the stairwell.

There were younger boys stationed at certain flights of stairs so messages could be passed from the roof down the stairwell to the bottom. When I was walking up, everyone stood aside and gave me priority to get to the top. In fairness, the roof of the Rossville Flats had no first aid cover and sending me up there was a wise decision.

I pushed open the door at the top, and about two dozen young boys were up there. Crates were lying everywhere, petrol bombs lined up against the roof's edge, ready to lift and launch below. As if the RUC were waiting for me to get up there, as soon as I walked out onto the middle of the roof, a wee boy was smacked in the arm by a gas canister.

"Oh Jesus! Are you alright?" I shouted out to him.

"Aye, I'm grand, don't be panicking," he said back to me, cool as a cucumber — pure adrenaline keeping him going. Although

I could see a nasty bruise brewing on his left bicep, he moved it freely so the canister didn't fracture his arm. I didn't see or speak to him again, but I knew that one would hurt in the morning.

I recognised most of the unmasked faces on the roof, the ones that were my neighbours doing their bit to protect our homes. There were more RUC there today, and it was a mild day. The RUC looked so small, like wee black ants running around the place, dodging being petrol bombed and the other debris flying their way. When people heard of the gasmasks, they were grateful for them, and gladly took them from me.

I saw Bernadette Devlin, with her bullhorn, at the barricade below, pointing and issuing instructions to the rioters. "Right folks! You boys here on the left aim at their heads; you boys aim at their feet." Then the rioters all cheered.

Beside one of the crates near the ledge on the roof was Hugh, wearing his pale blue jumper and black cords. When he saw me walking toward him, he put on his smiley face, lifted one of the petrol bombs and gestured to hand it to me, which brought about a laugh from the boys around him.

"Jesus Hugh, the only thing I can throw is a dirty look, mucker!" which got a wee bit of a cheer and a laugh from the other boys around us. The laughing quickly stopped when the thumps of the gas canisters were hitting the roof's ledge, the RUC timing their shots to when the boys were standing on the edge and preparing to throw.

Say what you want about the boys on the roof of the flats; they had hearts of gold. I knew plenty of them. They weren't violent scumbags hell-bent on destroying the area; these were my neighbours. I had the same fear as them: our homes and areas would be torched and destroyed by the people supposed to protect us. If you lived in the flats and were a wee boy over thirteen, you were on that roof; if you weren't evacuated like wee Caroline. It was purely the circumstances of the Battle of The Bogside.

The roof became frantic whenever a CS Canister landed up there; one of the wee boys had to grab it quickly to throw it back down whilst taking a second or two to ensure they were throwing it down toward the RUC and not their fellow defenders, on the ground. That gas was evil, and we were lucky to have masks, but we could still feel some of the effect.

I sat beside the stairwell door, and before long, Hugh came over and sat beside me.

"Jesus, this is madness, isn't it? Mind you, if my mother knew I was up here, she would go mad," he said, wiping sweat off his brow.

"What, she doesn't know you're up here?" I giggled back to him.

"No chance! There's me, Sarah, Bridget, Floyd and Bernard in the flat, and my Ma and Da. I'm my Ma's wee golden boy, you see, so I can't be up here. I have a reputation to keep down there you know."

"Is that right aye? I'm my Mammy's favourite too; there's only us two girls, me and Derek!"

Typical Derry, having banter and exchanging jokes at the worst of times. Even with the madness in front of us, petrol bombs flying off the roof, RUC-issued gas flying back up at us, Hugh and I chatted as we sat cross-legged on the roof.

"Where were you before you moved in here?" I asked him.

"We were in Pilot's Row, just down there." The Pilots Row houses aren't there anymore either, it is the location of a well-known local community centre now, but back then, it was a small street with two rows of houses facing each other.

"We were in Wellington Street, my Daddy died when I was nine, and Mammy wanted out."

"Aw, I'm sorry."

"You're lucky there's only you and Derek; there's eight of us. Our Olive and her husband Bernard live a couple of flats up from us too. Bernard Bonner is a gent; he comes out and plays football with the boys out the glass."

"Out the glass" was a slang term for the rear courtyard carpark of the flats.

"It's nice you are all that close, me and Derek are miles apart. His taste in music is shite too."

"It's like luxury here compared to Pilot's Row and Springtown Camp. We lived in a tiny hut for ages."

Back in the mid-1950s in Derry, families who struggled for housing ended up occupying and squatting in an old military camp, Springtown Camp. Old iron huts often had large families living in one room, and that's where Hugh was born. I have to say; if there were an award for living in the most famous Derry addresses, the Gilmours would win it hands down. Springtown Camp, Pilots Row, and the Rossville Flats.

The doors kept swinging open, and more crates of petrol bombs were coming up. The crowd on the roof swelled to about a hundred people. I was so busy talking to Hugh that a wee boy blinded by tear gas nearly staggered off the roof. Luckily he was Rugby tackled to the ground before he ventured over the edge.

There were no signs of the disorder becoming orderly soon, and from my vantage point on the roof of the flats, I could see that half of William Street was on fire at this point, as were some adjacent buildings on Rossville Street. It looked like half of Derry was on fire.

Hugh disappeared into the crowd, and I went back down the stairwell again. I just paused and looked at what was happening; it was surreal. I was so laser-focused on what was going on that it became this collage of madness. It was horrific, and I started to panic. I couldn't see any other first aiders; save for the odd time; I saw a couple running up and down Rossville Street with their gas masks on.

I returned to the first-aid post at West End Hall, which had reopened earlier in the day when more gas masks came, and the gas lifted slightly. By the evening of the second day, the RUC and the Paisleyites had gotten perilously close to St. Eugene's Cathedral but were driven back from it. More first-aid posts popped up, one at St. Mary's Boys Club and another in Creggan. The first aid posts were opening and closing more than Stormont, and keeping track of them all was challenging. The one near Bishop Street had closed early on the first day, Kandy Korner was intermittently opened and closed to allow the volunteers to go home and sleep, and West End Hall was in the middle of the gas cloud.

I was told that the Taoiseach, Jack Lynch, had come on the television to explain that field hospitals would be set up at the border by the Irish Army, and they wouldn't stand idly by while the police were attacking the Bogside. This brought massive relief to the first aiders because, after the first night, some volunteers thought that the first aid posts would be overrun, and we would be worthless if that happened. We were relieved; the Irish Army would help us, the battle would end, and we would all live happily ever after.

Thirteen

Day Three

The tension in the air lifted slightly, but the pungent gas didn't. Mammy, Derek, and I had tea and toast on the morning of the third day of the riots, and we were all relieved that the Irish Army would come in and protect us. Derek was coughing badly during the night, and even with all the windows closed in the flat, the gas still found its way in!

My bedroom light wasn't working, so I managed to master getting out of bed and throwing on my clothes without stubbing my toes on the bed or bumping into anything. There wasn't as much urgency to get to the first-aid post in my mind, the field hospitals were going up across the border, and the army would come any minute if they hadn't arrived while I was asleep the night before.

To cut a long story short, the Irish Army didn't come. The first aid post was jammed when I went down, first aid supplies were running low, the Knights of Malta Ambulance had sustained damage, and some other first aiders were wearing civvies with red first aid armbands because their uniforms were either soaked through with blood or singed by flames. Civilians were being used as stretcher-bearers to allow the first aiders to provide first aid, and local people were using their own cars and vans to take people to other first aid posts.

The Irish Army sat on their arses at the border, with bags full of needed medical equipment and medics that could help us. We kept saying to our injured, "the army medics will be here any minute, and they will bring us fresh supplies." But our faces must have told a different story, probably like when the Titanic Officers said to the frightened passengers, "don't worry, a rescue ship is coming," knowing fine well that they were fucked.

Some senior first aiders went down to Bridgend to try and get some supplies for us. The ambulance had been making trips to Letterkenny Hospital throughout the night and into the early hours of the past two days. The Irish Red Cross headquarters at Fowler Hall was visited, hoping to bring some supplies back. Sutures were gladly received since rioters, and other injured people, had been having their bleeding heads sewn together with rusted needles and thread.

Martha's shakes were back, so I had to keep myself busy. I was bandaging up heads, slinging up fractured collarbones and splinting wrists. Two volunteers had to stand at the door and even provide first aid on the outside pavement, only allowing the more severely injured to enter our treatment room. Some of our injured in West End Hall were sent up to Kandy Korner, but the ones we sent up were often sent back down again because their hands were just as full as ours.

Although blood injuries and fractures were expected, shock was a common thing we treated. Elderly people were terrified, and as a unit, we gave nearly as much spiritual aid as we did first aid. The gas rendered some unconscious. In three days, we went through around a year's supply of smelling salts.

Nowadays, the Battle of The Bogside is interesting from a historical point of view, but then we had no idea if we were in the middle of descending into a brutal civil war that would last forever. Today, people know how and when it ended. At the first-aid post on the third day, we hadn't the faintest idea how long these riots would continue.

I was utterly terrified, and now and again, I sneaked into the wee toilet inside the first aid post for a cry. What had I got myself into? "Daddy, make it all stop!" I said. "Daddy, make it all stop." Wee Caroline and her family had gone away, and the only comforting thing I had nearby was Mammy and my conversation with Hugh the day before.

We were struggling massively inside the first aid post. We were on the verge of collapse, yet I could still hear Bernadette rallying the rioters.

Everyone was so mature, graceful, committed, and dedicated to helping the distressed, and there I was crying alone in the wee toilet. I felt inadequate when people looked at me with wide staring eyes and blood gushing out of their heads. I wondered if they could sense I was afraid just like them, and I deduced that they did.

Given my recent death sentence, which prompted me to tell this story, I reflect a lot. I can't remember who exactly was there in the first-aid post with me; I can't remember everybody I treated, I can't even remember my grandchildren's names from time to time, but I can never forget how I felt.

I opened the door, and Marie was standing there. I was shocked to see her, and when she reached for my hand and said, "it's okay, Martha, we stick together, " I felt better. A bit of confidence returned to me, and I could get back into the treatment room again.

Word was circulating quickly that there was some RUC plot to burn St. Eugene's Cathedral down. I felt sick when I heard it, and the more experienced first aiders went toward the cathedral, and I stayed at the post. I felt utterly helpless; I wasn't that experienced and depended on the other Knight girls to help me.

The more severe injuries were taken away by Hugh Deehan in the ambulance, and luckily, we were getting through everybody in good time. We had developed a sound system of handing each other bandages, ointment, scissors, splints, smelling salts, water, gauzes, eye drops, and plasters (band-aids for the Americans).

To preserve the supplies, we made smaller bandages and dropped less into each eye. I even put two recently fainted people side by side to bring them around with the one capsule of smelling salts!

The capsule was a tiny glass bottle surrounded by cotton wool and metal gauze. When the gauze was squeezed, the acrid ammonia and alcohol mixture soaked into the cotton wool without the glass shards piercing through, and I placed it under their noses. Smelling salts are rank; every time I held them under somebody's nose, they jolted back to life.

Mr Day had started to enquire about more supplies, and we would all have to help if the rioting stretched into more days ahead. Throughout the morning of the 14th of August 1969, Leo Day was calling chemists in nearby towns and villages outside Derry to seek donations of first aid supplies. He also turned to other units to see if they could bring us anything they could.

The spire of our Cathedral is about two hundred feet high, and we looked out now and again to see if it was on fire. We couldn't bear to look; even though I wasn't very religious, I was thinking about Father Daly and hoping he was okay.

A young fella ran into the post and told us that two people had been shot and wounded in Great James' Street, about half a mile away. Hugh Deehan and the ambulance were gone. There wasn't a snowball's chance in Hell that a Northern Ireland Hospital Authority ambulance would come into the thick of the riot zone. Stretchers were needed, and two two-man stretcher parties left, leaving me and only three others at the first-aid post. When the stretcher parties returned an hour later, they told us that the RUC was on the verge of defeat. They had encountered two RUC officers lying in a heap in a doorway near Great James' Street. They approached to see if they needed help, but they ran on when they heard the cops snoring. The RUC had resorted to falling asleep in the street!

This gave us a bit of a chuckle, and a bit of relief, although it was unthinkable that the RUC would surrender to civilians. We drank a lot of tea that day and were making cups of tea for everyone we were treating, so much that it baffles me how we ran out of triangular bandages, but we didn't run out of tea bags or milk. In Derry, tea cures everything, the Opium of the masses.

A wee girl came in with a big cut on her leg, just above her knee, looking deep. She had fallen off her bicycle at the bottom of Westland Street, facing the first-aid post. She was only about ten, the most beautiful wee girl with a white and blue checked frock and matching ribbons in her hair.

"Miss! I fell off my bicycle when my tyre went over a brick on the road. Can I have a bandage for my leg?"

"Don't worry, wee love, but we have no bandages left. I will make you all better. Do you take milk and sugar?"

She nodded her wee head up and down, and I made her a cup of sugary tea and wiped her leg down with a rag until the bleeding stopped. After the cuppa, she was a new wee girl. Right as rain, she rang her bicycle bell as she slung her hook, and I waved her off at the front door.

I could hear more rapturous cheering from the porch than I had heard in the previous two days. When the cheers were heard inside the first-aid post, we all spilt out onto the street to see what was happening. Everyone rushed out with their injuries and cups of tea to see if the RUC had surrendered or if the Irish Army had come in to help us.

People ran over to us and shouted, "the army is here! We won!" Even some of the injured in our treatment room ran out toward Rossville Street. The rest of the group stayed behind to clean up the first aid post and wash all the cups, while I ran over to greet the army.

My name isn't wee Caroline, I didn't fancy men in uniforms, but with how scared I was in the previous two days, I was running toward the barrier and was planning on leaping over it and kissing them! We were on our knees treating people, and we had run out of supplies. Hospital care, first aid, and essential treatment weren't as advanced as now, so infections and sepsis were a genuine concern.

When I got over and heard the frightfully posh tally-ho English accents, I immediately thought, the British Army? This wasn't part of the script. The RUC were broken; they were like zombies walking around the inner portion of William Street beside Waterloo Place. It had turned from being a large-scale riot into a victory parade in only a matter of hours. The wee boys came down from the roof of the flats and sat on people's shoulders as they were paraded around the streets.

As a community, we were relieved, and the Army was coming to support us. Nearly forty-four years passed, and it is probably fashionable to say, "I was wary of the army from day one", but I was delighted to see them. So were many of us.

FOURTEEN

THE WHITE LINE

After three days of intense rioting, and the Army keeping some sort of peace, normality seemed to come back a bit. Wee Caroline came home, and Paddy Doherty ran Free Derry from his house in Westland Street. His home was the headquarters of the Derry Citizens Defence Association (DCDA), and he was the figure everyone turned to.

The barricades that had been erected along Rossville Street, and many other roads, remained. Free Derry was established, almost like a tiny, self-governed statelet within a country. We were like a poor man's Monaco. The Army didn't come in, they respected the barricades.

The atmosphere was fantastic, believe it or not, very little aggression was directed at the Army, and even when some jeers went their way, it bounced off them completely. It didn't bother them in the slightest. It was nice to have some peace about the place, the 12th to the 14th of August 1969 was surreal, and I still struggle to believe it happened. Not only that but also the fact there were no deaths.

Excuse the self-trumpet blowing, but over a thousand people were injured, and the Knights of Malta cared for and treated a considerable portion of them. We played a vital role, and I will always be proud of it. That first-aid post was mayhem, and we held it. We held out longer than the RUC. We were all volunteers with basic first aid training and ran a few pop-up first aid posts like battlefield hospitals.

Radio Free Derry worked wonders for morale, an excellent tool for everyone to stay informed of what was happening. If anybody or anything were needed at a barricade, the radio presenter would say things like, "Rossville Street barricade is weak, we need some volunteers. Tea and sandwiches are required for a barricade in Rosemount." Mammy brought down tea and sandwiches for the white armband patrolmen, and now and again, Derek went down to do his bit.

***

A couple of weeks later, the DCDA organised a Fleadh (music festival) for the Bogside. It was like a victory party. We couldn't believe it. We all went to it and danced in the street. It ran for three days, and there were donkey rides, toffee apples, music everywhere, and people having a fantastic time.

Was I doing first aid cover? Not a chance. I wouldn't miss this for the world. A concert, right where I lived. If I didn't explain it clearly so far, I love music. Music is my thing. In pub quizzes, I clean up during the music rounds.

The front of the flats was like a carnival; we all sang and danced to the fantastic music. Even The Dubliners performed! It was heaven for me. On a makeshift stage in front of the Bogside Inn, The Dubliners played for an entire day, no joke, a full day! The young people in the flats were out, and Hugh loved Irish music. In the breaks between songs, we chatted.

"When I saw all the soldiers earlier, it reminded me of something funny," Hugh told me. "When we lived in Pilot's Row when I was wee, I used to have this old British Army Helmet from the Second World War, and I used to play with it in the backyard. Now the army is in our backyard again!"

"Sure, it is all quietening down now; the craic is good, and where would you get it? There's nothing like this going on anywhere else."

"Exactly, and it's all down to me, so it is!"

Mouthy Martha came back, "is it aye?"

"Aye, it is! I didn't spend three days, and two nights on that roof for nothing, ye know? I got more of an education on the roof of the flats than I ever did at St. Patricks Boys or St. Brecans!"

"Aye, you probably spent more days up there than you ever did at school!"

"Aye, I went in the odd day. It wasn't that bad! Went in for my First Communion, Confirmation, Sports day, and some other days!"

"So, how did you stay up there all that time without your Mammy finding out or anybody else?"

"I just said I was going out, and when they asked, out where? I said, none of your business, and that was that."

I was keeping my composure as best I could, a couple of whiskeys were handed to me in the crowd earlier in the day, and I was only too glad to partake. I don't think he caught on. I was becoming good at hiding when I'd had a drink. I was always genuinely interested in what he had to say; I found him to be good company.

"Times like this, I wish Daddy was here," I blurted out. Around this time, I was starting to miss him, even though he had been dead for almost seven years. I bit my wee wobbly lip until it nearly bled; crying in public wasn't an option.

"I know how you feel; a few years back, a friend and I were swimming out in the River Faughan, and he drowned. I think about him often, and today. Anyway..." he deflected, "I don't think it will be too long before the Army starts trouble; some of the boys told me today that a couple of houses were raided already." More sceptical than I about the presence of the Army. I didn't press the issue about his wee friend that he lost.

"Sure, we have the barricades, we are penned in here like sheep, and we have our own police now. Them boys with the white armbands on. If your flat ever gets burgled, them boys will find them no bother sure."

The music started again, and so did the dancing, cheers, and laughter. I know Woodstock happened in 1969, but anybody that tries to tell me that Woodstock was better than the Liberation Fleadh, is seriously misinformed.

***

The following morning, I was awakened by a bang on our door. An electrical company was fixing broken electrics in the flats. My head was busting, and I had two pints of water quickly to bring me back to the land of the living. They told Mammy that we weren't the only ones having electrical problems and that they had to get a permit from the DCDA to enter Free Derry.

By mid-September, order was restored, the pubs closed on time, nobody was rioting, crime didn't happen, and Free Derry was probably the safest annexed statelet in the world. North Korea could have taken a leaf out of our book on how to keep the people reasonably happy. The army showed no real intention of coming in, and any time we left the barricade, they tipped their caps to the ladies.

James Callaghan, Home Secretary within the British Government, came to visit the Bogside. Crowds came to greet him, and, given that I wasn't interested in politics too much, I just watched the television and listened to records. I wasn't in the slightest bit interested.

Mammy was getting sick of the sight of the barricades as they made the streets look messy. I agreed with her; there wasn't anybody coming. We weren't going to be invaded. The army stood about twiddling their thumbs, smoking their fags, and then drinking in the city centre pubs at night before returning to the barracks.

Around the flats, people were debating about the barricades. Some Republican-leaning residents said they were desperately needed, and others thought they were an eye-sore. Paddy Doherty, Eamonn McCann, Sean Keenan, and the rest of the Free Derry leadership were getting complaints and to come up with a compromise.

Then the bright idea came, to remove all the barricades and replace them with a white line painted on the road where the barricades used to be. You didn't read that wrong; a white line was painted around the eight-hundred-and-eighty-eight-acre perimeter of Free Derry. Buckets and buckets of paint were brought in, and people painted our boundary line.

It was ridiculous. What astounded everybody was that the army respected it. Derek told me that the army searched Liam's car, and they had to tell Liam to move his vehicle forward slightly as the boot of his car was on the other side of the white line. It was a farce, and I found it hilarious that the army, with all their tanks and weaponry, was thwarted by this stupid fucking white line painted on the road.

The army seemed to be quite amused by the white line too. I was walking home from a first aid class on Clarendon Street and walked past a group of soldiers at the bottom of Rossville Street. I crossed the white line toward home, and one of the soldiers shouted, "Oi!"

I turned around, and he looked straight at me while his pals sniggered beside him. He theatrically pointed downward as he put the toe of his boot over the white line. He roared at me, "Go and tell them I was in Free Derry!" while the other squaddies laughed hysterically. I just gave him the middle finger and walked on.

***

We all met up at the thrupenny bits to go into the town. Wee Caroline, Peter, Charlie, Hugh, and I. We reached the end of William Street, and we crossed the impenetrable white line,

"What do ye think of the white line? Feel a bit safer now?" I couldn't help but ask Hugh.

"The army will be over the white lines in no time. I will paint white lines of my own one day, just you see." His claim of having white lines didn't make sense to me at the time, but it made sense later.

We went into the Phillips Music shop on Shipquay Street, and I had to get my records fix. I hadn't bought any in a while and needed to top up my collection. Wee Caroline's Mammy had a system, they were allowed to buy one record per week, and they had to decide among themselves who would get to choose the record.

Helen liked the same Bubblegum Pop as Derek, and it was her turn to pick the record. The tension in the record shop was unbearable; everyone stared at her. It was torture for them. When she picked up "(If Paradise Is) Half as Nice" by Amen

Corner, she looked at everyone's bewildered faces, sulked, and put it back down. Poor Helen!

I couldn't decide. The Rolling Stones had just made their big breakthrough, and I was never a fan. People who like The Stones only like them because they feel they must. Nobody will look back at the Rolling Stones like The Beatles and marvel at their musical genius. It won't happen.

"Dizzy" by Tommy Rowe, I loved it and picked it up. It was mine! I can't remember what other two records I bought that day.

A wee quip came from over my shoulder, "you would need to be dizzy to buy that!" Hugh always took any joke that was thrown in his path. He loved Irish music, and the Wolfe Tones were on their surge to popularity, especially in 1969 after what had happened. Even the music in the Irish Kitchen was becoming more rebel-orientated following the army's arrival.

We got the records, and Hugh stopped at a confectionery shop next door to the record shop and got a big bag of Dolly Mixtures. Martha likes her sweeties, so my wee grabby hands went toward the bag to try and take some of them from him. When my claw went over, he protected them like they were a bag of rare diamonds.

"Don't be lousy, share!" I said to him.

"Ye haven't a chance; they're for my Ma. Have to keep her sweet, you know?"

Jesus, my heart melted. I couldn't even argue with him because Daddy used to get me sweets, and I know he would never have given any of them away. A fifteen-year-old wee boy is getting sweets for his Mammy in the town. A beautiful quality; you wouldn't get that now. Even though I'm the forgetful one these days, my boys have forgotten my birthday several times. It wasn't a small bag either; it was quite a large bag.

"Here, where did you get the cash for all them sweeties?" I enquired.

"A boy Frankie Murphy from Creggan wanted to take our Sarah out last night; he wasn't taking her out for free, let me tell ye!"

We all burst out laughing; I had to ask, "Jesus Hugh, how much did you charge him to take your sister out?"

"Two bob. At least I know he's serious!" he replied proudly. Quite the businessman! "Sure, that will be nothing compared to what I will make working on cars; that's my plan." Sarah and Frankie are still married, so clearly the best two bob that he ever spent.

I said, "you're some craic; if you were able to charge him two bob, I could have changed Derek's boyfriend at least a fiver!"

One of the boys shouted to us, "ye hear that, Gilly? You undercharged him if she would have got a fiver!"

"Aye, I'm starting to think that now. Must hit Bernard Bonner for the money he owes me for marrying our Olive when we get back!"

"Gilly?" I asked him in shock, "the nickname committee must have been up all night thinking of that wan!"

Hugh stopped still in his tracks, "ye hear that, Charlie?"

"I did, Gilly, aye."

Hugh put his arm around me and walked with me, "I take his wee girl Martha out of the gutter, protect her home and family, show her life and all its possibilities, treat her as an equal! And what do I get, eh? She turns around and says hurtful things like that to me." He couldn't even keep a straight face as he said it.

"Aye, no gratitude Gilly!" Caroline, the wee witch, stuck up for him, I turned around, and she made a little mock kissing face to me.

Quickly changing the conversation, "so Hugh, I bet your Olive was a beautiful bride, bet you were as proud as punch with her in her wedding album?"

"Pfft, I don't do pictures, missus! You won't catch me getting into a photograph; what's the point? If anybody wants to look at this handsome face, they know where to find me. Twenty-three Garvan Place. I'm not even in my first communion photograph!"

"Snap! I wasn't in my first communion photograph, either." The truth is, I don't like pictures for no reason other than they reminded me of the day before Daddy decided to go." The family photo taken of us the day before Daddy died was in Mammy's room before I took it later on, and I kept it in Daddy's suitcase.

Hugh was a car aficionado; he would stop and look at the cars parked along the street. He would cup his hands around the sides of his face and look in the windows to see the car interiors.

In the flats barely anybody had cars. Thirty parking spaces, and a row of garages, for one hundred and eighty families, but only a handful of cars were parked in the courtyard of the flats back then.

When we returned, two boys were standing outside Molly Barr's shop. They were shouting at everyone around them, staring and pointing to the sky. Nosy Martha couldn't help but ask them what was wrong.

"Here, missus, a fucking army helicopter flew over here there now, so it did." One of the boys growled.

The other boy beside him was a bit calmer, "aye, it was clear as day, so it was, we both saw it. British Army helicopter."

I was a bit confused and asked them, "well did it land here or what?"

"Naw hi, they flew overhead. They flew over our airspace. There are laws against that, you know?"

I couldn't hold it in; I burst out laughing. I mean a proper cackling laugh. I was pointing at them and shouting in between my hysterical laughter. "You boys are standing there furious because a helicopter flew into our airspace. This airspace aye? Protected by that wee line over there? Give me strength this day."

They didn't know what to think, but when I said that to them, they looked at each other, knowing I was right.

***

Caroline and I were back at our regular first aid classes at Ozanam House on Mondays, and we decided to start the Home Nursing series of lectures. Marie had qualified as a nurse and was facilitating the course. Marie greeted us on the first day with her medicinal hugs, and wee Caroline and I were happy to catch up with her.

"Most accidents and sudden illnesses happen in the home. It is important to learn something about Home Nursing and to avoid maltreatment of the patient in the beginning. Prevention is always better than cure."

The Order of Malta Home Nursing service was what we availed of as a family. Even though it just so happened that Marie's wee brother was deaf, and their family could communicate via sign language, Daddy's main concern was depression. Daddy had lost weight after he was deafened, wasn't sleeping properly, and neglected his hygiene and grooming, as difficult as it is for me to say.

The syllabus of the Order of Malta Home Nursing Course was as follows; taken from a leaflet I received that night and still have;

1. Definition of simple Home Nursing. Knowledge necessary, Doctors orders. Simplc physiology.
2. Essentials for the sick room: ventilation, cleanliness, heating, lighting. The Bed.

Necessary requisites for Nursing:

1. Daily routine – pulse, temperature, respiration, excretions, toilet of room and patient. General observations of patient – symptoms, signs and reports.
2. Bed making and changing sheets.
3. Food and drink – invalid cookery, special diets.
4. Infectious diseases. Special cases.
5. General and special treatment – applications, medicines, enemata.
6. Surgical cases – sepsis, dressings, and bandages.
7. Sick Children, nursing, and common ailments.
8. Antiseptics, disinfectants, lotions, drugs, cough mixtures, sedatives, and hypnotics.

By the time of this course, I was a bit more mature. Still a mouth! But a lot more mature. The Battle of The Bogside meant I had to grow up a little bit quicker, as did we all, as a Unit. The ambulance corps needed to grow.

The army was on the streets, and of course, it was only a matter of time before the hostility toward the army would start to show. A Protestant man was sadly killed whenever there were clashes between Catholics and Protestants during a night of disturbances. I believe the poor gent was going out to bring his young son home when he was beaten to death. I found this news as sore as Sammy Devenney earlier in the year, another family like ours having to grow up without their Daddy.

Roads into the middle of Derry were closed at night, so wee Caroline and I couldn't do some late nights. We had to settle for ten shillings and go home by ten instead of the usual one o'clock in the morning. The tension was back, so the need to settle my nerves at night came back. They had to be settled in the only way I knew.

The Order of Malta recruitment increased, and we did a lot of fundraising and set up more first aid posts. Hugh Deehan agreed to stockpile first aid supplies in his home in Creggan Heights, and another house would be made available to us in Blucher Street in the Bogside.

As I worked in a pub, I agreed to take a bucket into the Irish Kitchen and keep it at the bar. Everyone respected the first aiders, and Caroline and I raised fourteen pounds on the first night. If I could make a guess, it would be the equivalent of around two hundred pounds in 2013 money.

I could have gotten drunk that night, but instead, I gave some of the "one for yourself love" cash tips into the bucket. I stuck to my limit that night, two drinks. However, the two drinks were two large straight gin doubles.

Everybody knows that the Brits like their medals and trophies, and wee Caroline and I were serving a table full of off-duty soldiers on a Saturday night. I wasn't used to hearing our punters speak with frightfully posh accents, discussing foxhunting, Morris Dancing, and other things rich English boys like.

One of them said, "excuse me, darling, that is a beautiful silk scarf you both are wearing."

I held on to my green silk scarf, "this here? This is part of my uniform."

"It is rather pretty," replied the half-cut toff. "May I have it?"

Before I could tell them to whistle Dixie, Caroline piped up, "Sorry, this is part of our uniforms, and we had to buy these ourselves. Our families are poor, and we live in the Rossville Flats in the Bogside. These scarves cost us half a crown."

I did well to hide my gasp. Wee bitch! I didn't think she had it in her! The scarves cost our Mammies one shilling and sixpence. A half a crown was two and six!

Nobody fancied an extra shilling more than me, so I played along, "aye, sirs; we are destitute. Sometimes when our Mammies can't afford shoes for us, they have to paint our feet black and lace up our toes."

The Brits conferred, and Caroline whispered to me, "fuck sake Martha, a wee bit less dramatic, we are already losing out because we can't do late nights anymore. Don't mess this up."

"Sorry!"

Guess what? They handed over two and six to each of us! All we had to do was go up to Woolworths and buy another scarf for one and six, and a shilling profit! The next day, we went up and bought three each. God knows what the Brits said about us when they returned to the Barracks!

As the weeks passed, we went to our first-aid lectures, raised some funds for the first-aid posts, and made a small side fortune selling our scarves. We made a spare ten pounds each in six or seven weeks. Mammy hadn't a clue, and it was great. Every night I would pretend to be disappointed, giving her my one-pound note.

The Home Nursing Exam was in early December, and we both passed! Wee Caroline liked it so much that she was more determined to become a nurse now. As she had the home nursing certificate and her first aid, it would mean that she would readily be accepted to the nursing course. A welcome lift in our spirits was short-lived, as the army started crossing the white line in their open-top jeeps.

FIFTEEN

THE GUILDHALL

Thump! Thump! Thump! I was trying to have my usual lie-in on a Saturday morning but was deafened by familiar thumps. I had a big fluffy dressing gown and decided to go to the balcony to watch the game. Hugh, his brother Floyd, Charlie, Peter, some other boys and Bernard Bonner played football in the car park below. Bernard Bonner receives his full title, as Hugh also had a brother called Bernard.

Hugh was standing in goal when Peter McLaughlin scored a rocket past him. Given that I had gotten to know Hugh better, I felt brave, shouting, "my oul' Mammy could have saved that!" Pity I called it just as she came out the front door, and she skelped me across the back of the head.

Several years later, I was told a funny story about an arranged football match between the Rossville Flats boys and another street. During the game, Hugh climbed up onto the crossbar and sat there during the match.

After I dressed and barged through wee Caroline's door, we went down to meet up with the boys. The doors in the flats were on springs, so you could push the front door open if it wasn't on the latch. I would nearly take the door off going in!

The McLaughlin family committee had passed a resolution that wee Caroline's keyboard was to be banned as too many people complained, and she couldn't even play it anyway! It sat in the hallway inside her flat with a sheet over it, with a sign on it, "DO NOT TOUCH, OR IT GOES OVER THE BALCONY". Poor Caroline.

When we went down, wee Caroline went over to an elderly gent sitting in a car. Peter and Charlie went over with her, and they were chatting away to this chap. Before Nosy Martha could investigate why they were talking to this mysterious figure in his fancy car, Hugh threw the ball at me quickly - but I was able to catch it.

"Ha! Safer hands than you! Call yourself a footballer do ye?" before throwing the ball back to him.

"Hold on a minute, plenty of football in my blood! My Da played for Derry City, you know?"

"Really?"

"Aw aye, before the war took hold, he was a superstar! Harry Gilmour. When he signed for Derry, it made the paper. Big centre forward, banged the goals in for fun."

"And there's you, who can't stop the goals going in!" I teased back at him.

"There was no stopping him. I remember seeing all the old newspapers; my Da kept them all. One was when he signed for Derry, and another was a clipping about his wedding day. Three Derry Players married within a few weeks, "Harry Gilmour marries Miss Catherine Boyle of Pilot's Row". The Germans were invading Denmark at the same time, but my Ma and Da's wedding made the paper!" he said proudly.

"Jesus, that's class! You're Derry to the core; all you're missing now is a drawer full of white socks and a greyhound!"

I was a wee bit jealous; his Daddy was practically famous, and he had three sisters, and I didn't havc any! We were both the youngest in our families, and we were both spoiled rotten. Derek was forever complaining that I got all the leeway and that I could do no wrong.

Bridie, Olive, and Sarah, Hugh's sisters, always looked lovely when they went to the dances. I didn't have sisters to do my hair or makeup or whose clothes I could steal. Olive and Bernard lived in a two-bed flat a couple of flats down from Wee Caroline.

He reminded me between his chuckles, "I've seen the Brits driving around the place, knocking on some doors. Since the B-Specials were removed, these boys are the new police now, by the looks of things. It looks like the British Government and the white line have something in common; they both mean fuck all!"

"That's true." I was seeing the army edging their way in more and more. By the end of 1969 and the beginning of 1970, the DCDA seemed to reduce its role massively. It was like a game of cat and mouse where a jeep load of cheeky chappies would cross the white line.

Being on the first aid posts later in 1969 wasn't all that exciting. Mostly, we stood around drinking tea and smoking our fags in a huddle outside the door. Now and again, people came in needing a bandage or a dressing. Mrs McCorkell drove around with a Red Cross sticker on her Morris Minor, and we could see her approaching a mile off.

Leo Day and Mrs McCorkell were both fit and athletic non-smokers, and a rule was issued that smoking at the door of the first-aid post was banned. So we had to stand up the street nearby. If we were at the door, we had to crush out the fags, and run inside when they were approaching. One day Mrs McCorkell arrived at the first aid post, caught some of us unaware, and reminded us all, "it is not proper for young ladies to smoke"—me standing there smoking like a smouldering hijacked Ulsterbus.

***

Speaking of other superstars, we had our own in the Flats. Rosemary "Dana" Brown! She lived in the same block as us, and her Mammy was a hairdresser who had a salon downstairs along the row of shops at the bottom of the flats. We knew she had been selected to represent Ireland in the Eurovision, and we all tuned in to support her on the night.

The Eurovision atmosphere was electric that night; that was back in the good old days when it was about the music. Everybody was rooting for Rosemary, and everybody tuned in. All the tricolours were flying out the windows; not everyone had a television, so we had a few stragglers in ours to watch it with us.

The Eurovision Song Contest of 1970 was held in Amsterdam, and the U.K. entry, Mary Hopkin, was the red-hot favourite. Julio Iglesias represented Spain too! Derry could have descended into a nuclear war that night, and I still wouldn't have put my white coat on. I was watching Dana, and that was the end of it.

When she won, the flats burst into celebration. One of our own had conquered Europe! It was terrific, and I remember screaming and clapping my hands when it was announced that she had won. Best about it, I don't, nor have I ever had an overly political bone in my body, but when Mary Hopkin and her fifty-piece orchestra had to settle with second, I was pointing and laughing at the television with my smug face on. The U.K. delegation had even organised a victory party because they thought it was a cert.

Even before Dana won the Eurovision, everyone was planning on throwing a homecoming party for her.

Mammy and I thought the flats would become a big tourist attraction because of Dana! The Derry version of the Cavern Club in Liverpool, a hotbed of global talent and artistic genius. Everybody wanted to become connected to Dana, even just for bragging rights. Neither of us got our hair done downstairs, so we had to become creative.

Dana winning didn't stop the lingering feeling of discomfort that the army had crossed the white line, but it did bring some colourful jeers from the wee boys who went down to the white line to shout at the army.

"Fuck Mary Hopkins! And fuck her orchestra too! Brits out! Booooo!" Some of the young boys roared. Jesus, me and wee Caroline were in stitches, and you know what? I could swear a couple of the Brits were dying to laugh. Typical Derry, any wee dig will do! The atmosphere was so great that the riots were slightly smaller in the days after Dana's win.

When the first aiders assembled at the canopy beneath block one of the flats on the Sunday after the Eurovision, we were all laughing at the young boys rubbing our Eurovision win in the Brit's faces. Even though they colonised eighty per cent of the world's landmass, we won the Eurovision that year, and they didn't.

We were excited that we might be able to do first aid cover at the Eurovision itself. We won it! So, the rules are that the winner hosts the following year. We could be on TV! Even though it was a long shot, the Dublin Units would probably end up doing it. Interestingly, 1971 was the year that Malta entered the contest for the first time.

Those days, Sunday the 22nd and Monday the 23rd of March, were quieter on the streets due to everyone's high spirits. The homecoming for Dana was planned, and we would be doing the first aid cover for that. We had already been told, and every last one of us was excited to be there. This was probably the most exciting event we have ever done.

We got our briefing on the morning of the 25th, Dana was coming home! She was flying into Ballykelly Airfield that morning and then on to Derry to have a reception at the Guildhall. Our unit was buzzing, and we couldn't wait to see her come home. Dana was the around same age as us at the time.

Ozanam House was near the Guildhall, so we assembled there on the morning of Dana's return to receive instructions for where we would be posted. When Mr Day told me and Caroline to stay up on the Derry Walls, I was fuming! I wanted to be so close to Dana that she would feel my breath on her neck.

Mr Day's justification was that because Caroline and I were Dana's neighbours, we would see her later that night anyway. He was right, but it wasn't much of a consolation at the time. The Derry Walls overlook the Guildhall; from our vantage point, we felt like we were miles away. So much so that we may as well have watched the proceedings from a mountain on the moon!

When Dana burst into "All Kinds of Everything", I sang my heart out. Even if somebody had a heart attack beside me, I would have been useless. I was so caught up in the moment. There were thousands of people there, to welcome my neighbour and best friend in the whole world back home from winning the Eurovision. Wee Caroline was demoted to an acquaintance for the time being.

Caroline was singing away too, she was an excellent singer in her youth. She was a former Feis performer, too, like Mammy. Don't get me wrong, wee Caroline couldn't lace Dana's boots, but she could belt out a number when the notion took her.

Just after Dana finished her song, a lady fell and hit her head off one of the monument cannons on the Derry Walls. Caroline and I extended our hands outward to disperse the crowd around us. She had split the back of her head open and needed stitches. I put a sterilised pad on the back of her head, and Caroline helped me to sit her up. The poor woman was dazed and had hit her head with an awful smack. We didn't have a stretcher near us, but luckily the woman came around to the point where she could get up and walk.

We gave her some water, and she managed to walk down the incredibly steep stone steps of the Derry Walls to Magazine Gate. Caroline stayed in front of her; I held up the rear. If the dizzy lady fell forward, she would take wee Caroline with her. I'm too young to die, I thought! Poor Caroline. We took her to one of the nurses to get stitches.

We missed Dana's speech, and I remember feeling disappointed. I was looking forward to hearing her speak, but it wasn't to be. Caroline and I walked home after the crowds died down and decided to disperse.

"I'm glad that wee woman was okay; that was a nasty one, wasn't it, Martha?" Caroline asked me.

"Aye, it was love! That was your singing that made her faint!" At this, we both laughed, and it lifted my disappointment slightly. What we got that night, though, was a real treat! Dana returned to the flats and sang "All Kinds of Everything" from the fifth-floor balcony.

I rushed out to see her and stood in amazement as the winner of the Eurovision, who was on television only a few short days ago, was singing on the balcony. It was our show, and I loved it — one of my happiest memories of the flats. Dana ran for election to be the President of Ireland many years later.

Politics is a dirty word to me, but I wanted Dana to become the President when she ran in 1999! The saying is true, you never remember what people say, but you always remember how people make you feel. That week, Dana made all of us, including me, unstoppable. A lovely memory of a troubled time.

The peace didn't last too long, though. The IRA had split a couple of months earlier, and trying to understand it was difficult for me. There was the Official IRA and the new Provisional IRA, but they were both the IRA. We had committees coming out of our arses for almost every cause back then. We loved a good committee, and I was too immature to understand the critical need for change. I was only sixteen, approaching seventeen.

Here is a short list of the committees and action groups of that time; The Derry Housing Action Committee, The Derry Labour Party, The Derry Citizens Defence Association, Derry Civil Rights Association, The James Connolly Republican Club, Northern Ireland Civil Rights Association, Derry Unemployed Action Committee, The Rossville Flats Residents Association (which Mammy joined), The Order of Malta Lourdes Committee (which I didn't join), and probably loads more.

The Official IRA had their Easter Sunday Parade only a few days after Dana returned home. The army had developed "snatch squads" and had arrested some people that day. Riots broke out, and it was like old times.

Part Four

"The two traditions must meet.
Derry has no future,
unless there is a change in the minds and hearts of people.
For Derry, is the mother, of us all."

John Hume

SIXTEEN

CROAGH PATRICK

We were all gathered at the thrupenny bits, and the young people within the Rossville Flats were getting quite close. There was a whole squad of us, and everyone came from all three blocks. Most of us had our friend groups and multiple friends at that time.

"What made ye join that Knights of Malta crowd anyway?" Hugh asked me.

"It might open more doors, later on, if I want to get into nursing or something like that; wee Caroline is on about nursing."

"You would have been handy to have about a few years ago when me and them boy used to play "The Alamo" when we were wains."

"The Alamo? What's The Alamo?" I enquired.

Hugh pointed across the street, "see them old houses there, us boys all used to go in there and split into two teams. One team would have to hide and barricade themselves in, and we would have to get them out."

"How did yee's do that?"

"Battering their barricade, booting it, throwing bricks at them and that."

"Jesus! No nice games naw? Me and Caroline used to skip and swing around a lamppost in Wellington Street, and there you boys were throwing bricks at each other."

Chris McKnight lived with his sister at 15 Donagh Place; he was good friends with Hugh as they moved in roughly around the same time. He shouted over, "aye, and one day he fucked a jar of bees in at us to get us out from inside our barricade!"

I didn't even laugh with the rest of them; I put on my serious but sarcastic face,

"Hugh, are you aware that some of them boys could have been allergic to bee stings? Quite an emergency, you know?"

"So? You know how it is, win at all costs! Sure, wait do you hear what me and Chris done one day, we made a massive banger. Bolts, screws, and a big box of red-head matches. We took it up to the roof and threw it off. You would swear a bomb went off! It was class."

"Tut tut! It would help if you were careful. By the way, the Knights of Malta has its compensations. Did you hear me and wee Caroline are going down to climb Croagh Patrick in a couple of weeks?" Reek Sunday day is the last Sunday in July, and pilgrims descend from all over the place to follow in the footsteps of St. Patrick up a mountain, miles away, in County Mayo.

"Compensation, aye? You would get more compensation for losing a wee finger!" Come to think of it, Hugh was right. If I could go back in time and choose between Croagh Patrick and losing a wee finger, it would be bye-bye pinkie.

***

I was all excited to go away. Mammy gave me extra money to bring back a relic from the trip, a set of rosary beads, or whatever else. Mammy had heard there was a gift shop at Lourdes and assumed Croagh Patrick would be the same. I packed two grey dress uniforms, and Mammy bought me a new pair of shoes. It was the least she could do after giving her my pound note every night I came in from work.

We wore our grey dress uniforms for first aid demos in schools, community settings, and whenever the Derry Journal or the Sentinel were sticking cameras in our faces. The white coats were just for the riots and so on. We had to look the part for going to Croagh Patrick, so we wore grey knee-length skirts, grey blazers, red ties, and a white leather belt across our fronts but still had our white linen first aid bags.

There was a big Maltese Cross flag that we had been encouraged to carry up the mountain by a priest that was coming with us for the trip. We thought it would be a piece of cake, no problem for us.

"Here, Martha, gone you take the flag?"

"Naw! You take the flag!"

"Naw Martha, you're stronger than me."

"Aye, because you're feeble. If I have to scrape somebody off the ground and throw them over my shoulder like a bag of coal, then you will have to carry the flag." I shoved it into her chest, and she folded the flag and put it in its little canvas bag.

The Cathedral organised a mini-bus, and we left after Mass around eight o'clock that Sunday. About twenty crammed into this mini-bus, and wee Caroline's bony arse was stuck on my knee. It was agony, and when I started to get a dead leg, I asked her to swap, and I sat on her and crushed her. We travelled in a wee Volkswagen Microbus, and I have no idea how we weren't stopped by the Gardai or the army on the border.

I hadn't been out of Derry before, so going to Croagh Patrick was as good as going to Barbados in my eyes. Somewhere new!

We stopped in Sligo for something to eat and walked around the town. It was so peaceful; it was a world away from Rossville Street. There wasn't a whiff of tension; everyone was just...getting on with it.

We eventually arrived at the foot of Croagh Patrick, and it was gushing with rain and wind. It was a day to sit in the flat with the gas heat on and watch television with a hot cup of tea. Wee Caroline and I helped unload all the pilgrims off the bus, and local boys were selling big wooden sticks that were supposed to be "mountaineering poles".

Some of our Derry pilgrims bought these sticks, and wee Caroline unfurled the flag and put it over her head. There were thousands of people there, and I thought, up this hill, back down, back in the flats in the morning. Easy!

A priest came to give us a briefing of some sort; he could barely speak with the wind and rain battering his bald pate but told us that the route would be slippery on the way up and to watch our step. The Rosary broke out, and I went to the back of the crowd to smoke a couple of fags with the mini-bus driver.

When I thought this torment couldn't worsen, the bus driver told me, "You know there is a Mass up there when you get to the top?"

"Are you having a laugh? Rosary, climb that mountain, then a spot of Mass at the top?"

"Aw, aye, it will be over in no time. In any case, I'm going to read the paper and have a sleep; see you when you get back, missus."

A priest came up to me and wee Caroline with two nuns and asked us if we would accompany them to the top of the mountain, and keep a close eye on them. They were stooped over and were at least two hundred years old. They could barely put one foot in front of the other at the bottom. Wee Caroline looked at me with her big sad eyes.

We set off with the shuffling nuns, and if my calculations at the bottom of the mountain were correct, we would get to the top by mid-December at the earliest. These nuns stopped about half an hour into the trek. "Don't you worry, Sister Bernadette, see if you want to go back; it's no problem; I will take you down for a cup of tea on the bus?" I thought I was getting out of jail for free. What did she do? She handed me her shoes to carry—wee black leather loafers. Wee Caroline's nun handed over her boots too.

These mad nuns walked up Croagh Patrick barefoot and put us to shame. I struggled, and wee Caroline complained constantly. "I'm freezing; I hate the cold; I can't wait to go home. Are we nearly there?"

The wee nuns were throwing dirty looks, and I wanted to grab Caroline's black pigtails and hammer-throw her off the mountain. I never heard crying like it; nuns in their nineties were trekking up the steep rocky path without complaint.

There was a wee cut on Sister Bernadette's heel. I asked her if she wanted it covered, but she held her hand up to refuse. A principle of first aid is that it can't be administered without the patient's consent.

We passed loads of mountain rescue people, Gardai, and fellow Knights of Malta from other units around Ireland. There were at least ten thousand there. When we got to the top, I was pretty pleased, then Mass started, and we were soaked through and shivering. That was the rainiest and windiest day I had ever experienced.

When Joanne and the boy she married went backpacking around India a while back, she phoned me one night and told me there was a monsoon, and it was a horrible day. I told her not to worry, and that one time forty years ago, we climbed Croagh Patrick in the wind and rain and survived. The wee nuns were phenomenal; they were made of sterner stuff. You don't see many nuns knocking about anymore, do you?

The bus trip on the way back was my final act of penance. Wee Caroline fell asleep on my knee, and my legs went dead. Eventually, I elbowed her and woke her up. We were about two hours from Derry,

"I'm bored, Caroline. What's the craic?"

"You woke me up."

"So? I've been sitting here with your bony hole sticking into me. I can't feel my legs anymore."

"I applied for the nursing course, you know?" She said to me excitedly.

"You kept that one quiet," I said to her.

"Another thing I kept quiet, last night at work, I got us free passes for The Embassy on Saturday night. My Mammy said I could go, so you will have to get the charm on with Bridie when you get home."

I hadn't been to the world-famous Embassy Ballroom yet. Derek was allowed to go, but I was soon seventeen, so surely Mammy would let me go. The owner of The Melville Hotel that housed The Irish Kitchen also owned the Embassy Ballroom.

When I returned to the flat early on Monday morning, I gave Mammy a pair of Rosary beads from my Croagh Patrick trip, and she was over the moon with them. After about ten seconds of handing them over, "Mammy, can I go to The Embassy with Caroline for my birthday?"

Seventeen

The Embassy Ballroom

After days and days of negotiations, I convinced Mammy to let me go to the Embassy for my seventeenth birthday. I bolted out of the flat, busted a left along the balcony, ran down the stairwell, and kicked wee Caroline's door down to tell her.

I got some of my birthday money, and we went into town to get some clothes. Mammy told me, "Martha, do not come home with a miniskirt!" I didn't; I left it in wee Carolines. I brought back a bag with a fancy, frilly frock that I had no intention of wearing. I got it for a few shillings in the bomb damage sale. Some of the stock was cheaper when shops were blown up, or damaged if the shop next door was blown up. After I came out and did a twirl for Mammy in the gammy dress, she told me I looked lovely and told me I needed to be back at midnight.

I had thick curly hair, and long straight hair was all the fashion. I needed to straighten my hair, and the plan was hatched. I wet my hair in Caroline's bath and lay on the floor in her bedroom so the gas blow heaters would dry my hair a bit. After this, wee Caroline lay the brown paper on her bedroom floor and put my hair on it, then a white cloth or towel over my hair. Me lying on the floor with Helen blasting "Chirpy, Chirpy, Cheep, Cheep" and Caroline was ironing my hair, the biggest fucking farce since the white line.

No matter how much she ironed or burned my head, it wouldn't go straight. Helen and May tried to help her, but it was a lost cause, even with a searing hot iron. Eventually, they got it straightened slightly. Of course, when Hugh, Charlie, and Peter came in, they thought this was the funniest thing ever.

Caroline cut the boy's hair and gave them all their trademark buzzcuts. Their hair looked the same. They all stayed to witness the straightening of my hair, which was much more entertaining than Saturday night television ever could have been back then.

"You boys are lucky; I might just shave my head too," I quipped to them. They would have been a bit younger than Caroline and me. Caroline was turning eighteen that December. I was ten months older than Hugh, his sixteenth birthday passing on the 1st of June 1970.

The boys had landed apprenticeships, Charlie was doing joinery with some crowd in the Waterside, Peter got into the labs at DuPont, and Hugh was starting in Northern Ireland Tyres as a trainee tyre fitter. Northern Ireland Tyres was close to the flats on William Street. Hugh loved cars, had it in his head that he would work with them, and didn't consider anything else.

We changed into the miniskirts we bought in the town that day and waltzed to the Irish Kitchen for a couple of drinks before going to the Embassy. Between Rossville Street and The Irish Kitchen, a distance of around half a mile, my hair returned to its curly form again.

In all my bravado, I went into the Irish Kitchen and ordered three straight gin doubles right away. Not one lady-like gin with a splash of lime to sip with a straw, like Caroline, three straight doubles. I downed them in the time it took to hand over the money and get the change back from the till.

As we were in company and going for a night out, I could leave the table, hang around the bar, and mingle. I wasn't a natural mingle-er, but I loved how the drink made me feel. It calmed my nerves when I was anxious and removed my fear of talking to other people that I wasn't overly comfortable with.

I timed my trips to the bar so that somebody different was serving. I asked for two doubles at a time as if I was getting them for other people, walked away out of view from the bar and downed them both. In about forty minutes, I had downed about six doubles. I felt calm, and when I got back to the table, I was the life and soul of the party.

Three men and the fiddle fired out their tunes in the corner; I was the first to sing and encourage others to sing too. As we worked there, I knew all their songs and all the words. They played the same set list every night. I dragged all the girls onto the dancefloor, and we were all loving life and laughing. I felt immortal. Nothing or nobody could touch me. That bar and everyone in it was mine. My head was slightly woozy, but I quickly mastered dancing because I had learned to walk in a straight line when I had a few.

One of the girls in our company shouted to one of the girls at the bar to bring a tray of Schnapps. I let out a big cheer, and when they came down, Caroline gave me hers, as did somebody else. The Embassy at that time was dry, with no alcohol, so the idea was to get tanked before I went in.

The fresh air hit me like a wet salmon when we got outside to walk toward the Embassy. It was still bright outside, I was swaying, and wee Caroline was giving me her look of disapproval.

"Martha, you have had far too much; you won't get into the Embassy."

"Ah fuck off you! You're a bore!" and wee Caroline opened her big green eyes as wide as they could.

I suppressed angry drunk Martha as much as I could, but when I saw her sad face I grabbed her, hugged her and said, "I'm sorry wee love, I didn't mean it, it's my birthday, and I'm sorry." After getting her forgiveness, I staggered on ahead of them. I was the loudest person walking along Foyle Street and the Guildhall Square that night. Back then, traffic drove through the now pedestrianised Guildhall Square, and I was nearly flattened by a bus that I had staggered out in front of.

When we got up to the door of the Embassy and walked up the red-carpeted stairs, the big right palm of the bouncer, Barman Duffy, greeted me. "You have too much in ye, sit there," and pointed to a bench beside him that two other boys were sitting on. The girls weren't having their night out ruined on my account, so they went on in. I was sitting on this bench, like a naughty child, until Barman Duffy felt that I and these other eejits were sober enough to go in.

Eventually, I got the all-clear to go ahead in, and when I got up to the giant circular ballroom, I went on a mission to find wee Caroline. When I staggered against one of the pillars beside the dancefloor, I felt a hand go up my skirt. I screamed, turned around, and instinctively slapped the boy as hard as possible.

"Here, love, no need for that; there's no harm in him," one of his mates said to me. I couldn't believe it. They all looked at me with disgust, as if I was the one that committed the crime of the century. I have no idea who he was or his mates who tried to justify him, but I don't care how drunk I was; he deserved it. I think there was an expectation for me to be flattered.

Men weren't supposed to behave like this; they were supposed to be kind and courteous like my Daddy. It was that second that I hated going out. This was in no way fun. I found wee Caroline and the rest dancing and told them I wanted to go home. I was instantly deterred, and I hated that night. It was like I hadn't drank a drop; I had sobered up, and Martha's shakes were back again.

I was crying, and wee Caroline came in with me to the toilets so we could talk,

"Some wee bastard put his hand up my skirt, and I hate him. Men are evil, except for my Daddy."

I got a hug from wee Caroline, she was having fun, and I felt I was ruining her night. It was only around ten o'clock, and when we walked out to the dancefloor, I insisted on going home. She didn't want to leave me on my own, and we went home together. It was late, and there was a riot at the bottom of William Street. The wee boys were pelting the soldiers.

I wasn't up to speed with events outside of Derry, but around that time, the Falls Road Curfew had been in place for a few weeks in Belfast, and snatch squads were arresting people and scooping them off the streets and roughing them up, in both Belfast and Derry. Relations between the Bogsiders and the Army were deteriorating rapidly.

A riot flared up, and wee Caroline and I crossed it in miniskirts. We got some wolf whistles from the rioters and perhaps a couple from the Brits. I was still feeling slightly half-cut and recognised one of the wolf-whistlers, who lived in block three of the flats and shall not be named.

I shouted to him, "here, mucker, want me to go and tell your mother you are down rioting? You weren't shouting "Brits Out" when your sister married one of them and fucked off to Scotland!" The top half of his face that wasn't covered by a white hankie mask went bright red. His mates turned slowly to look at him with disgust, hard lines, mucker!

Nobody gave me grief for treating the RUC during a riot or that my brother was gay because I would have cut them dead with words alone. Nobody challenged me; Mouthy Martha was known around the flats at this time.

Even when we were off duty, plenty of the rioters knew we were Knights of Malta, giving us a certain good standing. The Brits weren't doing anything other than standing behind the doors of their Saracen cars and watching the rocks batter them. They were dressed in helmets and heavy flak riot gear. No longer unarmed in crisp green shirts and green berets. Their uniform change alarmed me somewhat.

Even though I drank more than Caroline would ever allow, she didn't hold it against me after the pervert incident in the Embassy. I swore to her that I would never set foot back in the place, and I didn't.

We cut across the courtyard, and wee Caroline and I started squealing. A rat ran out in front of us, and the shock made us run toward the main door of block one. The rubbish chutes were only emptied once a week, and the significant build-up of rubbish was starting to attract rats. The caretaker greeted us,

"Address please?" he said to us.

"We both live here, 73 Mura Place," I slurred to him.

"Aye, 27 Garvan Place," Caroline chirped after me.

"You are in the wrong block for a start; there are no parties here!"

"But we live here!" we both pleaded with him, and we had no photographic ID that had our addresses on it. We didn't carry mobile phones then either, and we didn't know what to do.

"Caroline, what are we going to do now?"

"Hold on!" She walked around to block two, stood under the living room window of her flat, and roared, "Mammmmyyy!" "Mammmmyyy!"

Then replies started coming,

"Can you shut up, wee girl? My wains are trying to sleep!"

Then wee Caroline shouted, "Gone, get my Mammy to come down and get us!"

All I could do was light a fag and sulk while the caretaker stood with his arms folded. When Charlie came down to get Caroline, she went up the stairs, but I wasn't allowed up! So, there's me standing outside on my own, in a miniskirt that my Mammy would never let me wear in a million years.

I had to face the music; I shouted five floors up to Mammy; of course, she was sitting up. When she came to the window and saw me, I heard the sitting room door slam, her marching down the stairs, slamming the front door, and storming along the balcony and down the stairwell.

She dragged me back to the flat by the hair and battered me stupid. The hiding wasn't for being drunk; it was the skirt. The only time I felt pain close to that night was the recovery after my liver transplant in 1992.

Eighteen

Aggro Corner

The riots were picking up again toward the end of 1970. I, wee Caroline, and the rest of the unit found ourselves at the first aid posts and the surrounding area every day. Although the rioters were not "organised" or regimented like their enemies, they had a timetable.

The riots would almost always start just before four o'clock in the afternoon. This was seven days a week. Many of the young boys went to school, came home, changed, and assembled at Aggro Corner on time. They left around five o'clock when their Mammy's called them in for tea.

The riot would be at three o'clock on Sundays after Mass and Sunday dinner. They started an hour early because they had to have their Sunday night bath for school again on Monday.

The Brits would goad the wee boys, and bricks and bottles flew at them, but the Brits were suited and booted in armoured clothing whilst hiding behind armoured cars and a water cannon.

The army had advanced weaponry, state-of-the-art vehicles, a water cannon, baton rounds, tear gas, shields, and many troops. But no matter how well-equipped Her Majesty's army was, they could never quash a riot as quickly as Caroline and me.

All we had to do was shout, "run, boys! Father Mulvey is coming down William Street!"

I roared that one day and heard a rioter say, "aw Jesus, the first aiders are all into the chapel. They know the craic; we better clear off lads." And away they went like a fart in the wind.

Father Daly and Father Mulvey were more than priests; they were youth and community workers too. They often came down to the riots and encouraged the boys to go home. From what I saw, the rioters often listened.

The first aid posts were well run. They always had plenty of volunteers in them when they were needed. A house in Blucher Street acted as one of the posts, another was Hugh Deehan's house in Creggan Heights, and the post beside the Bogside Inn was the one I was more closely aligned with because it was near the flats.

Aggro Corner faced onto Rossville Street, where block one of the flats stood. Twice in 1970, rubber bullets went through living room windows. We were on the pig's back in block two facing away from the riots. We never had our window's smashed at any point.

Our role in the riots was to don our white coats and kit bags and treat any injuries caused during the trouble because we were under oath to serve all the Lord's sick, injured, and poor; this meant everyone. No rule said we could only treat the Bogside and Creggan residents. We all took this incredibly seriously. We were a lay Catholic religious Order serving as a first aid ambulance corps; we are non-denominational. The Salvation Army, in the Protestant faith, also must serve and accommodate homeless Catholics and did so in London, across the United Kingdom and even in America. When Daddy did stints over in

England, he found it hard to get digs, and The Salvation Army helped him out.

Even though we all wore the same thing, white coats and kit bags, everybody wore them and carried themselves a wee bit differently. I would learn everybody's mannerisms, walks, and small details. I became so close to my unit that I could tell them all apart, even wearing my gas mask during a riot, outside and in the dark.

The CS gas was the worst because it dispersed beyond the riots and even seeped into the flats, flaring up some residents' asthma. Before going home, I would have looked in on the older people on the upper balconies of the flats to see if I could help. When the rioting was intense, many of them were stuck indoors. Wee Caroline was bad with asthma, and the gas affected her badly. We learned that vinegar-soaked rags helped her immensely, so I carried a bottle, and so did she.

I feel it quite symbolic that we wore white coats, almost like we were ghosts. We were the ghosts of riots past, the ghosts of riots present, and the ghosts of riots yet to come.

Sometimes wee Caroline and I were out at the riots for seven or eight hours at a time. Most of us were, and we all came and went at specific intervals. Leo Day was very present; he wasn't like an army commander that issued orders whilst sipping brandy and smoking cigars in a barracks. He was out on the ground with us, and he could get up the gears for a man of near sixty years old! Many a time, I saw him sprinting up and down Rossville Street like a teenager. We were amazed at his athleticism; he was a champion sprinter in his youth.

I wasn't very nimble, and I would never have been able to outrun Mr Day. What I did notice was that he wore lovely shoes. The road was covered in glass, and petrol bombs landed around us when we were treating people. When treating somebody at the foot of Westland Street, a petrol bomb landed beside me and melted my wee plimsoles. Others stood on glass, and the battle-strewn roads weren't good for our parents' pockets; we all went through shoes like hot dinners.

I came home from riot duty one evening, and Mammy greeted me at the door with a rare smiling face. She had her hair done and got herself some new clothes.

"New do Mammy?" I asked her.

"Aye, love, but I've got something new for you too," she replied proudly whilst plumping her hair with her hands. She slipped into my bedroom, and I followed her to see a big box on my bed. I got pretty excited seeing her face. I was wondering what she got me. The box was too wee to be a nice pair of knee-high boots, maybe my first pair of high heels?

When I opened the box, I nearly died. The sight before me was ghastly, and I looked at Mammy's face. She was still delighted and waiting for me to throw my arms around her and spill my gratitude out to her.

"Mammy?"

"Yes, love."

"What are these?"

"A wee bit of gratitude wouldn't go a miss, you cheeky wee article! What's wrong with them?"

"There's nothing wrong with them, Mammy, but are you sending me down to work in the docks or what?"

"No, Martha, they are a sturdy pair of boots. I have bought you four pairs of shoes this past year, and you need sturdier footwear when you're out in the riots."

"Aye, I know. Thank you, Mammy. They're adorable, and I will wear them with pride every day." When Mammy sensed the sarcasm, she knew to smile and walk away. She left me with these steel toecap boots, which weighed a ton. I put them on my feet and walked around my bedroom. I walked around the room like a cat with Smarties tubes on its legs and feared falling through the floor into the flat below. Steely Dan was starting to come into the charts, and because I had steel toecap boots, I called them my Steely Dan's.

I wasn't the only one with big boots! Some of the other first-aid girls got Steely Dan workman boots too. So I wasn't alone, thank God. After a while, girls started wearing boots around the town and even to the dances. I don't care what anybody says; this wasn't a coincidence. We were trendsetters, and Bridie Bradley started it. Wee Caroline and I remained immature and sometimes kicked each other with the boots. She got me a belter in the shin one day outside the first aid post at the Bogside Inn and left me crying while she cackled at me. I vowed revenge.

Wee Caroline always had her guard up after that incident, but I was patient. Weeks passed, and the guard started to drop as she felt safe that no attack was imminent. I had her exactly where I wanted her. We were coming back from Ozanam House, walking down the Joseph Place steps beside the flats, when I stalled back to light a fag. She was a few steps down from me, and I took the opportunity to wind my boot. I drove my Steely Dan so far up her hole that it lifted her off her feet and felled her.

She lay on the ground squealing, and I felt a bit bad. She had her wee wobbly lip, and I helped her back to the flat. I knew I went too far, but at the same time, she knew not to mess with Martha. She walked a bit funny for about a week afterwards, probably a hairline fracture of her tailbone. She started it, so good enough for her.

None of us could run very fast with these boots on, and they took a while to get used to. One time I was carrying an empty stretcher down Westland Street when I tripped on a cracked slab and dropped the stretcher on my boots. It would have shattered every bone on my foot if I wore my old plimsolls, so I became grateful for them.

A particular evening riot at Aggro Corner had a lot of injuries. Hugh Deehan was up and down to Letterkenny Hospital, and the stretchers were ferrying people to Blucher Street, Candy Corner, and the Bogside Inn posts for treatment. A rubber bullet smacked one of the rioters in front of us, and we heard the crack of his leg shattering as it hit. Three stretcher parties had left, there was no stretcher with us, but we had another asset. One person that never needed a stretcher was Robert Cadman. He was a judo and swimming champion and could lift boys twice his weight.

Robert scooped this boy off the ground, threw him over his shoulder and ran away with him. No bother to Robert. It wouldn't be considered the textbook way to provide first aid, but there were times when we had no stretchers to hand; if Robert had already run away with someone, then we had nothing until either the stretchers or Robert came back.

Leo came down one evening to assess the situation, which again was terrible, and he stayed to help us out and provide a badly needed extra pair of hands. When he came down, I nudged wee Caroline beside me,

"Here, love, do you ever look at Leo's shoes?"

Caroline scrunched up her face, "what are ye on about?"

"Caroline gone look at his shoes, they are shiny as a new penny, and he has been wearing them the past six months."

"Martha, are you having a laugh?"

"Naw, I'm not! I wonder where he gets them? One day a petrol bomb landed beside him, and he jumped out of the way. He removed a cloth from his jacket pocket, wiped them down, and continued as if nothing happened."

Caroline didn't know what to make of this conversation at all. Nothing escapes Martha's eyeball. We all were stuck wearing our Steely Dan workman boots whilst Leo Day led our unit in his fireproof, riot-proof shoes. He must have polished them daily to the point where his shoes were mummified and immortal.

Mammy always got frightened and insisted that Derek avoid the riots on his way home. I have to laugh, though, that Mammy would fear for one second that Derek would be a rioter.

He got a job, was working a lot and was lucky to be working in the clothes shops. He worked around a few in the town and even had supervisory roles. He did stints in Bannon's Clothes Shop, John Morrow and Sons, and Austins. I loved when he worked in Austins because he was paid quite well and bought me records. I must have played "Love Grows Where My Rosemary Goes" about a thousand times when I got it.

Hugh was working every hour God sent him at Northern Ireland Tyres on William Street, and now and again I would walk back to the flats with him when he was coming home from work, and I was going off riot duty. When we got back to the block two balcony, he would burst through the door of 23 Garvan Place, and one of the girls always tried in vain to get him to clean himself up before dinner. I used to hang back to hear him shout, "naw! I'm starving, I will wash after. Gone leave me alone!" Pretty much the same interaction most nights, and I couldn't help but find it funny.

Floyd would wind him up, and said "go on, wash your hands and listen to your sisters will ye?!"

"Naw, I won't, Pretty Boy Floyd! Pfft, Pretty Boy Floyd. Nothing pretty about ye!"

He would be covered in oil and dirt because he worked changing tyres, exhausts, and car batteries throughout the day in the tyre yard. Sometimes, I noticed he even got it in his hair. I never worked out how somebody would get motor oil in their hair. Hugh was walking home on his own one evening in October when he was snatched and arrested. He just happened to be walking home covered in oil and dirt and accused of rioting. On an evening he wasn't rioting, he got arrested. All he did was insist that the army and the police contact his employer, and after they did, they released him and told him to go home.

He was quite shaken by it. I can't stress this enough. Hugh Gilmour was not politically minded whatsoever. He would have partaken in the riots because his friends were doing it and for his enjoyment, not because he was advancing any causes or ideas in his mind. It was just a bit of fun to him.

I was Knights of Malta, and we were taught to be politically neutral, so I think that is where Hugh and I saw eye to eye as we got a little bit older.

Even as a group, when politics entered the conversation at the thrupenny bits or up the town, Hugh would walk away or change the subject. Politics bored that wee boy to tears. Some young boys in the flats joined the Provisional IRA, the Socialists, and the Civil Rights Association. As he got older, he didn't get more involved in politics like others. All he cared about at that time was buying a wee car. That was his own goal, and he was sticking to it.

Now and again, when I was on the sidelines watching the riots, I would keep an extra eye on Hugh to make sure he was okay. On the days I wasn't on duty down by the riots, we went into town and tried to distract him somewhat. Some of his friends were very fond of a riot, and I imagine if I were Matthew instead of Martha, I would be neck-deep in the riots too.

Peer pressure is real; I knew Hugh had a heart of gold and wasn't a violent person at heart. Me and Hugh were sitting on the thrupenny bits outside our flat block when a young fella about the same age as us wearing a parka and a woolly hat, approached Hugh, "do you want to join the movement? Go over there to the Bogside Inn and tell them I sent you?" the boy brashly said to Hugh.

Hugh's cool response, "here mucker, see if you give me a piggyback over to the Bogside Inn; I'll sign up right away." The boy raised his eyebrow at Hugh, nodded in disbelief, and walked away from us. That was the end of Hugh joining anything.

"Jesus Hugh, you're nearly as cheeky as me! I said to him."

"Sure what money would I make in jail, or dead?"

As I am as hard as nails, it is tough to make me laugh. He had his wee way of making me giggle, a lovable rogue.

What really made me smile was how good he was to his Mammy. She was his queen, and he adored her. He always looked after her. When he got his pay packet from the tyre yard, he would always give some money to her, even though he wasn't making much as an apprentice tyre-fitter. When we were in town, any chance to buy her sweets or things she liked, he would do it.

I remember vividly seeing Chris McKnight and Hugh coming home from their travels near Fort George. There were days they would have gone fishing together for fluke and eels, and Hugh had spotted a collection of wild roses and insisted that they should be picked, wrapped in newspaper, and brought home for their mothers.

I always stayed around the riot until Hugh decided to go home, and I would walk home with him. I had water and bandages ready so that he could get the dust and dirt off his face, fingernails, and shoes. He always appreciated this; he didn't want to face his father's wrath, so he would go back into the house and, in his charming way, try to convince the family that he was helping little old ladies across the street.

"I'm getting a wee car soon," he told me. "I am going to start saving up my pay packets; I want a car to work on. Some of the boys in there bought cars, and now and again, people come in and try and sell them. I reckon I could get a decent wee car for about thirty quid."

"You better take me out in it!" I told him.

***

Caroline and I were sitting on the thrupenny bits one Monday evening after returning from a first aid class when I saw Hugh's window opening. He crept onto the canopy above the shops, then went arse-on-canopy and dropped to the ground.

"Alright girls," he said in his wee chirpy voice, about to meet his pals for a bit of stone throwing down at Aggro Corner.

I jumped off the wall and put my hand on his arm and said, "gone be careful, I'm not there, and if anything happens to you, go to one of the white coats. They will be standing about. If you're in bother, run back and meet me here."

Caroline piped up then, "Jesus Martha, who do ye think ye are? His wife!" Wee Caroline always waited in the wings to embarrass me back, when the chance came up. I was always worse to her, and she probably still had the make-up incident at the front of her mind.

"She wishes!" Hugh quipped back before smiling and running off down Rossville Street.

"I mean it! Be careful!" I shouted down the street after him.

Caroline had started to train as a nurse, and she was telling me all about it. She was going to dances and meeting new friends. I got a wee bit jealous! Because of her studies, I did see her slightly less. There was a home for student nurses beside Altnagelvin Hospital, and she split her time between the flats and the nurses' home.

Before Caroline could embarrass me even further, we were met with the sight of Mr Gilmour, decked out in his cap and long coat, bursting out through the door at the bottom of block one. "Oh Jesus," I muttered to myself. As usual, he sent his friendly smile our way and tipped his cap. Caroline and I just sat silently and smiled back at him.

Mr Gilmour proceeded down Rossville Street, with the most purposeful walk in the world, toward Hugh. Seeing him walk toward Aggro Corner and Hugh's back facing his approaching father was like slow motion. I couldn't watch. I just put my head in my hands, peeking through my fingers, and waiting for the moment Hugh would realise he was caught.

I saw Mr Gilmour tap Hugh on the shoulder, and when Hugh turned around, I saw him go sheet white from eighty yards away. He was marched back down Rossville Street unceremoniously and in full view of the other rioters at the barricade.

Hugh didn't even look our way when he was marching past us; Mr Gilmour gave us a little smile as he passed. Privacy was absolutely zero in the flats; I could hear conversations and instruments from my bed in the middle of the night. Hearing Hugh shouting "I hate that man! I hate that man!" from inside his flat was perfectly audible from the outside, especially when his bedroom window was only about forty feet from where we were sitting.

***

The poor political climate was starting to anger people greatly. As the riots continued into 1971, the Brits became much more aggressive.

The wee boys getting hit by rubber bullets were getting more common. In the preceding months, the Brits first fired the baton rounds at the ground to disperse the crowds, but now they had taken to firing them directly at the rioters. One of the bullets missed me by inches one day and smacked a wall beside Caroline and me. We just looked at each other in amazement.

A young boy came up to us and said, "here, hi! Can I have that?" pointing to the baton round that almost hit me. I was dumbfounded and handed it over. Some people collected riot souvenirs, like rubber bullets, and even sold them to the press!

The May Day Bank Holiday of 1971 was when I had to treat my most serious injury. Caroline and I went into town to buy new records and walked headfirst into a riot. We didn't even have our white coats on, and we weren't expecting a riot at two o'clock. They usually were later!

As we walked down William Street toward the city centre, a wee boy fell to the ground screaming after being hit by a rubber bullet. He was shot at point-blank range in the middle of the chest and was spluttering blood. The bullet must have smashed his breastbone; every time he tried to talk or breathe, blood was coming from his mouth.

I ran to a house nearby and asked if they could phone an ambulance for a wee boy shot by a baton round and needing a doctor immediately. Caroline was good at comforting people; she always had a lovely way about her when it came to administering first aid. Everyone felt at ease with her, making her a great nurse in years to come.

As it happened, that house had a car and offered to take him to the hospital. Two men carried the boy fifty metres to a car and told us they would take it from here. We thought nothing of it. The youngster lived to tell the tale, as I saw him rioting again a couple of weeks later. If we weren't there, that wee boy was dead.

As the wee boy was carried away, we bid farewell and proceeded around the riot. That day, I bought a Led Zeppelin LP, which still sits in my collection. "Whole Lotta Love" is my favourite song of all time, and I fancied Jimmy Page. By the way, Jimmy, I'm single again!

The wains got me tickets for the Led Zeppelin concert in the Millennium Dome in London for my birthday a few years ago. The tickets were in a birthday card that my wee granddaughter Rosie gave me, and even though I was fifty-six at the time, I squealed and cried my lamps out like I was seventeen again.

Strangely, I can't visualise it anymore. I know I was there, as I have the Led Zeppelin T-shirt that I bought that night framed and up in my living room where my wedding photo once was.

I held my new record under my arm, and there was an army checkpoint near The Diamond in Derry where civilians would be searched. Now and again, my Knights of Malta kitbag was searched, and one day a cheeky soldier tipped my bag all over the ground in the rain and called me an "IRA bitch". I had done nothing to him.

There were many occasions when the Brits were injured, and their "buddies" wouldn't give up their field dressings to treat their wounded partner. We had to do it!

There were soldiers at the checkpoints dotted around the perimeter of Free Derry, and the more the army presence increased, the more the white line was breached. We could tell them apart by their uniforms and beret badges.

The Royal Green Jackets, The Coldstream Guards, The Royal Regiment of Fusiliers, The Anglican Regiment, and pretty much every unit except for Dad's Army were in Derry by the early to mid-stages of 1971.

When Wee Caroline and I went home, the two soldiers at the checkpoint at Butcher Gate were Jackets. The Brits were the same to most, but we treated more injuries depending on who the rioters were opposing. We were always searched when we walked through Butcher Gate down to the Rossville Flats. On this day, we weren't

One of the soldiers had a wee slip of the tongue when we approached.

"Hello Caroline, go ahead, ladies!"

Sweet merciful Christ wee girl...

Nineteen

Altnagelvin Hospital

I turned eighteen in 1971. I didn't have an eighteenth birthday party believe it or not. I had been so deterred by some man putting his hand up my skirt that I didn't even bother to go out. Wee Caroline's eighteenth birthday was a scream; she had turned eighteen the previous December!

It wasn't usual for ladies to wear trousers to the pub back then, but wee Caroline did. She never drank, but she got plastered on her birthday. We were briefly in the Irish Kitchen and then went to The Favourite, a pub down the street. She got so drunk that she threw up through the open window and nearly hit people at the bus stop below. She never drank again.

When internment was introduced in August of 1971, public marches and demonstrations were banned, and street violence got to boiling point. If anyone was suspected of being a member of the IRA, it was automatic imprisonment without trial.

I would have heard around the flats that "so and so" had been lifted, and I was terrified. What if they lifted Derek, Hugh, or anyone else I cared about? I enjoyed my time with everyone much more, as I didn't know if they would be lifted and taken away tomorrow. The Ballymurphy massacre also happened in

Belfast; the Parachute Regiment murdered eleven people. The army was cementing itself as the enemy of the people across the Province.

There were bombings in the town, and some buildings were starting to get damaged. The place was a mess, and we went around William Street and the City Centre more and more just in case there were explosions and we would have to help. In the early days, I wasn't there when explosions occurred. I heard them from the flat or other first aiders at Ozanam House.

In August, the deaths were mounting. Soldiers were being killed, as were civilians and IRA Volunteers. All of them saddened me, but one, in particular, felt like a dagger through the chest. A young man, Eamon McDevitt, who was deaf, was shot dead by the Royal Marines in Strabane. It was so close to home, making me think about Daddy.

I spent more time in Daddy's room because people's daddies, brothers, uncles, and sons were being taken. It was almost like I had developed the ability to take on pain from every death reported on television, radio, or in the newspapers. I lay on the floor and sobbed. The pain was acute, and I was desperate for the pain to go away. I considered moving away. Derek had suddenly decided to go to England when internment came in. Given his sexuality, he was afraid of being interned and killed in prison, so he and Liam went off to London. We didn't have a party or leaving do for him because Mammy didn't want to attract attention to the fact that he was going.

One of the blackest days in our history came on the 6th of September 1971, when young Annette McGavigan was shot dead by the army during disturbances near Blucher Street. The first aid post was there, but she had been taken into another house in the street. She died almost instantly, and that was another day I spent a lot of time in Daddy's room.

Annette's death caused fury and outrage. The semi-jovial tone of some of the rioting had vanished. The fraction of a relationship between the Bogside and the army was gone entirely now after they had murdered a child. She was only fourteen.

Even though we were out every night, everyone had their jobs and career paths ahead of them. Charlie Glenn and Charlie McMonagle were training to be teachers, Majella worked in Crown Buildings in the Civil Service, Eiblin worked in the post office, Hugh Deehan was a van driver and a member of the Auxiliary Fire and Rescue Service, Attracta and Robert were training to be nurses, Dr MacDermott was a family doctor, Leo Day was a teacher at the Waterside Boy's School just to name a few. Some leaders and those in ranks above me had spouses and children.

Some worked in pubs or worked night shifts. Those working at night in their paid jobs often went to the riots during the day and went to work at night and vice versa. Despite this, we ran a reasonably robust healthcare network in the community. In the beginning, the first aid posts were a welcome last resort to help those who needed it, but concerns were raised about their use as time went on. Sometimes, at the posts, we would get drunks and a host of other domestic incidents and "accidents", where the poor ladies of the house "fell down the stairs" or "walked into something" after their husbands came home from the pub.

The last thing Mr Day wanted was for the community to think of us as an alternative to Casualty, but that was the way it was. Granted, we didn't have an x-ray machine and couldn't take blood, but there was very little we couldn't do. Many evenings we were resetting dislocated shoulders, splinting fractures, soothing burns, applying stitches, and even putting plasters on the knees of little children.

Even though Derry had spiralled into a war-torn region, the Order of Malta Ambulance Corps still hosted large gatherings where all the units from across the island would meet. First-aid competitions were very popular, everyone looked forward to them, and it incentivised people to stay.

The Derry Unit were always successful at the national competitions over the years, and won the 1972 Lodge Cup for the best overall unit. Charlie Glenn won the Men's Ulster Individual First Aid Cup in 1971, and Marian Griffin won The Cup for Home Nursing at the competitions of the early 1970s. Eiblin, Sofia, Geraldine, Antoinette and Alice formed a team that won another trophy in Dublin.

We took part in our parades, marching through the streets in our grey dress uniforms and flying our Order of Malta flags. This was the perfect way to show off our fancy uniforms and show people that we were a cause worth joining. Visibility was vital, and Leo Day led us on our marches. We went to other towns and combined with other units to make the demonstrations larger, but like every other demonstration, we were banned from doing it in late 1971.

I always thought back to the time before the Battle of The Bogside; we would stand at the back of the chapels and offer older adults water if they felt faint or unwell. We had innocent tasks in those days, and we were all innocent children, both in nature and in years. Then suddenly, we were thrown into the bloodbath that our city became. It caught us all unaware, and I feel I am only coming to terms with it now decades later.

I would never have admitted to anybody that I was frightened, confused, upset, or longing for the innocent days to come back. None of us did, although we all felt it deep inside. The only known antidote in those days was simply to get on with it, which didn't work. I had to self-treat all those feelings in the vile and toxic way that I did, drink. I compared drinking to taking medicine. I was settling my nerves because I didn't feel sad like Daddy was.

Ozanam house was a shared space, and when the violence escalated rapidly, we had to meet more often and sometimes at short notice. If we needed to meet quickly, we often went to Leo Day's house at 78 Marlborough Street. The drama was quite addictive, and I felt pretty important. We would be invited in and go to his front dining room. There he had a gold cloth armchair, a dark wood sideboard, and a piano in the corner. He would gesture for us to take a seat, and sometimes fifteen or twenty of us would be there. He didn't have a spare twenty chairs, so we used to sit on the floor and cross our legs like wains, including the married men and women.

***

My first brush with death came later in September when some wee bastard threw a nail bomb out in front of the ambulance when we were racing down Rossville Street. We weren't the intended target; I'm sure of that. I was sitting in the passenger seat, and when we saw a little fizzing can roll out in front of us, the ambulance screeched to a halt.

We had a woman in the back of the ambulance, as she had been hit in the ankle by a ricocheting brick, causing her ankle bone to contort and burst through the skin.

I could feel the blast, the windscreen cracked, and the ambulance jolted. I climbed over the passenger seat to the terrified lady lying in the back with a blood-soaked bandage around her foot. I reacted too quickly to be shaken or afraid; I had to comfort her and tell her that we would be back on the road in no time.

The two front tyres had burst. A nail bomb is a tin can filled with explosives, nails wrapped in tape, and a fuse sticking out the top. When it explodes, nails and bits of sharp metal fly everywhere. The ambulance having burst tyres was common; it had to drive over glass and shrapnel, so two spares were always kept underneath the bed in the back. Although, neither of us there that day knew how to change the tyres or use anything in the toolbox.

Luckily, we were beside Northern Ireland Tyre Service. Hugh was there, he was working on a car, and I dragged him out of the place.

"Where are you taking me? Hold on a minute, missus!"

"Our ambulance has two burst tyres, they were blown out, and we have a woman lying in the back bleeding with a broken ankle!"

"Oh dear, right! I'll get them changed."

The ambulance toolbox, jack, and two tyres came out. It was only a couple of minutes, and the two spare tyres were on!

"That was quick, no bother to you!" we were shocked at how quickly and efficiently he took the tyres off and threw the new ones on. Quick as lightning! We couldn't believe it; changing the ambulance tyres usually takes fifteen or twenty minutes. Hugh was as strong as a bull; he had developed an interest in bodybuilding by reading about Charlie Atlas in magazines.

"Fastest tyre-fitter in the west! People come in and ask for me up there, you know?"

"I would well believe it, well done you!"

"Right, missus, have to run and go up and wait for something. Dead exciting, I will show everybody later." So off he went, and we got to Altnagelvin Hospital.

I planned to visit Caroline in the nurses' home and said I would get my way back home afterwards to allow the ambulance to get back to the first aid post. I needed to enquire further about what she was up to, especially since the soldier blew his cover up the town. Caroline knew she would get quizzed and had avoided being around me. When I went to the nurses' home, I saw her wearing her wee nurses' uniform and a red name badge at the door. The student nurses had a traffic light system with their name badges; red were first years, orange were second years, and green were third years. Basically, big emergency or life-threatening ailment, avoid the red badges unless it was impossible to do so.

I didn't say hello to her to greet her.

"Milk and one sugar, love" then she went inside for a few minutes and brought out a mug for me and a cup for herself.

"So! You want to tell me the bars then?"

"He is called Joe," she said back to me.

"How did you meet?"

"A bus comes here and takes us down to Ballykelly. All the girls were going, and I went one night, men in uniforms and all that."

"Could ye not have gone for a fucking traffic warden instead?"

"Sure, where is the fun in that?" I was scared for her, but we laughed, drinking our milky, sugary tea.

"They have dances in the Barracks and drinks; you would love it, actually!"

Not that I was overly political, but I thought, no thanks. To me, love was always love. Derek and Liam were happy, wee Caroline seemed delighted, and I wasn't going to go to any dance. I wasn't having another man touch me up again. I didn't have a significant interest in boys; I was much too shy. The only time I talked to boys was when I was drunk. When any boy came near me or asked me out, I got defensive and refused. Mouthy Martha was all a front; I was a terrified wee girl that needed help from a drink to mix with others.

A belter about Wee Caroline: one night at a dance, in the pre-Joe era, she was kissing some boy at a disco somewhere. Somebody saw her and told her that what she was doing was a sin. Wee Caroline disagreed and asked a parish priest if kissing some boy in a bar or disco was a sin.

According to the priest, "kissing does not constitute a sin, but passionately kissing should certainly not be something done by young girls, especially unmarried young girls your age.. To us, kissing was a broad area because I kissed Mammy and Derek on the lips back then. It wasn't unusual in our family one bit. Daddy always kissed Mammy in the mornings before he went to work.

Caroline said, "The priest said that passionate kissing was everything over one minute. So, I always count and stop when I get to fifty-nine seconds!" Jesus, we laughed sore, my sides were busting, and I realised that I missed her because we hadn't spoken in a while. I didn't want us to drift apart. A lot of the group of friends we had in the high flats were going their own way, and I didn't want it happening to the both of us.

"Awk Martha, he is lovely; I don't see him as a uniform. He plays rugby, has a few wee nephews, and is the same age as us. He says that if he were born and bred in the Bogside, he would also throw stones at the army. He doesn't want to be here, only here because his family were all in the army, and he had no choice".

"Two sides to every war, eh?" We both nodded and agreed.

"It was wile funny; he came and sat beside me the first time I went. The Protestant girls here are far more comfortable in the barracks than I was. I recognised a couple of the soldiers from the Irish Kitchen. He came up to me and asked me to dance; I said no at the start, but I gave in and danced with him when he asked why I was at a dance."

"As long as you are happy, wee love, I'm going to be moving up to Donagh Place soon up to the bedsits with the other spinsters and bachelor uncles."

"Aye, Martha, you need to get your act together."

"Marriage? Wains? Shitty nappies? Naw, thanks!"

Wee Caroline decided to go home, and we took the bus together to the Guildhall from Altnagelvin and walked along Rossville Street. When we got to the balcony, the Gilmour's and wee Caroline's sisters were standing on the balcony. They were looking nervously out into the courtyard, and I had to ask,

"What are you all doing lurking around here?"

I think May said, "Gilly said he has something to show everybody."

We waited for about fifteen minutes and were greeted with the sight of three wee boys pushing a rusty white Mini towards us. A couple of mutters, "oh Jesus," and some tuts came out. Hugh was proud as punch in the driving seat, having his mates push the car into the flats carpark while he got to steer it.

He had saved up his wages, definitely a few weeks' worth, and was proud as punch with his new car. The sills were rusted, there were dents on it, and given that nobody drove it back, the thing didn't even run. I can still see that car clear as day.

"Look at that!" he exclaimed to the bewildered crowd. We didn't know what to make of it.

His Mammy asked, "how much did you pay for that son?"

"I only got it for forty pounds!" I thought she was going to faint. "It will be up and running in no time, just you see."

I don't think we held on to a lot of hope. I would go out to the balcony, and the car was parked just below the Garvan Place balcony, and I could see him holding the bonnet open with one hand.

The football matches were still an all-day affair. Bernard Bonner was out all day with them, and every time the ball went near the car, Hugh would bark at them, "watch my car, boys!" The matches, at times, would go on from nine o'clock in the morning, and the only thing that stopped them was a burst ball. Hugh idolised Bernard; and always talked about him.

The days passed, and the car still wasn't going. He was getting annoyed, and I went down.

"No joy?" I said to him.

"Naw, it's wile annoying; I put a new battery in her, changed the water pump, and still dead! The boys in the tyre shop told me to get one of these because the parts are cheap, and they are easily fixed. If I don't get her going, I'm either selling it or putting a match to it."

Some of the other tyre-fitters had mechanical experience teaching him some repairs. He loved it and was doing exactly what he wanted to be doing. I told him to go to my flat and offered him Daddy's tools to try and get the car going. He went upstairs and came down with the two toolboxes. He didn't have a lot of tools of his own, as tools were costly back then, and the tyre yard wouldn't loan the tools outside of the workshop.

I was given the noble duty of holding on to the wee tiny bonnet while he worked away inside, tightening all the bolts, checking the radiator, and putting in new spark plugs. When he got inside the car and turned the key, the damned thing spluttered into life. He was revving the Christ out of it and started beeping the horn.

It was the feeblest horn I've ever heard in my life. I just about heard it, and I was standing beside it! He could drive it a bit, as some of the tyre-fitters were teaching him to drive. Although, wains came out of the womb quicker than that car.

The boys and Hugh's brothers looked at the car with their eyebrows raised. None of the dials worked, except for the clock. Hugh was sitting still in the carpark with the handbrake on, and the speedo said he was doing twenty miles per hour. He urged a few of the boys to come with him to get a jar of petrol for the car; he didn't risk driving it because he didn't know how much fuel was in it.

They ran down the Strand Road for a gallon of petrol, and I wish I had been there. It wasn't a wise decision to be a couple of Catholic wee boys carrying a jar of petrol towards Rossville Street back then. Did the army stop them? Of course, they did.

"Excuse me, young man - name and address?"

"Hugh Gilmour, 23 Garvan Place."

"Would you mind telling me where the fuck you think you're going with a jar of petrol?"

He was still dressed in his work clothes and clattered in oil and mechanical muck.

"I got this new car, a wee Mini; I have been working on her and getting it going. She is up and running now, and I am taking her out for a run." He was talking so passionately with this soldier, to the point where the boys swear on their lives, the Brit was dying to laugh.

"Yes, indeed, young man, now may you remind me why you need to have three fellows with you to purchase a jar of petrol?"

This stumped the wee boys, and they all looked at each other, but Hugh stuttered out, "I didn't want to go on my own, in case somebody tries to steal it from me. They are here to look out for me!" and all the wee boys nodded and went along with it.

Unsurprisingly, the Brit ended up sniggering. He lost. "Go ahead, go on! Fuck off!" he told them, and they strolled back to the flats to fill the car. Even when I saw them put the petrol in it, the fuel needle didn't move a millimetre.

About seven wee boys piled into this mini, and they didn't have a driving licence between them. I could hear the cheers from inside the car. There is a famous circus trick where a pile of clowns fit into a mini, and this was an identical scene. They all got to take turns driving the car. This wee white rust bucket of a car went around the Bog, the Brandywell, Creggan, and everywhere that didn't have a checkpoint asking for a driving licence.

About three hours later, when I was having a cuppa and a fag on the balcony, I was greeted by the wee boys pushing the car back again, of course, Hugh in the driving seat steering it. The wee boys were sweating buckets, and they had pushed the car back from lower Creggan about a mile away. I didn't go down, but their comical arguing was hilarious. They had to guess how many miles they got for one gallon of petrol; when that wasn't the right strategy, they had to try and guess how far a mile was on the road with a broken speedometer.

This became a regular sight in the flats, a group of hopeful wee boys piling into this car after getting a jar of petrol and pushing it back again when it ran out. Nonetheless, it was Hugh's pride and joy.

A lot of the other seventeen- and eighteen-year-olds in the flats were starting to socialise and go to dances more. I didn't do drinking other than in the Irish Kitchen. Hugh didn't drink like some of his friends; he was more preoccupied with work and this wee car. There was a disco every Sunday night in The Embassy Ballroom, The Diddler's Disco, and he went there on Sunday nights.

Mostly, The Embassy played country and western music. I fucking hate country and western. Even worse when Derry folk wear cowboy hats and brown shoes for the country and western nights. The only exception is Johnny Cash; everybody else can do one as far as I'm concerned. Derek liked country and western, and so did Mammy. She got some old Marty Robbins records, and I scoffed at her every time she played them in the flat.

The car was in the process of getting a makeover when I went down to see the group one afternoon. They were painting the car black! Honestly, it made it look worse! There were some suspicious dings, dents, bumps, and scrapes that the black colour wouldn't remove.

"Remember I said about my own white line? Look there." And Hugh pointed down at freshly painted white lines in the carpark that said, "Gilly Parking".

"So, you have your own parking space now?" I asked him.

"Aye! It's my space, and nobody will park on it." It was just in front of the garages below block two.

"So, none of the other parking spaces were good enough for you?"

"Naw, they aren't! This one has my name on it."

I counted the cars in the carpark; there were three other cars. There were thirty parking spaces. He wanted a parking space that was right below his flat balcony.

November of 1971 wasn't just a turning point in my life but in the narrative of Free Derry itself. Kathleen Thompson, a mother of six, was shot dead by the army in her back garden in Creggan. After this, the barricades went back up again like they were in 1969. A woman was shot dead. Would it be me next?

Soldiers were getting killed too. I couldn't stand all the death and dying; I was afraid I would become desensitised to it. I was so conflicted; of course, people would join the IRA. The murder of civilians is despicable, and courageous people wanted to do something about it and stand up for their communities. I just felt like a helpless coward. My unit was so brave; I wasn't. I spent a lot of time crying in the toilets of the first aid posts. I developed the habit of squeezing a roll of bandages with my two hands across my front to stop my hands from shaking.

It was time for work again, and wee Caroline was waiting outside her flat. Anytime she wasn't in the hospital, she worked extra hours. She was the busiest of the two of us. I was always excited about work, and tonight was no different; I needed to get my sneaky fix. I realised that when I drank, I slept much better. When we arrived, the Melville Hotel was in flames, and the street was cordoned off. The windows burst under the immense heat. Wee Caroline started to cry, and I held her while she sobbed like a wain.

Tragically, two firefighters were killed tackling the blaze. It wasn't due to an IRA bomb or anything, but stories of how the Melville and the Irish Kitchen burned down have been subject to speculation. We ended up going down to The Favourite, and after that, I remember nothing.

Twenty

The Briefing

We were at the first aid post in Blucher Street at the turn of the New Year. I remember being with Wee Caroline, who had just come down from the newly established first aid post at St. Mary's in Creggan. Hugh Deehan's house in Creggan Heights and St. Mary's were now fully operational first aid posts.

Disturbances and gun battles between the Provisional IRA and the army near Creggan were common. As we were first responders, it was unreasonable to take someone from the top of Creggan down to the Bogside if they were wounded.

I tended to my first gun battle injury a few weeks before Bloody Sunday in early January 1972. We could hear a gun battle raging on William Street and were starting to know the difference between the boom of a baton round and the crack of a live round. When we heard cracks, we went closer to the sound, and it took us to William Street.

When we got there, a young IRA volunteer was lying on the ground, clutching his leg. It looked like he had been shot at the top of the thigh and was lying exposed on the footpath. I shouted to him, "crawl over behind that wall beside you!" He dragged himself over, leaving a trail of blood behind him.

He was wearing a long parka, fur hood, and balaclava mask. When he was in cover, we went over to him. Wee Caroline unbuttoned his trousers, and we saw the round had gone clean through, a neat circular hole at the top of his leg and a ragged exit wound at the back just above his knee. I applied cicatrene powder, an antibiotic, into the wound to clean it.

The fella was about eighteen or nineteen, no more than twenty. When I started to tourniquet his leg, he said, "thank you, love, thank you, love," in between his shallow breaths. The firing had stopped, and he slumped forward. He had fainted and had lost a fierce amount of blood, but he was still breathing.

His pulse was slightly thready, but not so worrying that I thought he would die. Wee Caroline said, "we can't leave him lying on his back. Go you and run for the ambulance, and I will prop him up against this wee wall."

"Good idea! Back in a minute," I scuttled to the end of Abbey Street. After running about twenty paces away, I heard a shot and wee Caroline shrieked and crumpled to her knees beside the fella. I dashed straight back over to her, "Fuck! Fuck! Fuck! Are you alright wee love?"

Wee Caroline was crying; she wasn't hurt, but when she tried to shift the young fella, she dropped him down sharply, and the revolver in his pocket went off. The gun blew a hole out the side of his jacket pocket, which was open, luckily, the barrel was pointing outward, and the bullet smacked a building across the street. Neither of them being seriously injured or worse was a miracle.

The boy came around and was extremely apologetic and upset. He was an awful grey colour, and I gave Caroline and him a glug of water before sprinting back for the ambulance. No doubt this boy would live, but he needed the wound treated in the hospital. He thanked us, "God bless yees, God bless yees."

This boy was around the same age as us, and before he was taken to Letterkenny Hospital, he asked for our names. Instinctively, when we said our names, we gave our addresses too because the army had stopped us so many times. A couple of days later, Caroline and I had a delivery of flowers to our doors. My card read, "For Martha, With Gratitude", and no name for who they were from.

Meanwhile, during the riots later that week, there was another incident in which Robert Cadman grabbed a lit petrol bomb out of somebody's hand before they could throw it. Leo Day just happened to be standing behind him.

This was quite a serious incident, and we had a meeting in Ozanam House on a windy Monday evening in January; Leo Day took to the front of the room and instructed everybody,

"If you are treating a casualty in the street, always ensure that they are not holding a weapon of any kind. This is not a public reprimand but something we had not foreseen. If an IRA Volunteer, a soldier, or the police are felled, ask their partner or comrade to ensure that their weapons are taken from them and that the safety mechanism of their guns is on. This is the same for nail bombs; we can only administer first aid if it is safe. We are there to treat injuries, not cause them. If you encounter armed casualties, you must find a telephone and call for an ambulance. We are not insured or protected in such situations, and the Northern Ireland Hospital Authority paramedics are."

We all nodded and took this incredibly seriously. All marches and processions were banned until the end of the year; we had all heard on the news and radios that morning. A protest march was planned for Magillian Strand on the 22nd of January. As the march was to walk down a private laneway and onto the beach, it was probably lawful as the law said there were to be no marches on public roads or pathways.

At protests and demonstrations, the participants were often battered by the security forces, and it was a good thing that we were there. There wasn't a policy for us to be present at marches, but ambulances wouldn't come unless they were called for. Leo Day wanted us to have as discreet a presence as possible. We were not to be at the front nor be seen as part of the march.

The march at Magilligan Strand went ahead, but because it fell on what would have been Daddy's birthday, I didn't go. Daddy's birthday was a sore day in our house, and we always marked it.

Mammy told me a lovely story of when he asked her to marry him. He bought flowers and had saved up his wages to buy a lovely side of beef from a fancy butcher up the town. He had asked her Mammy and Daddy for their permission and if he could make her something nice to eat in their kitchen because he still lived with his parents. Granny Moran insisted on helping him, but he had none of it. God love him; when Mammy came in from her work at Tillie's factory, she was greeted by the smell of a burnt round of beef. He had cremated it and given her the flowers.

They laughed at this burnt awful meal, and then he asked her to marry him, and she said yes. Mammy never told me this story before, and we had a wee cry together. Jesus, I fucking idolised that man, and the void in our flat was always there. We learned to live with the void, and yes, it did get easier, but even now, the void is still there. Daddy's suitcase in my bedroom is as close to Daddy's Room as I can get now.

I told Mammy I was going for a walk into the town to buy a new record or two. She was happy to let me go because she would have had a wee cry on her own. I had to go somewhere I had never been, the cemetery, to visit Daddy himself. I had no intention of going for a drink; I wouldn't have gone to a pub alone.

Daddy's grave could have been anywhere in the City Cemetery, so I walked along the graves, looking at their dates. I scanned along and got as far as 1961 when Daddy lost his hearing. Then the January 1962 graves came into view. I walked along the graves, and my breathing got much shallower as I got to the August 1962 graves.

Bradley is a common name, and when I saw the name on the foot of some headstones, I shuddered and became almost relieved that the Christian name wasn't right. A couple of men around a grave nearby gave me a bit of an odd look when they saw me.

Eventually, it came into view at the end of the row. I had no flowers on me, as I didn't know that leaving flowers down was the done thing. I crumpled when I saw Daddy's headstone,

In Loving Memory of

Francis Christopher Bradley

Died 2nd Oct 1962

I went over and threw my arms around his headstone; I cried my heart out in that cemetery. I must have cried for about ten minutes solid. I squeezed the monument in my arms as hard as I could, "I hope you're okay, Daddy, wherever you are. Derek is away in London with his "friend" Liam. My work burned down a pile of weeks back, I'm in the Knights of Malta, people are getting killed. I can barely sleep the nights I'm not working because I don't take a nightcap."

I poured my heart and soul out to Daddy's grave. I just kept talking and talking. I stood there for an hour and kissed his headstone before I left. I walked down the Lecky Road to go home, and the temptation to buy a drink after walking past several pubs was immense. I didn't want to disappoint Daddy, so I didn't.

More graffiti was appearing around the flats, political statements, recruitment statements for the Republican movement. Walking up the slope between blocks two and three, when I stopped and looked at the place, I realised that the high flats were starting to look unsightly.

Speaking of unsightly, Hugh and the boys were pushing the wee car into the car park again. After weeks, they still couldn't determine what a mile was on the road or how long a gallon of petrol would last them. They pushed the car back into Hugh's parking space and scattered away into their flats. Hugh and the boys went up the town, and he bought a pair of brogues and had them "tipped". For young people, men used to have metal bits hammered to the bottom of their shoes in those days. I heard him walking around the balconies. Everyone did! You could hear him from a mile away with his ballet dancer brogues! He loved these new shoes; they were his new pride and joy.

Whenever he went for a wee bit of stone-throwing of an evening, it didn't matter a damn if he had his entire face covered. Anyone would know him with those clicky brogues; they are a fond recollection of mine and his friends. He didn't care what anybody thought about him. If he thought something was funny, he would do it! Purely for his enjoyment. It took me years to develop the same mindset as him; it is a nice way to be.

That night I heard the news about the protest march at Magilligan Strand and that the Paras had battered and beaten those who were there. Hugh Deehan went down. Not because anybody was ordered to be there, but because he wanted to go. He brought the first aid trunk with him. The Paras were so ferocious in their firing of baton rounds and their baton charges that some of their own men needed to restrain them. John Hume confronted them and demanded they stop firing rubber bullets at them. It was horrendous, and part of me felt guilty for not being there, even though the 22nd of January was a sacred family day.

The following morning, I heard about a march organised for Sunday the 30th of January 1972, and I already told Mammy that I would go to make up for missing Magilligan Strand. People were knocking on the doors of the flats to drum up support for the march; they wanted large numbers. Flyers were posted through letterboxes, posters went up in the stairwells, and everybody was talking about it.

Wee Caroline had insider info,

"Was with Joe last night, and the march came up."

"Oh! What did he say?"

"There was talk of blocking the march from going to the Guildhall and putting roadblocks up. Big row! The Jackets have been here a while, and they told command that it was a terrible idea!"

"Sure, they will have to let the march pass, wee love! There will be too many. The whole town is going, and all the politicians are going to speak at it."

"What if they bring the Paras in, Martha?"

"They won't; them boys are all on the naughty step after last week, love! Don't worry about it. Mystic Martha knows the craic."

Jesus, that was an emotional sentence; I am writing as I think, and whoever gets their grubby hands on this to edit, this isn't to be removed. This is incredibly hard to write about. Trying to capture a festive mood of hope pre- the 30th of January 1972, versus now knowing what happened on the day, is impossible for me.

We were all to meet at Ozanam House on Monday, and it was here that we got our briefing for the 30th of January 1972. All of us were expected to be present on that day. There were thirty in the room, and our first instruction was to get into pairs and stay in our pairs whilst on the march. Naturally, wee Caroline was my partner. The younger volunteers were all going on the march; the older volunteers would remain near the first aid posts. Leo was very fit and active, so he was coming on the march.

As there were thousands expected, we needed to be prepared for the disorder of any kind, and we were told we would be issued three shell dressings that day instead of the usual one. Plus some more bandages, ointment bottles, sterilised pads, and antiseptic creams. We were getting our supplies from the Irish Army then, and more supplies were ordered in preparation.

Leo told us to avoid walking on the road with the march. As this was deemed an illegal procession, the Order couldn't afford to be fined or face prosecution. Therefore, we were told to walk on the footpath alongside the march.

We were to meet at the Bishop's field at half past one for the headcount and then disperse along the adjacent footpaths at specific intervals from near the front of the march to the rear. When the crowd was on the move, we would walk alongside on the footpath.

Hugh Deehan was to pick the ambulance up at half-past one on Sunday, and I felt we were somewhat prepared even if bad things happened. He was to remain in Creggan with the ambulance in a workman's hut with a telephone. Should the ambulance be called for, he was to take the ambulance down to act as a mobile first aid post if the other posts were overrun.

The nerves were setting in by the weekend; I didn't have an outlet for drinking since the Irish Kitchen burned down. Although, strangely, the night before Bloody Sunday, I slept as well as I had in the past year. Daddy must have known I would have needed it.

Twenty-One

Bloody Sunday

Whenever I got up on the morning of the 30th of January 1972, there was an air of excitement, believe it or not. The atmosphere around the flats was electric; the city would later take to the streets to demand civil rights. Technically, marches were banned several months before, but we couldn't wait to go out in droves and give the middle finger to the establishment.

Although I would be joining the march as a first aider, I was very aligned with the sentiment of the civil rights movement of that time. The spirit in the flats was still very much there, but the substandard construction was starting to become apparent. As I had my breakfast that morning, there was a metal bucket in the kitchen to catch drips from a leak in the ceiling. Drip. Drip. Drip.

You could hear a fart from five flats down, so hearing everyone's excited voices was very easy from where I sat that morning, at the table with Mammy.

"Now Martha, you watch yourself today. Do you hear me?" Mammy said sternly to me.

"Mammy, it will be okay; I heard that the IRA are staying away completely. Heard it in bed last night. The march is going to be peaceful. There might be the odd wee brick here and there, but sure that's life! That's why we are going to help."

All around the flats, people were buzzing, and rumour had it that over twenty thousand people were going to march the roads.

I took my cup of tea out to the balcony around eleven o'clock. I liked to walk around and give my legs a stretch. I walked along the balcony, saying my good mornings to everyone, and came to the point on the balcony of our block where I could see across the car park and into the adjacent Chamberlain Street.

There were two Saracens, a ferret car, squaddies unfurling barbed wire, and the soldiers lifting wooden planks on the far side of Chamberlain Street, which led onto William Street. That was when I thought, *isn't that where the march is going?* Even at first glance, I didn't think anything of it.

As this was a large march, and I was needed for first aid cover, I got to miss Mass that morning. Mammy went without me, and I threw on my white coat and kit bag. Most of the flats were at Mass, and the place was very peaceful as I walked down to wee Caroline. She was a bit more fearful; she had insider information due to her lover boy Joe.

"Martha, Joe told me last night that they are putting barricades up because it is an illegal procession. Command insisted on it. The boys all protested, and they were all shocked. They are asking for a riot!"

"Aw Jesus Caroline, now I'm thinking of it; I saw rolls of wire and planks carried out of army cars at the Chamberlain Street junction of William Street."

We started to get slightly worried, but we went downstairs to be up at St. Mary's Chapel in good time.

As we were leaving wee Caroline's, Hugh came out onto the balcony, closely chased by Mrs Gilmour. She was shouting at him, "you wrecked those good jeans! I got those jeans in Paddy Bannon's!" The style back then was bleached jeans for the boys.

Hugh had tried to bleach the jeans himself, bless him. He gave her fifty pence and told her, "I will give you more later when I get back." It was her birthday the following day, and he had every intention of treating her.

We left about one o'clock and turned right to cross over the rubble barricade that stretched across the entire road on Rossville Street, from the entrance of Glenfada Park directly across to around halfway up block one of the flats, save for a small gap in the middle. We continued down Rossville Street, turned left up William Street, past the Cathedral, and up Creggan Hill. Crowds were leaving Mass, and we found ourselves walking with others as we summited Creggan Hill. The carnival atmosphere was still alive, and people had talked about the march for the past couple of days. I vividly remember somebody saying, "sure; the Brits had a PR disaster at Magilligan last week; they will be on their best behaviour today; it's a wee cert."

Jesus, even recalling that quote gives me the urge to vomit.

The Knights of Malta are always visible, so the clump of white coats was easy to find among the ever-growing sea of people gathering at the Bishop's Field, adjacent to St. Mary's Chapel. The coal lorry was there, so the organisers could stand on it as the march proceeded on the route through Creggan, down the winding hill of Southway, left onto the Lone Moor Road, right through the Lecky Road, left up Westland Street, right along Laburnum Terrace, and down William Street towards the Guildhall.

I have a haunting memory of that morning. A house on Iniscarn Road, across from the chapel, had all the windows open. Caroline and I walked around saying hello to people we knew, and I heard their radio. I will never forget it.

Blasting out the radio was the number one hit in the UK charts on that day, The New Seekers – "I'd Like To Teach The World To Sing".

Caroline was singing, "I'd like to see the world for once, all standing hand in hand! And hear them echo through the hills, for peace throughout the land!" as she pointed at me and pointed to the massive assembly. Jesus Christ, my beating heart...

There was a big blue banner with "CIVIL RIGHTS ASSOCIATION" behind McGlinchey's coal lorry, and everyone was in jovial spirits. It was a lovely clear morning, bright but cold. Even in the thick white Malta coat, I was eager to set off as my feet were getting cold.

The organisers were shouting on the bullhorn, "please stay behind the coal lorry!", and cheers were erupting now and then. This was very much a family event, women had babies in prams, and those who were elderly were there too. It wasn't a bunch of men riled up for a fight, the spirit of that morning was infectious. So much so, that at two o'clock we still hadn't set off.

Mr Day came to Caroline and me, looking slightly worried,

"Can you two remain near the front of the march, please? Don't forget to remain on the footpath. We are going to spread out as there are so many people."

"Yes, Mr Day," we both responded and took our positions just to the right of the coal lorry. Men with white handkerchiefs tied to their arms were the march stewards, and there didn't seem to be that many for a march this size.

"Martha, what if those stewards can't manage everybody?"

"Awk don't you worry sunshine," I said to her. "Mr Cooper said he will give me that bullhorn, and I will put everybody right." A trademark "Mouthy Martha" quip, didn't reassure her at all.

The coal lorry fired up, the NICRA banner flew aloft, and with two blasts of the lorry horn, we set off just after half past two.

The crowd erupted, and away we went. Older people on their porches were applauding us. As we approached the downward winding Southway, we felt unstoppable.

A group of girls behind us started singing our national anthem, Amhrán na bhFiann, as we walked down the hill. I turned around with Caroline, and we looked at all the homemade signs that people made, "END SPECIAL POWERS ACT NOW", "NO INTERNMENT", and placards with names of people who had been scooped off the street and imprisoned without trial – anybody who remotely looked like they were a member of, or supported the IRA, was taken.

The atmosphere intensified as we got closer and closer to the Guildhall, the singing and cheers got louder, and all the way there we got support from everybody standing on their porches. I hadn't experienced anything quite like it before, as people we had enough of being cast aside and treated like lepers on our own patch. As we marched up Westland Street and turned right onto Laburnum Terrace, the crowd erupted in song,

"We shall overcome! We shall Overcome! Someday!"

As we proceeded down the long straight of William Street toward the Guildhall, I noticed young people running out in front of us. The stewards were attempting to call them back. Some returning, and others running forward. There were words and whispers that a British Army Barricade was ahead, and we were marching right into it. More pockets of hankie-faced wee boys were starting to run past us, and out beyond the front of the march.

I heard Marie's booming voice coming from behind us, "Martha!" "Caroline!" We turned around, and she shoved her way through the crowd, bumping from side to side like a pinball. The white coat always caused people to step aside, but she was coming toward us quite slowly due to the sheer volume of people.

She was battered when she got to us and confirmed, "there is a barricade down at William Street! The route has been blocked! Go down to the barrier and meet up with us later!"

Caroline and I started to become frantic halfway down William Street. The stewards shouted, "turn right down Rossville Street, don't confront the army! This is a peaceful protest!"

It was in vain; we knew at this point that confrontation was inevitable. The stewards ran forward to try and divert the marchers and stop some of the youths running past them toward William Street. There were too few stewards, and I realised that the march would lose control.

"Stick together, Martha, this is a big crowd, and there will be a lot of anger."

I just held out my hand and held wee Caroline's. I nodded, and she felt a bit reassured. We walked down the right-hand footpath of William Street holding hands, and I squeezed her hand to stop my own from shaking.

The coal lorry was blaring the horn and trying to signal everyone to turn right to pass the Rossville Flats and gather at Free Derry Corner. The coal lorry disappeared off to our right down Rossville Street, and we walked down William Street into the abyss.

When we walked down toward the junction of Chamberlain Street and William Street, I saw the Royal Green Jackets manning a barrier and could almost hear their gulps as we walked toward them. The crowd started roaring when the barricade came into full view, with barbed wire and wooden barriers and about twenty wearing visors. We stayed behind a twelve feet high "CIVIL RIGHTS ASSOCIATION" banner, which two men were carrying.

There looked to be some RUC officers behind them standing at the bottom of Waterloo Street beyond the barrier, and Caroline and I ran out in front of the march alongside the stewards. We all held hands to try and push the crowd back, but there were only three dozen of us to attempt to hold back around four or five hundred.

It was no good; Caroline and I took up our positions outside McCool's newsagents, and we saw others from the unit near us. We had a perfect view of the initial confrontation between the soldiers and the stewards. I heard their commander saying, "this is an illegal procession." I knew the riot would start at any minute as soon as those words left his lips.

I looked at them all individually. Even when angry marchers were reaching over the barrier at the soldiers and spitting at them, the soldiers didn't shout back at them. Eventually, they retreated behind the doors of their vehicles. When the rumbles were getting louder, the arc of a bottle flew out from the crowd toward the soldiers. A few seconds later, a brick followed and knocked an RUC man's cap off his head. Bottles were starting to fly, bricks were flying toward the soldiers, and we could see the Jackets loading baton rounds.

We were too close to the barrier, so we decided to keep our heads down and cross the street whilst the booms of the baton rounds were being discharged toward the rioters. We saw video cameras, photographers, and the press. Caroline shouted to me amongst the rioting, "at least the cameras will be able to show people what happens here."

After we reached the other side, the tracks of the water cannon were rumbling up to the barrier. When people saw it, they retreated and ran back up to the junction of William Street and

Rossville Street. The cannon was blasted out, and the water had a tinge of red or purple.

The most vivid sound from when the water cannon started spraying everyone was the sound of women screaming. The water cannon had dispersed almost everyone, save for around sixty or seventy. We didn't see anybody we knew there, and a group of young fellas arrived with a corrugated sheet to act as a shield. Gas was filtering through the air, and we heard some people choking. I went to a lady around twenty metres from me and handed her a drink of water and a vinegar-soaked rag to help her come to her senses. The soldiers battered the corrugated sheet with baton rounds, but it became slightly quieter after about ten minutes.

"Right, missus, this is dying down. Will we make our way around to Free Derry Corner? I think the wee boys are getting a bit bored now," I said to Caroline.

Before Caroline could reply, a group of soldiers started gathering at the barrier; I heard their commander, or whoever he was, shout to the men.

"When you cross this barrier, men, do *not* chase them down Rossville Street! Go get them! Go on the Paras!"

"Oh fuck!" Caroline blurted to me before turning to the rioters, "Run, boys! the Brits are coming forward, go!"

With that, the wee boys all scattered down Chamberlain Street, back up William Street, and we turned to run back up toward Rossville Street. I looked over my left shoulder, and the Paras ran out to the barrier's other side.

We took a sharp left onto Rossville Street and slowed down. We thought the soldiers wouldn't advance any further as we heard them being ordered not to chase anybody down Rossville Street. It made sense in my mind, as there would be nothing to separate rioters from peaceful marchers due to the sheer volume of people.

Three Saracen cars were driving into Rossville Street, and Caroline looked at me, bewildered. "This isn't what is supposed to happen," she whispered. When the doors flung open, the red-capped paras jumped out and were doing exactly what they were ordered *not* to do, chasing people down Rossville Street. I didn't know much of the following was happening on Bloody Sunday itself, but I was able to piece it all together in the years since.

As we jogged further down Rossville Street, past the Eden Place waste ground to our left, we saw a soldier standing over Charlie McMonagle lying on the ground. His kit bag was tipped out, and he was getting back to his feet. There were a few more white coats around, and the disarray was beginning.

"Oh God, Caroline, Run!" I yelped to her, so we ran down Rossville Street toward the flats when I heard a sickening crack that stopped us in our tracks.

"That wasn't a baton round or a canister of gas!" Caroline was almost hyperventilating at this point, and so was I. A wee boy, who I learned later was Jackie Duddy, was lying on the ground on his back at the rear of the flats. Father Daly and Charlie Glenn were there, praying and trying to give him aid.

Rosemary, another Malta girl, was shot in the face with a baton round from about four feet away. She was wearing her gas mask, but the round had injured her jaw and loosened some of her teeth. I started roaring, shouting, and losing my temper. I roared over, "we're first aid! It's a war crime to attack us!"

A man beside me grabbed me and said, "don't antagonise them, missus, they're shooting real bullets."

The Paras were running amok around the courtyard of the flats, one of them was swinging his rifle like an axe and smacked a wee old man in the face with it. I ran toward him, and he was very shaken and bleeding from his nose. I pulled out a little patch of bandages from my kit bag and told him to hold the bandage to his nose with his left hand and pinch the bridge of his nose with his right. People were frozen in terror and unable to move.

I was used to rioting and the odd bit of trouble at Aggro Corner, but my legs felt incredibly heavy, and I was trying to control my breathing to keep calm. It was impossible. My hands were shaking, and my eyes were welling up with tears.

There were more volleys of cracks, we ran toward the rubble barricade, and we saw people taking cover on the ground. Caroline was facing the flats carpark and roared,

"That army car just fucking ran over that wee girl; it drove straight at her!" She ran off to help, and I ran alone to the rubble barricade. Hugh was there, and he stood up after lying down in cover. Just as he turned and ran a couple of paces toward the flats, he jumped up and shouted, "I'm hit! I'm hit!" clutching his left arm but remaining on his feet and running toward the block one entrance door.

"It's alright wee love; it's only an arm wound! Keep going!" I roared to him, and he ran on. He started doubling over just as he got to the door of the flats, and two men grabbed him by each arm and took him around the side between blocks one and two.

Cracks and volleys were flying down the street, and I could almost hear the whoosh of the bullets as they passed. Eventually, I dived into the corner between blocks one and two of the flats. There was a collection of people huddled inside the red telephone box.

Hugh was lying on the ground, and people were talking to him. There were about twenty people so I couldn't see him. He was being seen to, so I didn't worry. There were frightened civilians and a couple of other white coats coming in and out of Joseph Place.

I peeked around the corner and saw a clump of people at the gable wall of Glenfada Park, including Father Bradley; they were tending to Michael Kelly, who was shot just after Jackie Duddy, while I was running down Rossville Street.

I saw a wee boy stand up from a bending position at the barricade. A crack rang out, and the wee boy fell to the ground screaming. He was shot high in the chest. I learned this wee lad was Willie "Stiff" Nash. He had nothing in his hands.

Two other boys, John Young and Michael McDaid, fell in quick succession as they ran out to help; it happened in seconds. They had nothing on them except their intentions to help the wounded Nash.

Mammy came round the corner and begged me to go upstairs into the flat. She was tugging my coat, and I said, "people needed our help; we are all they have! Ambulances won't come near this place. Hugh was shot in the arm! There are three wee boys shot over there, plus I saw another one in the back carpark." Mammy stayed nearby and wasn't letting me out of her sight.

Around the corner and out of my line of sight, a wee boy was crawling on the road toward block one. He was struck by a bullet from behind and dragged inside. Jim Norris, one of our unit, happened to be coming down the stairs looking for someone to help him treat somebody who was smacked in the face with a CS canister. Jim helped carry the wounded wee boy upstairs, and another bullet struck the main door of the flats while he was doing so. The poor soul was Kevin McElhinney.

While this was happening, Willie Nash's father was also shot and wounded whilst trying to go to his son's aid at the barricade. I didn't see this either, but I remember people shouting, "they shot that wee old man too!" If I had seen that, my heart would have shattered there and then, and I wouldn't have been able to go on.

The shots and the army shouts were one thing, but the sound of my neighbours whimpering and crying inside their flats was profound. It was pandemonium. Doors were slamming inside the flats, children were crying, and I heard some alarms going off.

Some people huddled at the corner of the flats had cuts and bruises, and a few of us patched up and reassured the petrified people. There was an inconsolable older man there; all I could do was rub his back and offer him water. Other unit members were carrying people into the houses in Joseph Place, just beside block two. I started retching when I saw two Malta men taking Alana Burke into one of the houses. An army jeep hit her.

A young boy of about fifteen was crawling past one of the thrupenny bits in front of us. I heard a window fly open above my head, and a woman shouted, "lie still, son!" The wee boy did just that and turned his head to his left to face me. People were taking cover behind the thrupenny bits. I looked at him; he was so close that I could see a tear running down his face — sheer terror. Every time there was a crack, he closed his eyes and flinched. Eventually, the youngster rose to his feet and bolted toward the gap between blocks two and three. I was relieved he escaped.

Some other volunteers were around me, and I saw commotion across the street in Glenfada Park. I stood up from a crouching position and was seething was rage. I was angry, furious! I looked at the clump of white coats beside me, and they almost read my mind and were pleading, "Martha, don't!"

I peeked around the corner, and Marie put her arm around me. "Martha, if you go out there, they will shoot!" I shoved Marie out of the way and left cover; I was completely exposed as my legs took off across the rubble barricade.

The stinging cloud of CS gas, the volley fire, and the screams of the people merged as zipping bullets flew out continuously now from beyond the veil. I heard the bullets zip past my hair and arms, and I stopped at the gap in the middle of the barricade.

I pointed toward them and roared, "stop fucking firing! We are unarmed!" There were two soldiers beside an open Saracen door, and one slapped his partner's rifle barrel downward. I am convinced they would have shot me dead if that hadn't happened.

The place seemed to fall silent, and some more cracks of gunfire flew past me as I stood still. I then heard a snobby accent roar to the men, and I will never forget it, "Do not fire back for the moment! Unless you identify a positive target!"

As soon as he shouted that, I ran into Glenfada Park. As I passed, I looked at the three innocent wee boys. They were all dead. I took cover at that gable wall, just opposite where the Museum of Free Derry is now and looked over toward the flats. I put my hands over my ears and was coming down from the adrenaline rush.

I seldom prayed, but I remember shaking and whimpering out loud, "if you can hear me, Daddy, please help me, If you can hear me, Daddy, please help me."

Three men were lying in Glenfada Park along the far left-hand fence in front of the maisonettes. They were moving slightly, and I could tell they were seriously wounded after being shot in the back. William McKinney, Joe Mahon, and Jim Wray. A crack rang out, and the man lying closest to the alleyway between Glenfada Park and Abbey Park jarred and lay still. The Paras had shot Jim Wray again as he was lying wounded on the ground;

I was frozen in terror. I struggled to breathe and wanted to scream, but I couldn't.

Further through the gap, beyond the alleyway, another clump of first aiders surrounded a man and a boy on the ground, Gerard McKinney and Gerald Donaghey. I didn't recognise Gerald that day, even though we both did some of our growing up in Wellington Street. Robert Cadman was leading the group that looked to be giving the man CPR and rescue breaths, and I assumed at that time that they were helping someone who had a heart attack. Both were carried away into houses in Abbey Park. I could see Mr Day through the gap. He was in his full-dress uniform and easy to spot among the crowd. Throughout, the Paras were constantly shouting at us and training their rifles on us

After the shooting stopped for about a minute, Eiblin ran out from the gap of Glenfada Park and shouted, "Red Cross! Red Cross! Don't Shoot!" A thump hit the wall beside her, and I started crying sore when the bastards shot at her. She fell to her knees and was holding her leg. The bullet had torn her trouser leg, and it was a miracle she wasn't hit. Mr Day came back through the gap between Glenfada Park and Abbey Park to assist with carrying Jim Wray to a house in Abbey Park. Sean McDermott was part of the group that carried William McKinney in the same direction. I noticed Leo wearing what I thought to be a lady's shoulder bag, but as it turns out, it was William McKinney's cine-camera bag. Someone had handed it to him, thinking it was one of our kitbags, and he looked after it.

People in Glenfada had been injured by debris and even bullet fragments. My hands were shaking as I put bandages on and wiped dust out of people's eyes with my water-soaked rags. Whilst this was going on, some people were being carried through the north-western alleyway.

A wee boy, Michael Quinn, wearing a bright orange jacket was shot in the face, and people were shouting for him to run up to Blucher Street to the first aid post. He stumbled through the alley, and off he went before I could get to him.

There was a lull in the firing, and it stopped after some minutes. Ambulances started to arrive and were putting the dead and injured into them. I saw a couple of Knights of Malta going into the ambulances with them. I saw Jim Norris and Bernard Feeney helping to carry Kevin McElhinney to an awaiting ambulance; just after they prayed and placed him in the ambulance, the Paras opened fire again, and they fell to the ground. I crumpled to my knees and two men helped me back up again, I could see them lying there and thought they were dead. When the firing stopped, they got back up again, and I was beyond relieved.

I crept across the barricade, and the three bodies that were once there had been lifted. I assumed they were put in ambulances at the time. I heard afterwards that they were thrown into the back of an Army Pig. The whimpers from everybody around haunt me to this day; people stayed in cover for what seemed a long time after the firing stopped. Around Glenfada Park and toward the waste ground at Eden Place, people were standing facing walls with their palms to the wall and being arrested!

I reached the other side of the barricade and was back with the rest of the Knights of Malta. Most tried to put on brave faces, but we all held hands, hugged, and wept. Some of their white coats were stained with blood, and some even carried their own injuries.

I looked over to where Hugh was lying and felt my soul leave my body. Somebody was draping him with the Derry Civil Rights Banner, staining it with his blood, and he wasn't moving. There was a pool of blood by his left side; I hadn't realised earlier on that the round had passed through his arm and had entered his side or if he had been shot a second time as he was running toward the flats.

My knees buckled, and Mammy ran over to me and threw herself to the ground beside me. I screamed, cried, and punched; Mammy took every single blow. She was praying in my ear, and I kept looking over at Hugh until he was put on a stretcher by paramedics and taken away in the ambulance.

There was another body near Hugh, Barney McGuigan, who was shot trying to go to the aid of the wounded Paddy Doherty whilst waving a white handkerchief. Paddy Doherty and Barney McGuigan were shot dead while I was on the other side of the street, but Mammy was there and saw everything.

I was worried about Wee Caroline and was in full panic, wondering if she was okay. She had gone towards Chamberlain Street and helped to assist those shot and injured who were carried into the houses from the street. Wee Caroline came over, and she was cried out. We all were at this point.

She told me that a child and an older gentleman had been shot. John Johnson and Damian Donaghey, and that Damian Donaghey was only fifteen. John Johnston would be the fourteenth victim of Bloody Sunday; he passed away five months after being shot. Damian Donaghey was seriously wounded but pulled through, as did Joe Mahon, who was shot in Glenfada Park.

Majella and Charlie were over in Chamberlain Street and treated Peggy Deery, and we were all shocked that the army had shot a widow with fourteen children. The last time I saw Charlie, he was getting battered by the Paras. After that, he immediately went to help those wounded and was taken to the houses on Chamberlain Street.

I couldn't speak; I don't think I told her that Hugh was dead because I had gone into shock. Wee Caroline linked onto my arm, and she and Mammy had to help me up the stairwell. My legs turned to jelly, and my mind became somewhat blurry after this point. I was helped into the flat, and Mammy cradled me on the settee. I didn't talk; I just cried. Mammy turned the television on, and an army commander said four gunmen were shot dead in Derry on the six o'clock news. I leapt off the sofa and roared at the television,

"Fucking gunmen? No gunmen down there. Are they trying to say Hugh was holding a gun? Murdering bastards! Fucking tramps! Tramps! Those wee boys at the barricade had nothing in their hands!"

This was the only time Mammy didn't reprimand me for swearing, "I know love, three at the barricade, three at the side of the flats, the wee boy carried out of block one."

"Aye, and I would say four or five more from the Glenfada side! That's twelve or thirteen. Where the fuck are they getting four from? I saw them firing from the hip and dropping to their knees to shoot!"

Mammy started sobbing, and I hadn't heard her sob like that since she found my Daddy hanging in the scullery in Wellington Street ten years prior.

"I knew Mr McGuigan, a lovely man. Around the same age as your father and I roughly. Paddy Doherty was also trying to crawl behind a wall when he was shot from behind. People tried to help, but the soldiers kept shooting. I saw Leo Day with him too."

I told her what had happened to Hugh. He was running back toward the flats and shot from behind while running away. Mammy was distraught, and when the phone rang, all she said was,

"Hello, Derek, Martha and I are okay. Will call you back later?" and hung up the phone.

After this, I hauled myself up from the settee, held onto the staircase's handrail, went down to Daddy's room, and shut the door behind me. I just lay in the foetal position on the floor. I cried and cried and cried. I couldn't stop. My hands and legs were shaking, and Mammy came in and lay on the floor beside me the entire night.

The Knights of Malta were everywhere that day. Most of us were only young, under the age of twenty-one. We treated whoever we could and prayed for the people we couldn't. What struck me as I lay on the floor in the foetal position was that it was Mrs Gilmour's birthday tomorrow.

Twenty-Two

St. Mary's Chapel

I remember little but the silence that Monday. Everyone remembers that horrific silence that descended upon us. Most people I talk to about Bloody Sunday say that the following days were a blur. I lay on the floor in Daddy's room and didn't eat a bite. I only left to go into the toilet and was dry retching because I hadn't taken any food or drink.

Mammy came in with a Valium tablet and a glass of water. It made no difference other than taking my memory of that day away. I remember it being one o'clock, thinking Hugh was alive twenty-four hours ago. Now he is gone and must be waked on his Mammy's birthday.

Typically in Daddy's room, I could hear people bickering in the next flat or above us. The window faced out onto Free Derry Corner, and I could see clumps of people, but I couldn't hear anything due to all the hushed tones. I thought about Daddy, so many people were talking, yet I couldn't hear anything. It was horrific.

Years later, I heard that Floyd and Bernard Gilmour went to the hospital on the evening of Bloody Sunday to visit Hugh as they believed he was shot and wounded. They got to the window of the nurses' station in Altnagelvin Casualty and said they were there to visit Hugh Gilmour. The nurse just said, "morgue!" and slammed the window on them.

According to Joe, again telling me years later, there was an almighty punch up in the barracks in Ebrington that night. The Paras had been pulled out of Derry, and the sentiment among the army was that the Paras should have their lives put on the line patrolling the streets after what they did. It was a fair point, the Paras did the murdering, and the other units of the British Army had to pick up the pieces.

Memory is a fickle thing. I know now that my memory is going, I know now that I have little memory of the days after Bloody Sunday, yet I remember some things so vividly. I am still in touch with many old friends from the flats, and they recall very little. Mammy came over to visit me a couple of weeks ago, and we talked about it.

"I don't remember anything. I don't know what I did. I don't know what you did. It was just dreadful," she said.

Only one word for it, trauma. We were all traumatised that thirteen people were murdered in the streets; there were reports in the newspapers that the army had won an IRA gun battle.

Joe told me years later,

"When I saw the newspapers the next day, some of us were pretty upset. If anyone knew who the ringleaders were in the riots, it was us. None of the portraits in the paper were any ringleaders or big players we knew.

Some of the boys at the barracks were very clear in that what they saw in the Bogside was murder. Many of them told command that the Paras were firing from the hip and had murdered six children under eighteen, three men not far off eighteen, a twenty-six-year-old Derry Journal worker with a camera, and three married men with young children.

They were preparing to leave and return to the barracks because the rioters were bored. When the paras came and started running amok, the boys became enraged. One of my fellow Jackets was in the group of soldiers who witnessed Father Daly and the group of men carrying Jackie Duddy along Chamberlain Street, and he was deeply affected.

Plenty of The Jackets and the Coldstream Guards at the barricades made it clear to command that the murderous behaviour of the Paras was a stain on the security forces. The cover-up started that night after thirteen men were murdered, and many others wounded and carried into houses."

Hugh was the least political person I knew. It is repeated throughout my recollection of him because it is the same recollection as the rest of his nearest and dearest friends group. He wasn't part of anything; he didn't want to be either. He fended a lot of peer pressure and did what made him happy. What sticks out in my mind is not looking anywhere near his parking space in the flat's carpark. I couldn't face it and never did. It was like my brain protected me from looking at it.

It was the same as the funerals at St. Mary's where the march had started; I remember very little, we all had to stand outside, and it was pouring. There was a speaker outside so we could hear the funeral mass, but the audio was so muffled I could only pick up a few words between the weeps of the massive crowds surrounding us.

It was forty-one years ago, but in my mind, Bloody Sunday, 30th January 1972, was five or six years ago.

The day itself is so vivid. I can smell the gunfire, hear people screaming, and feel the rage still. The anger was regarded by many, as there was a queue right the way up the stairwell of the flats with young men and women wanting to join the IRA.

A week passed, and we all had to give statements about what we saw; the Order of Malta Command wanted reports from all of us, and we gave them on the 8th of February. There was a mass for us at St. Eugene's Cathedral, and everyone was given a bronze Maltese Cross medal with their name and "1972" engraved on the back.

***

Lord Widgery had commissioned an inquiry into the murder of Hugh and the twelve others in February. It was to take place in Coleraine, practically on the other side of the world to us at the time, and tons of statements were taken from those who had witnessed the events of Bloody Sunday.

It was over as quick as it started. Over about six weeks, only thirty or so civilian witness statements were allowed as evidence. The Gilmour's were one of those few. Olive had witnessed Jackie Duddy being shot dead in the courtyard of the flats as it was just below the flat where she, Bernard, and her young children lived at the time.

As a family, they prepared statements, trying to recall all they had seen that day. Olive saw Mickey Bridge being shot and wounded and Paddy Doherty lying on the ground at the front of block two, which would have been below her sitting-room window.

Bernard Gilmour was called to the stand, and after confirming that he was Hugh's brother and that he had identified him in the mortuary of Altnagelvin Hospital, he wasn't asked any more questions, which was pretty much it.

The report came out in April that year and cleared all the soldiers of the blame, with blame directed at those who had been murdered that day. Another sickening element was that Gerald Donaghey was "discovered" to have nail bombs in his pocket when his body was taken to a British Army post. After the car he was being taken to hospital in was seized, the driver, Raymond Rogan and Leo Young, the brother of John Young, were arrested. Leo didn't even know that his brother, John Young, was dead.

I only learned later in the evening of Bloody Sunday that Gerald Donaghey had died, or maybe I knew the following day.

Leo Day was in that vicinity at the time, he helped carry Joe Mahon through the alleyway of Glenfada Park to Abbey Park whilst Gerald Donaghey was lying on the ground. Robert Cadman gave rescue breaths to Gerard McKinney, and Mr Day oversaw the first aid effort being administered to both of them. As Captain, there wasn't a snowball's chance in Hell that Mr Day would permit anybody to render aid to anybody who had one nail bomb visible on their person, never mind more. The protocol would have been to clear the area and immediately call for an ambulance. None of us saw any weapons of any kind on anybody. Leo was the calm voice of reason for us on Bloody Sunday, even though I wasn't in his ear or eyeshot for almost all of it. Seeing him nearby was enough.

That wee boy didn't have fucking nail bombs in his pocket. End of story.

The army denied shooting at the first aiders, which, may I add, is a war crime; they shot at Eiblin. I saw it, and there are bullet holes still in Glenfada Park to prove it. Rosemary Doyle was shot in the face with a baton round. Charlie Glenn was battered and arrested after carrying Jackie Daddy up to Waterloo Street to await an ambulance that was phoned; Charlie McMonagle was battered and had a rifle pointed into his chest. He had to point frantically at his Knights of Malta emblem to convince the Para roughing him up not to shoot him dead.

Even when some of the first aid girls went forward to the Paras to ask for stretchers or to let ambulances through, the troops jeered at them, whilst having rifles pointed at them. Majella had her kitbag thrown away after treating the woman they shot, Peggy Deery.

Not to mention Jim Norris and Bernard Feeney had to throw themselves on the ground under gunfire whilst helping to take people to ambulances. The Derry unit treated all of those who were mortally wounded, all of them! There aren't many photographs of Bloody Sunday that don't show them treating the mortally wounded and injured and at the epicentre of everything. All their statements were ignored by Lord Widgery.

Even if nobody was murdered that day, the paras should be brought in front of The Hague for War Crimes for how they treated the Knights of Malta that day. That is how strongly I feel about it. These were my friends, my colleagues, and my heroes. This book is about memory, and everyone has different experiences when it comes to Bloody Sunday.

Wee Caroline wanted to go to England, as did Joe. The opportunity was there to leave, and she had every intention of taking it. I had no job anymore; wee Caroline had finished her nursing course and could walk into a hospital anywhere. She was making arrangements and had remained friends with another girl that had worked in the Irish Kitchen with us, Stella.

Going to dances and discos was a joy for wee Caroline; for me, it wasn't. We were sadly drifting by the end of 1971 and the start of 1972. She was meeting with Joe, and I wasn't going out. In March of 1972, she and Stella left to go to England. I was upset that she was going, but I didn't trust myself to go. I didn't want to be far from home or Daddy's room.

I have always been the type to become homesick quickly. On my honeymoon, with that boy I married in 1980, we went on a cruise around Australia, New Zealand, and Samoa. After about a week, I wanted to come home. I never went on holiday for more than a week at a time.

With wee Caroline gone and not policing and giving me dirty looks about how much I drank, I was starting to go into off-licences to buy drink. I would buy a bottle of lemonade in Molly Barr's and a bottle of vodka in the Bogside Inn. I would pour half of the lemonade out, and half of the vodka into the lemonade bottle. Mammy hadn't a clue either. She didn't say much to me; I was always going for "walks" or going somewhere.

Drinking in a pub on my own wasn't an option, and when the notion took me, I was going to the off-licence but still quite some distance off drinking every day at that point. Wee Caroline had my phone number, and she would phone me every night to cheer me up. She told me they were living in a small flat in London, and both had jobs. I missed her terribly; she was my closest friend. I got a job in The Favourite, the pub where wee Caroline leaned out the window and threw up on everybody at the bus stop after her eighteenth birthday. By then, the Brits didn't dare drink or go to the dances in the pubs. Before Bloody Sunday, it was reasonably common, it got less common in 1970 and 1971, but by 1972 it just didn't happen.

In retaliation, more soldiers were killed, more IRA Combatants were killed, and the widespread anger and death were just too much to bear for me. The usual thing happened when I was at work, "one for yourself, love", and I gladly gulped them. At the end of my shift, I was starting to take "one for the road", which was always three straight vodka or gin doubles.

I strayed slightly from the Knights of Malta, as another Bloody Sunday could have happened any day. I went now and again, and by that time, the Order of Saint Lazarus was taking over the Bogside First Aid Post at the Bogside Inn, and becoming more active in Creggan.

When I went to the first aid post, I stayed there and didn't go out into the riots as much. I did some stints at St. Mary's and even up in Creggan for a change of scenery. The Brits were firing rubber bullets at the wee boys, and rubber bullet injuries were coming in daily. These "non-lethal" bullets did kill. Being hit with them could crush bones and cause severe and life-threatening injuries.

I became friendly with two of the first aiders from the Order of Saint Lazarus, Damian McClelland and Alex Wray, the brother of Jim Wray, who was murdered on Bloody Sunday. They were best friends and had joined together. They were the equivalent of wee Caroline and me, just two muckers looking to do their bit. Despite his brother being shot twice in the back and murdered, Alex being a first aider was very admirable. Shows his true strength of character.

Hugh Deehan was involved with establishing the Order of Saint Lazarus at the Bogside first aid post, and he drove the ambulance for them too. He was incredibly busy and helped them to set it up. Nobody talked much about the Knights of Lazarus then, or even in the years since, but I promise it existed. Their uniforms were black dress uniforms and white coats, and the Knights of Malta were grey dress uniforms and the same white coats.

The emblem of the Order of Saint Lazarus is green. On their white coats, they had the green cross badge. The Knights of Lazarus is similar in make-up and style to the Knights of Malta. Their full name is the Order of Saint Lazarus of Jerusalem, also known as The Leper Brothers of Jerusalem. The Knights of Lazarus weren't a result of any form of a split in the first aiders; it wasn't like the "Continuity Knights of Malta" or "the Provisional Knights of Malta"; it was simply another first aid organisation, as Derry had descended into anarchy by mid-1972.

I always struggle with language when describing conflict-related deaths, so I have always done it; if either side of the conflict were killed by the other when off duty and unarmed, it was murder. Civilians and children were always murdered. And, either side killed in a gun battle were killed in active service/ line of duty, as is the preferred language of the Republican movement and British Army. There will never be universal agreement on language and terminology, and I don't mean to offend. Still, I was genuinely politically neutral, and death was one thing uniting all sides.

Daddy never liked politics, and neither did Mammy, and it descended to me.

The deaths and killings didn't stop. In May, Provisional IRA Volunteer John Starrs was killed on active service in the Bogside. It was a massive funeral, and I learned that he had been in the Irish Army before joining the Provisionals following the events of Bloody Sunday. This was the effect that day had on him.

Manus Deery, a fifteen-year-old wee boy, was murdered from the walls by the Army, around the corner from the first aid post at the Bogside Inn. He had eaten a bag of chips before being killed by a single shot to his head.

A Derry Catholic from Creggan, Ranger William Best was also off-duty and murdered by the Official IRA when he came home on leave. He had been in the Irish Rangers, spent time in Europe as part of the peacekeeping efforts, and was roughly the same age as me. This came two days after the murder of Manus Derry on the 19th of May. Even though he was warned not to come home, it didn't excuse what happened to him in my eyes. I can't stress enough that each death affected me, especially when those deaths were close enough in age to me or lived or grew up near to me. At the end of May, the Officials called their ceasefire.

Derry Catholics joined the British Army before the conflict escalated; many left, and some remained. Whilst joining the army back then may have been met with a queer look and some nasty comments, it wasn't a death sentence like it would have been in 1972. Manus and William are buried next to each other in our cemetery, which is a memorial to how complex the conflict in Derry was at that time.

Wee Caroline was phoning almost daily, and I think she was getting a little homesick. She missed me and asked how the Gilmours were, and I told her that we didn't see much of them as they valued their privacy as a family, and everyone in the high flats respected it. I hated talking about Hugh in the past tense. My heart couldn't take it, and I still didn't look at the parking space outside.

We reminisced, wee Caroline and I,

"Remember when block three was being built? I used to play around the balcony and see Gilly climbing up the scaffolding of block three. Mrs Gilmour and Olive used to go out and shout at him to come down. Jesus, he was climbing about sixty foot up and if he lost his grip or slipped, he would have been fucked!"

My heart swelled, and I started to laugh. This was precisely what I needed. "God, it seems so long ago."

"That wasn't all," she continued.

"His old party trick, standing high up on the scaffolding and taking a running jump to another block of scaffold about four or five feet away. One day Bernard Bonner was sent to try and convince him to come down off the scaffolding and was pleading with him to come down. Gilly looked at him, took his run-up, and grabbed the other side with one hand before turning around to face Bernard and scratching his armpit like a monkey!"

Christ almighty, we laughed and laughed. Then when my wee sniffly tears started to come, I changed the subject to find out how they were getting on.

"Aye, London is mad! Joe is being sent back soon, he thinks that we might be coming back. Stella is a star turn, so she is! We were walking to mass in the rain one day, and she stopped some boy driving past and made him give us a lift to mass. Even better, she got a job in a bookie's, and I went in to do the interview for her! She says the footballers come to a door out the back to place their bets! She is in a bookie's near Tottenham Court Road."

"That sounds like wile craic; I wish I were there. If I can move the high flats and Daddy's room over there, I would come over in a shot. It's awful over here."

"Joe is the one Martha. I want to marry him, but because he might be going back over, he doesn't want to leave me as a widow."

"I went on a date a couple of nights ago, Caroline."

"Fuck off did ye, who with?!"

"Never you mind! I had a couple after work, and a boy asked me out. I woke up the next morning knowing I had a date and couldn't remember what the boy looked like. I got new rags up the town, and Mammy ironed my hair. When he came to the door, I asked my Mammy if he was good-looking, and she said, "well.... he has all his features". God love him. I ended up getting tanked and going home early."

I must say, after a few drinks, I was feeling braver around men. After work, I started going to parties with some of the punters and people I worked with, and I won't say too much more because I have wains and grandwains that will have to read this. Just throwing this wee bit in to answer the question you might be asking, did she not go with anybody? We love the bars and gossip in Derry, and I have loads! But you aren't getting any!

"Aw Martha, I feel for ye; happened to me many times; it's all about getting back on the saddle, wee love."

"Pffft, you need to get off the saddle you!"

"Miss you!"

"I miss you too, gone come home."

"I think there's going to be something big happening over there; Joe can't and doesn't say too much. However, I think it will get worse come the summer love. I have to go because this is a payphone and we have been talking shite for ages, love you, bye!"

A couple of weeks later, I got a knock at the door; wee Caroline was there! I squealed when I saw her, and even though I was completely hungover, I was so happy to see her. Nothing could take away how glad I was to see her.

She said in a sinister tone, "The war is coming, Martha"

PART FIVE

"They say her flower has faded now, hard weather and hard booze.
But maybe that's just the price you pay for the chains that you refuse.
Oh she was a rare thing, fine as a bee's wing
And I miss her more than ever words could say.
If I could just taste all of her wildness now.
If I could hold her in my arms today.
Well, I wouldn't want her any other way."

Richard Thompson

Twenty-Three

Operation Motorman

Mammy knew that I liked going out to parties after work. For every one time she noticed that I was drunk, there were ten more times she didn't, either because she fell asleep in the sitting room waiting for me to come back or the fact that I had perfected the art of lying straight to her face, walking in a straight line, and not tripping going up and down stairs.

The dampness in the flats was starting to become a real problem, and the wallpaper in Daddy's room was beginning to feel wet and peel away from the wall. There was a small fire in the flat next door, and the man of the house stuck his boot through the asbestos sheet separating our flat and theirs. It wasn't replaced.

When we all used to go to the cinema on Friday nights, one time Hugh had a black eye. I was concerned that he had gotten into a fight and that somebody had punched him. As it turned out, their flat never had the asbestos sheet separating them from next door. His bedroom was the bedroom that should have had the asbestos sheet behind the door, and a wee toddler had waddled into his room and smacked him with a bobo when he was sleeping.

Mammy developed a strategy to get me away from partying; she bought me a car. It was a black Ford Anglia; it had nice, big, plush leather seats and was in remarkable condition. She went to the credit union and took out a large quantity of the money I had given her over the past three years, which amounted to over £300. I was delighted with it.

The radio worked in it, and sometimes I would start the car and listen to the radio in peace. I had some driving lessons and took to it right away. I was a natural, even though he had to keep telling me to slow down. I think I terrified the driving instructor on a couple of occasions.

There was no theory test back then, thank God! But I was so good at it that I decided I was ready for my driving test. I flew through it and passed it on the first attempt, only a few weeks after I got the car. I loved taking myself for drives and was even taking Mammy out. One day we were stopped by a Provo barricade near the flats.

I rolled down the window, and the masked man said, "name and address please?"

Mammy leaned over as far as she could, her head coming level with mine, "Excuse me, son, do you want me to tell your mother what you are at? Or I will get out of this car and skelp your arse myself!"

The boy shat himself and let us return to the flat's carpark. Mammy was increasingly involved in the resident's association, and they were pleading with the Housing Trust to get repairs and maintenance done to the upper flats.

The first story level and Garvan Place seemed to be okay, but further up where we were, there were more issues. The housing trust had an office in the flats, 37 Garvan Place, but after Mammy and the resident's association kept annoying them, they moved out and left the flat empty.

The graffiti on the stairwells was disgusting, the lifts stank of urine, and the place quickly became very run down. Wee Caroline didn't seem to have any issues in her flat; she always had her lights working, her asbestos sheet, very little damp, and never recalled any problems. I always went down to her flat because I was getting a bit embarrassed with ours.

We went back to the first aid meetings on Monday nights, but we all knew the shit would hit the fan very soon. We didn't know what "it" was, but "something" was coming. The army was planning something big.

Bloody Friday had taken place in Belfast. A series of IRA bombings killed nine people and wounded over one hundred others. It was horrific, and after that, I stopped watching the news. I couldn't take it anymore. Things had gone too far, the army was going to invade, and everybody knew it. It was just a case of when.

For what would eventually come to be known as Operation Motorman, we didn't get orders or instructions to set up any first aid posts. We were to always stay in cover unless we were sent for, and because Caroline and I lived in the Rossville Flats, we were told to stay where we were. If I were a Brit Commander, the first place I would have attempted to invade would have been the high flats, given how strategically sound it was for the Battle of The Bogside.

On the 30th of July, everyone was cleaning their flats. I went down to wee Caroline's, and her Mammy was cleaning like it was Christmas Eve,

"Mrs McLaughlin, you know the Brits are going to come in here and ransack the place?"

"Yes, I know, but I am not having the soldiers coming into a dirty flat!"

Sound logic, I thought. Everyone had heard that ships were landing in Belfast, with tanks, more vehicles, and thousands more troops, plus weaponry. The Republican factions within the flats were nowhere to be seen. They all knew that standing up to the full might of the British Army would only result in a colossal loss of life, nothing else.

The hours passed, and everyone was waiting around. The ladies were coming out onto all the balconies, right up to Donagh Place, in their big fluffy dressing gowns and wondering where the soldiers were. Then we heard them coming. I dusted my white coat, made sure I had a ton of supplies, and ran down to the car to have a couple of swigs of vodka that I kept in the glove compartment.

When I read about Motorman or even the troubles in general, they all say that the Saracens and APCs "rumbled". It was more than a rumble, they burbled, hissed, and spat their way down Rossville Street, and I ran around the corner of block one.

The scale of it was unfathomable. There were troops everywhere. Tanks and armoured cars rolled in, and a helicopter came and landed on the roof of block one. It was terrifying. A big, armoured bulldozer burst through the barricades, and soldiers ran into the flats. Along all the balconies, there were pillars. There were two soldiers for every pillar right the way along all the galleries of Garvan Place, Mura Place, and Donagh Place.

I think the IRA factions knew that the flats would be taken from the top to the bottom. One way in and one way out were the entrance doors on each of the three flat blocks. The place was surrounded in a matter of seconds. There were two Pigs in the carpark that had turret-mounted rotating machine guns on them. If a gun battle commenced, The Brits could have sprayed all three flat block galleries in no time.

The only time wee Caroline and I were called into action that night was when the soldiers grabbed some wee boy and threw him over the balcony. It was like slow motion, there was a soldier on each arm, and they flung him out to the railing; he went head over heels off the railing and landed on the row of garages below Garvan Place on block one.

Wee Caroline went over the railing in a flash, and I laboured over a bit because I was a bit "touched". We dropped about ten feet from the balcony to the top of the garages and the stricken wee boy. Thank Christ he was okay, just winded, with no broken bones as he landed flat on his back. He didn't seem dizzy or like he had taken a blow to the head. He could stand up, put his arse on the edge of the garages, and drop down to the carpark.

The way it worked was if the soldiers didn't have any intelligence on you, they knocked on the flat door. They would put their boot through it if they did have a word on you. It was so fast that I saw doors flying off the springs and the male occupants being dragged outside. There were only two ladies in our flat, me and Mammy, so the Brits didn't kick our door in, but I went upstairs when they made their way up the stairwell.

The soldiers who came into the flat weren't the worst. One was a high-ranking type and older; the young fellow beside him seemed like a fresh-faced recruit. The fresh-faced ones were always a bit more civil at checkpoints; then, as the years went by, they turned into hateful bastards. As does anybody in any job working with the public, I suppose.

They tried to make small talk, but we didn't give them a lot of small talk back. One-word answers or less. More words were added when they went into Daddy's room. I saw red. The soldiers were touching all his things, and I walked up beside him, "get away! Those are my late Daddy's tools!"

"Oh really? We had a similar story at a property search before and found bomb parts," he said sternly. I wanted to go for his throat. His partner put his hand on my shoulder and moved me back from him.

"You have done your duty, now get the fuck out of our flat! We aren't the people you are looking for!"

"Language Martha!"

When I started shouting at the soldiers, they started ransacking.

"Naw, Mammy, they are ransacking the place now!"

The soldier stopped and looked at us, "you might not be who we are looking for, but how do we know you are not hiding who we are looking for?"

Mammy and I looked at each other, and from their point of view, we couldn't argue back with them. People were always hidden in safe houses; for all they knew, we were a safe house too.

"I apologise for the inconvenience, ladies, " the Brits said. "Although, young lady, you may want to have a drop or two less the next time we come and visit," then sniffed hard twice. Mammy went bright red and reached for me, but I got out the door before she could get to me or the Brits could leave.

The whole thing was over in a couple of hours, and I had to go in and face Mammy.

"Martha, have you been drinking?"

"Naw, Mammy, I wasn't; our kitbags have alcohol disinfectant, and that was probably what the Brits smelled."

She roared at me, "Martha, do not tell lies to your mother!"

"I'm not Mammy!"

"You will end up on the bloody street!"

"Mammy, naw I won't. I was just nervous, and I settled myself down, there I said it! I can stop whenever I want, I'm sorry."

She grabbed me by the shoulders, "There is a word for that, Martha! Alcoholic! If you are going to continue to drink, Martha, you will not be living under my roof."

"Mammy, sure you take Valium now and again. What's the difference?"

She didn't even respond, her wee lip wobbled, and she stormed up the stairs in the flat and slammed the sitting-room door. The thought of never drinking again was too daunting, I wouldn't be able to survive without it. I was only a week away from my nineteenth birthday, and I may as well say, I knew at that point that I was an alcoholic.

It is too easy for people to assume that The Troubles was the cause of my drinking problem, but I hope you know it loud and clear, my drinking started long before Bloody Sunday. I was already an alcoholic and had been from the age of fifteen. I don't think it would have mattered if the deaths didn't happen; I was susceptible and felt invincible when I drank. The pattern of drinking to dull pain wasn't my experience. I was drinking to "feel like Martha".

Somebody was writing a book about Motorman about ten years ago. There was a call out in the papers for anyone present during Motorman, and I came forward with a statement to the author. Attracta Bradley (Simms) also prepared a report but the book didn't go to print. To avoid it being a waste of her time writing it, I thought I would include it in my book. In Creggan, things were much more eventful, and here is her statement.

Attracta Bradley (Simms)

I woke up, on the morning of the 30th of July, feeling the tension in the air. I lived in Creggan Street, which was on the periphery of the Bogside, Creggan and Rosemount. It was just opposite St. Eugene's Cathedral, very close to Derry City centre. I knew, like everyone else, (as my mother would say, "even the dogs in the street knew") that The British Army were going to come into the "No-Go Areas", dismantle the barricades, and put an end to them. There was a lot of army activity about, with extra army vehicles being drafted into the city. I was a third-year nursing student and a member of the Knights of Malta, a first aid organisation.

We were not given instructions to open a first aid post that day or night, but I became very concerned that we were leaving the "no go" areas without any First Aid cover. After discussion with another first aider, we decided to ask permission from one of our senior members, a Knight. Our pleadings were to no avail. He told us to go home because that night was going to be unsafe for us and he wouldn't take responsibility for our safety.

Being young and unafraid, we didn't give up. We proceeded to our Captain's house where, after persistent pleas from us, it was agreed that we could go ahead and open the First Aid Post. A hut in Balbane Pass became our base, as it had been used before. We erected a first aid flag above the door and prepared it for the night, hoping we wouldn't need it. As there was a restricted entrance to and from the area, we treated minor injuries during the day and early evening.

It wasn't until the early hours of the next morning that all Hell broke loose. From a distance, I could hear the army vehicles making their way into Creggan. Small explosions were followed by gunfire in the distance. I was standing at the entrance to the hut, with the other first aider and my boyfriend (now my husband), when the shooting appeared to be getting closer. Some instinct made me drop to the ground, pulling the other two with me, just as a bullet hit the top of the well-lit doorway in which we stood. Two of us were wearing white coats, and standing below the First Aid Flag, so we hardly posed a threat to the British Army. The bullet must have hit a piece of metal, as it ricocheted into the hut. We lay on the ground, terrified, not knowing what would become of us. If we moved, would we be shot? We couldn't see who had fired at us.

A short time later, as we lay face down on the ground, I heard a woman's voice from one of the houses across the green, shouting to us to get away from the brightly lit hut and crawl over to her home. We didn't need any encouragement as we quickly made our way over the grass, then across the road, to the safety of that kind woman's home. There we lay on her floor, along with the rest of her family. It seemed that no one had gone to bed that night, as they were too scared of what was going to happen.

It was sometime later, in the dawn light, that I heard a loud rumbling, then saw a Centurion tank, appearing from behind the houses on Creggan Heights. It was being used to bulldoze the barricades. Lines of British soldiers appeared, with guns at the ready. Local men and youths gathered in the area and began stoning them. The army responded by charging at the crowds, in an attempt to disperse them. This began a "cat and mouse" battle between them.

Later that morning, during one of these set-tos, when the youths were retreating, I saw a soldier drop to one knee, take aim and fire, hitting one of the youths as he was running away, and in mid-air, as he jumped over a fence. The boy fell immediately, and I could see a group of adults running to his aid and carrying him into a house. At this, an eerie silence descended on the area. I was terrified and unsure of what to do. I could see only armed soldiers. Everyone else had fled and I was in a house a short distance away. Then, out of the silence, someone shouted, "Is there a doctor about?" then, "Is there a nurse?" At that, my boyfriend helped pull me up and I knew I had no choice but to go and help. Looking back to that moment, it was the longest walk of my life, as I had to pass the soldiers with their rifles pointed at me. But my adrenaline kicked in and I started to run, with my white first aid bag over my shoulder.

There were a lot of people in the house, trying to help the boy, who looked about sixteen or seventeen. I took over, assessing his condition. He was breathing and conscious, so I got someone to ring for an ambulance. I kept reassuring him as I applied field dressings to the wounds in his right buttock and front pelvic area. I used splints to immobilise his legs, as I was unsure how much damage had been done. The ambulance seemed to take forever to arrive but, eventually, he was taken away to the hospital, or so we assumed. I later found out that the British Army had held the ambulance at their checkpoint, and it was several hours before he reached the hospital.

After that incident, my memories of the rest of the day are vague. I couldn't go home, as I lived outside the barricades. My parents did not know that I had spent the night in the middle of a warzone, so I went to my boyfriend's house on Creggan Broadway, where Mrs Bradley asked no questions. She just put me to bed and let me sleep.

That night saw the end of the "no go" areas in Derry and Operation Motorman was written into Derry's history.

Twenty-Four

83 Donagh Place

By the end of 1973, I was drinking every day. I didn't drink in the morning, but I drank every night. I bought a wee perfume bottle to keep on my person and strong breath mints. I had to become more creative with Mammy too. I feigned illness when I was lying in bed with dreadful hangovers, and of course, she took me to the doctor, who told me there was nothing wrong with me.

I was still going to the first aid meetings but always rushing to get home. Marie knew something was wrong, and I denied it whenever she asked. I was functioning quite well. I could drive, work, and attend first aid, but when I got home at night, I was drinking myself to sleep in my room.

Working late meant going to parties, but I became upset when I woke up in random places and had to make my way home in the morning. Mammy and I had gotten distant to a critical point, so I had to start drinking under her roof on my own. I would sneak the drink inside, always in my tote bag, never in my first aid bag. I worked out that a litre of vodka would last me four nights, so it was only every four nights that I had to go to an off-licence. By Easter of 1974, a litre was only lasting me two nights.

Wee Caroline asked me where I was hiding, and I told her so many lies that I can't recall them now. I think I told her I had a boyfriend and was meeting him. I didn't have a boyfriend, and my only love was drinking. Mammy let me bring the record player into my room, and I would drink, listen to music, cry, and fall asleep.

"Martha, how come you are falling asleep in your clothes?" Mammy enquired,

"I just be that tired Mammy, a lot going on around the place in case you don't see it."

She knew something was going on, "Martha, I am telling you now for the final time, if you continue to drink, then you are out!"

I was caught in a vicious cycle. I'm nervous; I need a drink. I am happy and want to celebrate; I need a drink. I think I am a disgusting piece of shit; I need a drink. Mammy took the gentle approach and made me swear I would stop drinking. I didn't do it, and she didn't bother battering me stupid because she knew it wouldn't work.

Many people were asking Mammy why I hadn't found a man, gotten married, or anything else. She told people I wasn't well or hadn't met the right person yet. The truth is, I met loads of the right people. The drink was the only man I needed and wanted; it made me feel good when I wanted a lift. My relationships were casual because men and boys came into my life and left again, and the drink didn't go.

Mammy didn't tell Mrs McLaughlin about my drinking either, Mammy was always a private person, and she barely spoke about Daddy anymore, except to say to me how disappointed he would be if he knew what I was up to.

"Your Daddy would be terribly upset looking on you now, Martha. Your Daddy would love to see you happy, with a husband and children. We reared you better than this, Martha."

When I started to cry, she would stop.

After these talks, I decided I would try and stop. When I went to work, I did wee Caroline's old trick, having lemonade with a slice of lime in it and telling the person who bought it for me that it was vodka. I was shaky. One morning when I was driving to the post office, my trembling hands on my car wheel caused me to reverse into another car. On another occasion, I dropped two trays of pints in the bar in one night. I had no confidence.

For about a week, I was throwing up bile into the toilet in the flat. There weren't any windows in the wee toilet room in the flats, and the smell was putrid. I'd never felt as ill in all my life, it was hell, and the drink was pulling me back toward it. Surely a wee sip to get me over the sickness won't harm me, would it?

I don't think I spoke to anybody; I had a rotten head and wasn't very pleasant or chatty with other people. I told wee Caroline I had gastritis, or some dirty awful lie that I don't remember. She was a trained nurse who commented that my face always looked red.

"Hot flushes!" I used to say to her.

"Hot flushes, aye? At twenty-two years of age?"

"Mary had a wain without doing the deed, love, stranger things have happened!"

When she laughed, I won. The conversation changed. The mouthy quips were always a ploy; when I am a Smart Alec with somebody, I am deflecting from the situation. I still do that to a certain extent. She was a trained nurse, she knew.

After nine days, I couldn't take the pain anymore. I didn't talk to anyone other than Mammy, and I barely slept. When Mammy met a friend for tea and cake, I went to the Bogside Inn, got a smaller bottle of vodka, and pinned it on the way back to the flats. The secret drinking pattern had returned.

When she came home again, Mammy said, "Gosh, Martha, you are back to your old self again."

"Aye, Mammy, sober as a judge!"

I was drunk.

***

There was violence on the streets on all sides, but crime had increased. One night when I came home from first aid training, somebody was trying to open our front door, and I chased him away. The landing lights on our balcony had failed, were not fixed, and it was a glorious opportunity for burglars. Despite this, the residents were defiant and kept their doors open at night, against advice from the Housing Trust.

Caroline was saying that Joe was back and that it was getting harder to meet him as they weren't allowing girls into the barracks anymore for security reasons. They had to meet under cover of darkness, often in strange places, and I had agreed to lend them my car. I wasn't using it much anyway, other than to take Mammy some places to keep her sweet.

The drinking intensified as Mammy built trust in me to go out and meet some friends and leave me alone in the flat. I had to drink as much as possible to take the edge off, but not too much that she would notice when she returned. I needed more and more.

***

When the Provos got wind of anti-social behaviour in our neighbourhoods, they took matters into their own hands. Wee Caroline and I were on the first aid post beside the Bogside Inn when I was preparing to go home. We heard four pistol shots right beside the post, and then someone slapped the window at the front four times before running off.

We went out and saw that two young fellas were kneecapped, a round fired into the back of each of their knees with a pistol. I recognised one straight away, the wee bastard that had tried our flat door handle. I treated seven or eight kneecappings over the years, and they never seemed to scream as you would imagine in dramatic depictions. It was short rapid breaths, wide-eyed stares, and unable to speak over their breathing.

The process was simple, a bandage soaked with antiseptic Boracic Ointment, a field dressing, and a wrap-around application on each knee. The wee boys were lying in their underwear, as wearing trousers could mean that bits of cloth or fabric could get into the wounds, cause infection, and lead to amputation.

On that first kneecapping I saw, I realised I was desensitised somewhat. It was either because I had become used to it or because I knew I had a stiff drink waiting for me whenever I went back. Hugh Deehan wasn't around that day to drive the wee boys, and I agreed to take them because I was the only one with a driving licence.

The Malta ambulance was a wreck, it had seen so much abuse, and it wasn't easy to fundraise for a new one. Republican fundraising was much more effective than our method of shaking buckets in pubs and the street. So, we had to try and conserve the ambulance until it was necessary to replace it. We asked the wee boys if there was anybody we could phone to take them first, but when they said no, we didn't have much choice.

There were two beds in the back, and we put them on each bed. I was always a good driver, but my nerves were in bits taking two casualties to Letterkenny with Caroline. She was a trained nurse applying more field dressings to one of the wee boys, as the round to his left knee hadn't gone clean through. The bandages weren't changed but more applied on top.

The road to Letterkenny was a nightmare, it wasn't lit as well as the Derry roads, and I hadn't driven in the dark. There was an army checkpoint at Coshquin, just before the entrance to County Donegal. The siren didn't work very well, but the blues and twos lights on the roof did work. They had a sign on the road that said, "PREPARE TO STOP", but I wasn't for stopping. Luckily, we were waved right through when the Brit stepped out onto the road.

My hands were shaking at the wheel, and I was starting to stray into the other lane now and again.

"Martha, watch the road!" Caroline would shout in from the back before I jerked the wheel to the left to stay in our lane. I needed a drink; this was an inconvenience because all I wanted to do was go home and listen to "Ain't no Sunshine When She's Gone". I heard that song for the first time on the radio on the night of Bloody Sunday and only recalled it that moment behind the wheel of the ambulance.

We got to where we needed to go and rallied back up the road. The Ambulance was kept just behind the first aid post in the car park, and I was breaking out in cold sweats. If I didn't start drinking around nine o'clock at night, I was beginning to get irritable and intense.

We walked back towards the flats; the army was patrolling Rossville Street. We went past the Bloody Sunday Monument, which was placed where the thrupenny bits once were, and up the steps of block one. Youths chose the stairwell in our block to drink and smash bottles in because it was around the side between blocks two and three and more secluded.

"Martha?"

"Yes, love?"

"You're very shaky."

"Aye, I'm not used to all this yet, you know."

"I want Martha back."

"Awk, wise up you! Look at me; I'm still here, aren't I?"

"Aye, but the Martha I left behind going to London differs from the Martha of now."

"Me and Mammy aren't getting on."

"Why?"

"She wants me to move out, get married, and squeeze out a pile of wains."

"I've known Bridie B all my life, Martha; there isn't a hope she would throw you out for no reason!"

"You don't know her as well as me, but how's Joe?"

"You're changing the subject, Martha!"

"Awk shut up you!"

Just as our little disagreement was starting to escalate, a man walked toward us on the balcony of Garvan Place. Wee Caroline was standing a bit behind me, when the man stood right up in front of her nose and said, "we know what you're doing! For your sake, I would advise you to break it off!"

The man walked away calmly, and wee Caroline cried and pushed her spring front door forward and slammed it behind her.

I ran to the flat and went to the door to tell Mammy. "Mammy!" "Mammy!" she didn't respond. Things were lying everywhere. Daddy's tools were strewn all over the floor, the wee toilet room had towels and toiletries thrown around, and upstairs the airing room cupboard door had been ripped off and was lying beside the sitting-room door.

The television was destroyed, I stepped into the kitchen with the ever-leaking roof, Mammy was crying at the kitchen table.

"It's okay wee Mammy, we will get the place ready to go in a couple of hours, and all will be well again!"

"No, it won't, Martha!"

"Why would the soldiers come back and raid us, for there are only us two birdies in here?"

"No, Martha, I am glad it happened!"

"Why is that Mammy?" I was pretty confused, but I still didn't catch on.

"The same soldier who came around during Motorman came back, the older chap. Do you remember him?"

"Naw, Mammy, I don't; I see that many soldiers, so I do." That was a lie. I remembered him clear as day with his sharp cheekbones and pencil moustache.

"He said, "I have found what I am looking for, Madam." Then Mammy leaned down to her right and put four empty vodka bottles on the kitchen table. I had forgotten to throw them down the chute before going to the first aid post.

"He said he had an alcoholic father and remembered you, Martha."

"Mammy, I promise I will stop, I swear, please!" I pleaded with her. She stood up from the kitchen table,

"Come downstairs with me, Martha!"

I followed on behind her, and she opened the door of Daddy's room. His leather suitcase was sitting in the middle of the room, open and empty.

"Mammy what are you doing?" I started bawling and crying.

"I want you to pack your things, and I would like you to be gone tomorrow evening. My decision is final Martha. Feel free to visit, but if you have taken drink, don't you dare come near my door!"

"Mammy! No!" I crumpled, grabbed onto her apron, wrapped my arms around her legs, and pleaded with her.

"No Martha, you have betrayed my trust and lied to me. You have to go, and whenever you stop drinking, my door will always be open."

I went to the Housing Trust up the town the following morning and told them I was homeless. I was offered a bedsit at the top of the flats because there weren't that many people living up there due to the leaks caused by the roof. Over time, the guttering and the roof had weakened, causing rainwater to penetrate the concrete. Mammy always discussed it as a critical issue in the Rossville Residents Association meetings.

Many of the older people living in the bedsits in Donagh Place had been rehoused, and some of them went to be cared for by their families. As the lifts were often broken, they were trapped up there if they had mobility issues. If there were a fire, it would make rescue pretty much impossible — housing older people at the top of gallery access flats, Jesus Christ Almighty! The rationale at the time of construction was that children needed places to run about, and younger families were housed in Garvan Place.

She handed over the key to me, and I went back toward the flats. I walked up the slope connecting blocks two and three because I didn't want to bump into Mammy. I was put on the eighth floor, at 83 Donagh Place. The graffiti up there was horrendous and much less inviting than in the lower galleries. When I got to the door, the key was hard to turn in the lock, but after fiddling with it, I pushed the door open.

Right ahead was a small hallway, a living room with a kitchenette, and a bedroom adjacent to it. Curiously, the bathroom and the kitchen in this one-bed flat were the exact sizes as Mammy's flat. The urine smell was disgusting, and the tilt and turn sitting room window overlooking Free Derry Corner had a snapped handle and could only be opened about an inch. Some old furniture was there like the previous elderly occupant had left in a hurry.

The wallpaper was peeling, the bed was crooked, the gas heating spluttered like an asthmatic dog, and the lights flickered. There had been between little and zero maintenance done to this flat. I went down to Mammy's flat and packed my things. I was raging with her; I didn't want to beg her. I thought, *she can go fuck herself!*

I loaded my things into Daddy's leather suitcase and took some of Daddy's things too. I packed in the first aid stuff and took the record player. I told Mammy, "that's mine! I am taking it with me." Although she knew I would take it anyway and didn't put up a fight.

I bought a bottle of vodka and drank it all that night. I woke up the next morning covered in my vomit.

Twenty-Five

The Angel of Death

Whilst the riots around Derry were spreading like a rash, Caroline and I took up our stations at the Bogside First Aid Post along with the Knights of Lazarus volunteers who regularly occupied it. It was pretty business-like. I didn't drink every morning, but I drank on the mornings I wasn't needed at the first aid posts.

Even though I was friendly and well-acquainted with the Order of Lazarus First Aiders, I seldom addressed them by their names. I always wondered why this was, and I have the remnants of a theory. Farmers don't tend to give their livestock names. You will never see a farmer have a cow named "Daisy" or a pig called "Arnold". I wasn't interested in making friends or getting close to anybody, just in case they would all be taken away from me.

A scrawny masked youth ran to the door of the first aid post shouting, "help! a wee boy got burnt; come quickly!" This was seen as a minor inconvenience to the nurse and doctor, so they gave Caroline and me the nod to investigate what was happening.

My head was sore from the night before, so I sighed and jogged behind the youth to see what was wrong. We turned right at the exit of the first aid post and headed toward the bottom of Westland Street. This was a typical "flashpoint" for rioting, as this was the main thoroughfare for the RUC and the British Army to get to their barracks and stations.

I felt like my stomach was in knots, and my mind wasn't even focusing on what I was about to see, only the next drink to settle my throbbing hangover.

When I got around the corner, we saw a youth lying on the ground, squealing like a stuck pig. He had dropped a lit petrol bomb and set himself on fire. He was gravely injured; his leg was roaring red, and his clothes were charred.

Petrol bomb injuries were reasonably common, but we hadn't seen one as bad as this. The smell of that wee boy's flesh is stuck with me; it put me off red meat for a long time.

"What's your name?" Caroline asked the youngster calmly,

"It doesn't matter, Jesus Christ!" he snapped back at her. Caroline, being the picture of cool and calm, applied some water and bandages onto the charred leg and directed me to run back to the first aid post to bring the ambulance around.

My brain was sloshing around inside my head, and when I returned to the first aid post, I just blurted to the nurse and doctor that we were taking a burnt petrol bomber to Altnagelvin. I didn't even give them the chance to reply; I grabbed the Ambulance key and went to the rear of the post.

Ambulances in those days were a fucking nightmare to start. They took so much abuse that they would often go wrong. We used Ambulances that weren't purpose-made; ours was on an old Bedford van that somebody had painted "AMBULANCE" onto. It had a stretcher in the back, and the rear doors were often stuck. Only the left one would open easily, and I would have to go in and kick the other one out from the inside.

It took three turns of the key for the thing to splutter into life; I pulled out of the car park and reversed the ambulance back to where the wee boy was lying on the ground. As we rolled him onto the stretcher, the wee boy was still squealing and saying, "gone fucking watch it, will you?" Caroline was stuttering her apologies and reassured him that we would get to Altnagelvin as quick as we could. I didn't have time for abuse; I ignored them half the time. I didn't say a word.

It wouldn't have been unusual to take the rioters to Letterkenny hospital to avoid being arrested by the RUC. In this case, it was easier to go to Altnagelvin and much quicker. With burns, infections and blistering can occur more rapidly and need immediate attention. Sometimes going to Letterkenny could take close to an hour.

With my heavy right boot, I could get to Altnagelvin in about twelve minutes. In fact, I could get to most places in Derry in twelve minutes before the doctor took my driving licence off me. One time a few years ago, I got from the Foyle Road to the Europa Hotel, Belfast, in fifty-six minutes.

I shoved the gear stick into first and jolted the ambulance forward down Lecky Road. We hurtled down the long straight thoroughfare, slaloming through rows of derelict houses and swerving to avoid glass and nails scattered over the road.

When we got to the end of the Lecky Road onto Foyle Road, I turned right so hard that the wee boy on the stretcher was crashing into the interior sidewall of the ambulance. "Jesus Christ, missus, will you calm down? You're going to get us all killed," he shouted.

I saw red and pulled the handbrake up in the middle of Foyle Road, "Martha, what are you doing?" Caroline gently asked me. I gave her a look that nearly burnt a hole in her face, and she put her wee green eyes into the footwell where they belonged.

Luckily, there wasn't a car behind us. Otherwise, I would have been up the creek without a paddle.

I shoved open the driver's door and slammed it so hard behind me that the ambulance wobbled. I marched to the ambulance's rear and opened both doors almost simultaneously; I nearly tore them off the hinges. The wee boy was sheet white, lying on the stretcher with a blanket over him. He still had a white hankie mask over his face, and his eyes doubled in size when they met mine.

"Do you want to drive your fucking self to Altnagelvin? Go on! Away ye go. See that big bridge over there, walk towards and cross that, walk up the hill in front of you, and there's a sign on a big building saying Altnagelvin Hospital ye can't miss it," I shouted at him.

Of course, he started stuttering, "ahh, ahh, ahh". The more he tried to talk, the worse the stuttering became. He lifted his hands as if to surrender when he saw my "Mouthy Martha" face. Everyone did. It didn't matter how "hard" they were or how much "street-cred" they had. When my demon face came on, you were in trouble.

"Ssssoorryyyy," he whimpered.

"Aye, of course, ye are. I am giving up my time to help you, and what do I get, eh? Wee mouths like you! You can't even be trusted to hold a lemonade bottle, and you're giving me grief about driving. Give me strength!" then I slammed the door on him again.

When I got in and looked at Caroline, she smirked in my face, and we both burst out laughing in the middle of the road. When a car behind us beeped the horn, we knew we had to get going.

I was driving over the Craigavon Bridge, and my hands shook at the wheel. I could feel them, and Caroline was staring at them.

"Jesus, Martha, you're shaking like a leaf," she laughed. I don't remember exactly what I said back to her, probably because what I said to her was a lie. I needed a fix, and I needed it pretty quickly.

We arrived at Altnagelvin casualty, and I pulled off a stylish handbrake stop in front of the door. I went around the back along with Caroline, and the wee boy flinched when we opened the door. I needed to let the wee boy know the drill,

"Right, mister, first you take that rag off your face. We will take you in here, and you tell them you were picking daisies for orphans when a petrol bomb came out of nowhere and landed beside you, okay?"

"Aye, aye, aye, okay!" the wee boy whimpered back at us. He knew I meant business. Even after I became a paramedic years later, he ranks as one of the biggest clowns ever to find himself in the back of Martha's ambulance. Trust me; I had every single famous Derry character in my ambulance at one point or another.

Wee Caroline, the eternal lady, frowned at me when I said things like this.

"A wee bit of professionalism wouldn't go a miss, ya mouth ye!" she scowled.

I always used to tell her, "Aye, but Caroline, you have to speak to people like that in their language, trust me! They are grateful for it." This served me well in my combined forty years of driving ambulances for both the Knights of Malta and the Northern Ireland Ambulance Service.

Caroline worked in casualty at the time and knew the other nurses and doctors there. They brought the wee boy in and gave us tea. I was still shaking in casualty; I lied my knickers off and said a brick hit the ambulance on the way over and I was a bit shaken. I think this was when Caroline realised that her best friend had a drinking problem; she knew the lie.

We devoured the free cake, drank a gallon of tea, and shimmied out of Altnagelvin and into the Ambulance to leave it back to the first aid post. I clasped the wheel as tight as possible to stop my hands from shaking.

"Martha..." the little voice from my left said.

"Yes, love," I quipped and smiled back at her.

"Are you alright? Seriously though, are you okay? You don't have to be mouthy Martha all the time, you know?"

"Awk, I know, but sure you know me, hard as nails love."

I am disgusted and embarrassed at how convincing I became. I knew when Caroline wasn't sold and could deflect the conversation perfectly. I became so good at it that I probably would have made an incredible politician.

Mammy once said to me, "Martha can you make me one promise that you won't ever get into politics or stand for election?" When I inquired why she wanted this promise made to her, she replied, "because you would win Martha, and then we are all in trouble."

When we got back to the first aid post, I threw the ambulance keys in the door, and I was pacing toward the flats. "Jesus Martha, what's the hurry?" Caroline shouted from behind me. When I turned around, a man had burst out through the Bogside Inn, grabbed her and shouted in her face, "we aren't going to fucking tell you again! This is your last chance."

She just pushed him away and walked toward the flats with me. It had been ages since wee Caroline was warned last, all talk we thought. Nobody would ever harm one of us. I had my vodka waiting for me when I was to get home. I left Caroline at her flat and ran up to mine. I don't think I even checked on her or hugged her. I threw her in the door, and up I went.

Addiction is strange; elderly alcoholics walk for miles to get to an off-licence, and it doesn't faze them. Because I was on the top floor, I ran up the steps, going as quickly as two steps at a time. I could scale the steps rapidly and wasn't even out of breath.

Visiting Mammy became less and less of a priority, and I didn't visit at night as much anymore. I had a habit to feed! The vodka was hidden in my "hidey hole", a broken piece of plaster from the last time I was raided. There were bottles all over the place. They were accumulating in my flat quicker than I could throw them all down the chute. Seeing all the bottles strewn about reminded me of one of Hugh's business ventures. Back then, people got money for returning glass bottles to pubs, shops, etc.

Floyd Gilmour told Hugh about this, and hearing of it, Hugh's mind went into overdrive. Making a fortune from returning glass bottles. At one stage, he had filled his room full of bottles he was planning to sell back to a pub. Floyd told him exactly where to go and who to talk to.

Eventually, it was time for Hugh and his muckers to take these crates to the pub. Along the way, they laughed and speculated how they would spend their fortune. I can't tell the stories about Hugh like his closest muckers tell them, but all I can do is try. Hugh burst through the door of the pub, and the conversation went like this.

"Hello, how ye doing? Would you like to buy these bottles from us?"

"Aye, son, let me have a look." The barman brought a little book over to the bar top and sat it in front of him. "Right, what is your name, son?"

"Hugh Gilmour."

"Right, right, Hugh Gilmour, from where?"

"23 Garvan Place."

"Okay, son, I will take these bottles off your hands now."

Hugh was rubbing his hands together and spending the money in his head. Although, a few seconds passed, and the barman wasn't very quick to hand over the money. Which prompted Hugh to hold his palm out.

"Tell me this, son, are you anything to Floyd Gilmour, also of 23 Garvan Place?"

"Aye, he's my brother!"

"Right, right. As it happens, Floyd Gilmour bought a carryout in here last week on tick and hasn't paid for it yet. So, see that ten bob, take it up with Floyd Gilmour! Have a good one, lads, cheerio!"

Jesus, he stormed out of that pub, stormed along Rossville Street and didn't even wait until he got back to the flat before confronting Floyd! Hugh shouted up from the carpark below the balcony where Floyd was standing,

"You owe me ten bob, Floyd Gilmour! You owe me fucking ten bob!" I think Floyd just shrugged and went back inside. Sure, that's what big brothers are for, passing on the tricks of the trade. However, there was one time when Hugh had one of his finest victories.

When the main man came, Hugh and the boys were playing football out the back. In Derry, the main man is the Maine man, who sells lemonade door to door in a small flatbed lorry with stacks of clinking crates. Glass bottles of lemonade from the Maine man were always a treat on a summer's day. If we were sitting out the back of the flats, we all refreshed ourselves with Sarsaparilla, Cloudy Lime, and Cream Soda.

There was a wee boy that sat in the lorry too, who was the Maine man's helper. After the Maine man disappeared to the upper galleries with lemonade crates, Hugh kicked the ball to Bernard and ran over the lorry. "Here, hi! You owe me a fag," Hugh demanded of the Maine man's wee helper. The young fella shouted out to Hugh that he didn't have any fags on him, and Hugh paused in thought, "well can ye give me a bottle of lemonade instead?"

Seeing this as a fair deal, the wee boy got out of the lorry and looked up toward the Donagh Place gallery. When the Maine man was out of sight, he handed Hugh a big bottle of lemonade. After completing their business transaction, Hugh shared the bottle of lemonade with the boys. Hugh got the last gulp and kept the empty bottle.

When the bottle was finished, and the Maine man drove off, Hugh ventured around to Molly Barr's shop at the bottom of block two. When he entered the shop, he asked if Molly would like the big glass bottle from him. She agreed and turned to open her till to give him a tuppence or whatever she paid for bottles.

"No thanks, Molly. Can I have a single fag instead?" In those days, you could buy individual cigarettes, a single. Without hesitation, she handed it over. So he ended up with the bottle of lemonade *and* the fag.

Whenever I would down the vodka, I would say, "forgive me, Daddy, please forgive me." Jesus, my Daddy would have been ashamed of me, and I don't blame him. Mammy and Caroline knew something was going on but didn't know the extent. They probed, and I deflected. When wee Caroline asked me why I moved out, I said it was for my own space and no other reason.

I fell asleep at my kitchen table and was awakened by a rumble. I didn't know what this was and thought I was going mad. The flats started to crumble from within, but I didn't think they would collapse. Although my eyes were blurry, I knew this wasn't a usual side effect of my lonely binges.

"What the fuck is that?" I heard from next door. I put on my dressing gown and staggered out of the kitchen toward the front door. Something was badly wrong. I realised when I reached the door that I had terrible hiccups, so I turned back toward the kitchen.

I did my usual trick, pinched my nose, and took five big gulps of water without breathing. I waited to confirm they were gone before going to the balcony to see what was wrong. Other front doors were opening and closing, so this was not the flats, nor my sanity, collapsing.

Pulling open my creaking front door, others were talking loudly and wondering what was happening. My eyes hadn't adjusted, and I could see the blurry outline of people standing around the balconies on all three blocks. There was tension and fear, and it felt the same as it did the day of Motorman.

Something was coming, but at that point, I didn't know exactly what. It was pitch dark outside save for the lights of the flats. The rumble was familiar, but it was much louder this time. I placed my hand on the balcony railing; it was ice cold and it trembled somewhat.

Then arose in my eye line, an evil shrouded figure. She frightened every single person that looked at her. The light she emitted was blinding, and she flew over our heads. The gasps and shrieks of everybody filled the air. Her propellers deafened us, and blew my matted curly hair all over the place.

She flew in from the west, came almost level with the top of the flats, and jolted upward. Children started screaming and crying as the Angel of Death flew in and landed on the roof of block one.

Twenty-Six

"HM Prison" Rossville

The Brits were making themselves very comfortable up on the roof of the Rossville Flats and quickly became my neighbours. They had occupied some empty flats up there; their commander seemed to have a flat of his own, and the helicopter pilot did too.

In a failed community relations stunt, the Brits told the rest of the residents and me that the disruption would be minimal and that they would communicate to the other observation post at the top of The Embassy Ballroom using a Morse lamp. That was all well and good, but they did their fucking shift change using the helicopter. As the crow or helicopter flew, the Embassy Ballroom was only five hundred metres away.

In my flat, when six o'clock came, I would hear them running about and getting into the helicopter. They left the blades turning for about fifteen minutes; when many families were having dinner, the helicopter flew to The Embassy, returning about forty-five minutes later with new guards.

The guards stood along the top balcony of the flats and just walked around. They looked slightly bored, and nothing was going on. They had their rifles by their sides, smoked their fags, and the place had become fully patrolled by mid-1975. This was when the famous graffiti appeared near the main entrance of block one, "HM Prison Rossville".

I hadn't spoken to Mammy in ages, and I went to work one evening only to be told that I had been sacked the night before. I was too drunk and had started to use foul and abusive language around the punters. I was so disappointed in myself. Although half a litre of vodka that night removed the disappointment.

Wee Caroline came to visit me now and again. She knew, like everyone else, that I was a full-blown alcoholic. I came out at night and started shouting at the soldiers. I bought a record a few months before as it had a song that reminded me of Hugh, "The Bogside Man" by The Men of No Property. There was a riot in Rossville Street, and Hugh started singing it one night, and everyone joined in singing it with him! By now, we were far from those days past. Wee Caroline grabbed me while I was roaring and singing at the army,

"Steady on your aim with the petrol bomb! Don't throw it son til the peelers come! I am the Bogside man! We are all browned off with the midnight raids. Every man to the barricades! We are the Bogside men!"

In the end, wee Caroline shoved me back through the door and threw me on the fag burned sofa. She sat with me until I fell asleep, left me a glass of water, and pulled the door behind her.

Marie had come to visit me too and urged me to seek help. I was glad to see her, but I hurried her out of my flat. I wasn't interested; I just wanted to drink. On her way home, Marie would stop by and bring me something to eat, and I was glad of it. If I answered the door, great! If I didn't, she left it at the door. I didn't eat it if it was left at the door because what if the soldiers poisoned it? I also stopped drinking the tap water in the flat; what if The Brits tampered with it? I started sleeping with the lights on.

I never dared to drink on Monday mornings or afternoons; it was first aid meeting night. I couldn't look anybody in the eye, and some of my friends were asking me if they could help, but I said no. When anyone from my unit came to visit, even to try and cheer me up, I turned them away and told them that the soldiers might have bugged my flat.

The IRA had called a truce earlier in 1975, but that didn't stop the riots at times. Raids were becoming very frequent, antagonising people more and more.

Wee Caroline wasn't there, but I was in the first aid post when somebody came in and asked for assistance. He had been split pretty severely on the back of his head by a rioter who was too far back and had hit his own man at the front. He had two stitches put on the back of his head, and I offered to walk him home.

When we got to the junction of Abbey Park and Rossville Street, I was looking at the flats to my right, then all of a sudden, I was looking at the clouds above me with the rain landing on my face. The sounds of everything around me slowed down like a record playing at half-speed. The impact of that plastic bullet took my breath away and, as I would learn recently, took my memory away too.

A man came out of a house beside where I was lying and sent the wee boy back to the first aid post. I was driven to the hospital. I had been struck right in the middle of the forehead and was in and out of consciousness. I was taken to Altnagelvin, and Mammy was sent for.

Mammy was told that I had haemorrhaged and had started bleeding from my ear. She sat with me all night and did crosses on my forehead after dipping her thumb into Holy water. A nurse had told her to get out, and Mammy refused. The next day I came around, and Mammy was asleep on the chair beside me. I was drenched in a cold sweat, and I was shaking.

The doctor told Mammy that I was stable and that I would be okay after a few days. There were no brain scanners then, and I was doing all the exercises with the doctor, following his finger with my eyes. Mammy gave me a wee kiss on the forehead and went home.

I didn't sleep after I woke up the first night, I went berserk. I was shaking, and almost leaping off the bed. When the nurses came in, I roared and shouted at them, "get the fuck away from me!" "Get the fuck away from me!" Those poor nurses, I yelled, slapped, scratched, and spat on them. I screamed the ward down so hard that they feared I would tear my vocal cords.

An aura came over me, almost like a feeling of peace, before I started fitting like a caught mackerel in the bed. The nurses had to pin me down and strapped me to the bed. With the straps on, I screamed louder, and porters wheeled me out of the ward. I was put in an ambulance and sent down to Gransha. I stayed there for two or three days. They thought that I had taken a breakdown; nowhere on my medical records did it say "alcohol abuse" at that time. However, they learned it when I was in Gransha.

The consultant came to do a ward round and asked one of the nurses,

"Martha Bradley, what is the story with her? Is she mad?"

"No doctor, just a drunk."

"Ok then, not for psychiatry, send her home.."

The doctor came in, clearly annoyed that a drunk like me was taking up one of his beds. Post-Traumatic Stress Disorder (PTSD) hadn't been invented in 1975, which was contributing to my drinking problem. Mammy didn't even know that I had been transferred to Gransha, and nobody was allowed to visit me.

This is the entire conversation concerning my discharge from Gransha after having been treated for severe Delirium Tremors secondary to alcohol withdrawal, and a traumatic brain injury,

"Martha, stay on the straight and narrow now! No alcohol! No driving until you haven't had a fit in a year. I will prescribe you Fentanyl pain relief and one more question for you."

"Yes, doctor?"

"Have you a lift home?"

"I can get one organised."

So, I phoned Mammy, and she arranged for somebody to take me home, although I can't remember who it was. When I came out of the hospital and went to see Mammy, she started to cry. I had dropped down to around six stone in weight over the past year.

She insisted I eat. I barely ate a bite in the hospital, and now that I was out, the evil demons were coming back to me; time for another drink. She offered to let me stay with her, but I said no.

I wanted to go and rest, so I asked Mammy if she would sell my car for me because I couldn't work or get a job. She did, the day after I got back to my flat, and she got £265 for it. Her big mistake was giving me the money. She thought I would be sober because I had withdrawn from the drink for a few days. I got a bottle of Mundies and a straw that night.

Migraines were killing me, and the Fentanyl painkillers weren't helping much. I was taking them with vodka, and that helped a bit. I brought my record player into my room and was drinking, listening to my records, and taking occasional breaks to go to the toilet to be sick. I was waking up on the floor, at the kitchen table, and I was extremely vulnerable.

Wee Caroline always knocked on my door. If I didn't answer, she knew to walk away. This time I brought her in, and the flat was at least presentable as Mammy had cleaned it for me while I was in the hospital.

"Martha, love," and she held my wee shaky hand across the table. I knew it was coming.

"Caroline, don't! Please!" then my wee blubbery tears came on.

"Martha, I have to; Joe will be stationed in Germany. His tour is over here, and I am going with him. I'm lucky I haven't been put out or tarred and feathered. You know I've been warned, I'm on thin ice, and I can't stay."

"What if you get married without me being a bridesmaid?"

"I won't. I promise."

"You fucking better."

"But Martha."

"Don't say it."

"I'm saying if you don't stop drinking, you will die. If you are drinking by the time of my wedding, you aren't coming."

"Aye, I know, you're worse than Mammy."

"Bridie misses you wile."

"She knows where I live."

"She can't look at you, Martha! She thinks she is going to come up here and find you DEAD! MARTHA! DEAD!"

"Only the good die, young Caroline; I will live to ninety."

"I am going tomorrow. First thing, we are flying to Gatwick, and onward from there. I bought you a present." The wee sweetheart bought me a phone, so we could still phone each other.

I hugged her and didn't want to let her go. "Love you, Wee Caroline!"

"Love you too, Martha."

I watched her walk to the end of the balcony and through the stairwell door. When I went back in, I drank myself into oblivion. I was full of hate. I decided to grab my empty bottle and stagger out of the flat to confront the soldiers occupying our homes. The helicopter had just returned,

"See you! Get the fuck out of here!"

"Would you not like to come up with something more original, Martha?" one of them smugly returned. They all knew me because I was that much of a pain. I was roaring and shouting at them, more ferociously than I had ever done.

A voice from the balcony below shouted, "Martha! Stop shouting, please, you are frightening my children."

"Aw fuck off, you Margaret! Do you want to tell Mickey about them men in your flat when he's working in England?" There were no men in her flat; I wanted to inflict maximum pain for no other reason than to take my anger out on her.

An elderly man came out of his flat, four or five down from me, "it is okay, Martha, love, just go in and calm down."

Even he got the third degree, "who do you think you're talking to, you miserable bastard!? Gone in and mind your own business!" He tipped his cap and shuffled back into his flat. There was a chorus of tuts from the galleries below me, and everyone was coming to see the scene.

Mammy burst through the door at the top of the stairwell,

"Mammy! Get down to your fucking flat! This has nothing to do with you."

She stormed up to me, and two soldiers walked behind her. She stopped about six feet from me.

"Martha, I am your Mammy, and I love you. Please go back inside as you are frightening the old people and the children."

I lifted my empty vodka bottle and launched it as hard as possible at the soldiers, which shattered off one of their flak jackets.

"See them boys, Bridie Bradley; they are fucking cunts! Fucking murdering tramps!" The searing sting came across my left cheek, and it felled me, I fell back against my front door, and Mammy dragged me by the hair back into the flat.

She just stared at me; I stared back at her and said,

"Should be you in that fucking grave instead of Daddy." Then she turned around and left.

Twenty-Seven

?

The two years, after wee Caroline left, are a blur. She kept phoning, but there was no sign of a wedding come the summer of 1977, even though they had been together six years. Both families approved of each other, but Joe was travelling a lot, and she was working a lot. She worked in a couple of army hospitals but didn't like travelling.

I was an entire bottle of vodka a day drinker. I had drifted away from first aid gradually. I didn't buy another car or get another job, but I hadn't had a seizure in a year. My Knights of Malta friends came to see me less and less because I wasn't nice to visit. I met a boyfriend who was a bastard. Not the bastard I eventually married, the one I was going with before him. Mammy hated him and stopped coming near me completely.

Birds of a feather flock together, and he had a drinking problem like me. Our relationship was as toxic as the drink. We drank and fought, he would hit me, and I would cry. He would say sorry, and I would forgive him. One night he hit me with a broken chair post. I grabbed his long hair, pulled him to the ground and kicked the living fuck out of him. That was him off the scene after that.

The neighbours complained that I was playing my records too loudly, the army raided me, and it was all hopeless. I hadn't been to Ozanam House in over a year and spent most of my time in my flat on my own. My Knights of Malta coat and kitbag were in Daddy's leather suitcase, but I didn't bother looking at them because I knew he would be disappointed in me.

I became a regular at Casualty in Altnagelvin. I would venture down for a packet a fags, fall, and bust my head open. I fell getting out of the bath, lost some teeth, broke my wrist, and I was a wreck. I didn't even look at myself in the mirror, I don't remember caring about my hygiene, and sometimes the soldiers would jeer at me.

Birthdays, Christmas, and most other things were a blur to me. The only day I ever abstained completely was on Daddy's anniversary. I couldn't do it to him. In 1977, he had been dead for fifteen years. I went to his grave again; it was only the second time I had ever been.

The wind cut through my ragged skin and bone frame. My shoes had a hole in the toe, my clothes had cigarette burns, and my hair was matted because it hadn't been washed.

***

The 19th of November 1977 was the day I decided to kill myself. I was going to leave and join Daddy. I had it all planned out. I was going to take all my painkillers, down a bottle of vodka, and slash my wrists in the bath. I would stab into the mid-forearm and down, not horizontally across the wrist. I bought a jotter and pen and was going to write Mammy, Derek, and Wee Caroline letters.

I had become a burden, and now dread becoming a burden to my children and grandchildren, as my memories and faculties fade away. Back then, I was just a nuisance. People were finding me in a heap outside the shops at block two and carrying me up to the flat. As I was Knights of Malta, people tolerated me. They must have thought that what I experienced was the precursor to my drinking. It wasn't. I resorted to knocking on flats and begging for money. I was at an unrecoverable low. I got a sharp kitchen knife in a hardware shop, picked up my Fentanyl Prescription, and my usual litre of vodka.

I was sober that day, and I went to visit Mammy. She opened the door, and I stood there crying,

"Mammy, I haven't drank today, I promise."

"Okay, wee love, come in."

I went up the stairs and into the sitting room. Mammy's flat wasn't holding up well. She had changed the wallpaper, but the dampness was very much on the floors. Since their helicopter lived on the roof, The Brits deterred anyone from coming and doing repairs.

"Mammy, I miss you. I'm sorry for everything I did and said." My aim for that visit was to say bye to Mammy. Daddy left without saying goodbye, and I was at least going to say goodbye to her and tell her that I loved her before she buried me with Daddy. I was sober; I hugged her and promised to make a change.

I only told Mammy about this recently, as she was the one who told me to write down all my recollections. I never told her about my plan, and that my visit that day was to say goodbye to her. She had no idea. I got Derek's number from her and phoned him. He knew what I was going through, and I wept when he told me that Liam had been diagnosed with Hodgkin's Lymphoma. Mammy didn't tell me because she wasn't sure how I would handle it, and she was right to do so; I took it poorly.

Mammy and Derek had become close via phone, and now and again, he came to visit, but I wasn't aware of any of the visits because I was a drunken mess. Derek had a caring role for Liam now; he was only twenty-six. Mammy knew what it was like to care for somebody, and it brought her closer to Derek. I bid my farewell to Derek on the phone and said goodbye to him.

Wee Caroline told me when I phoned her that she was getting married in April of 1978. My heart shattered as I knew I wouldn't be going. I had become a master in the art of deception, and we talked for an hour and a half about what the wedding would be like. I remember Caroline saying to me, "and we are getting married in a Baptist Church, love, don't you be asking for Holy Water now!"

"Aye, no bother, I can be an awfully posh lady of the manor when I so choose!" and we laughed.

I was sober, and I felt myself a wee bit again. Even though the bottle of painkillers, the vodka, and the sharp knife were sitting on the kitchen countertop. The longer I waited, the more painful it would become, so I told her I loved her with all my heart and soul and that I would see her soon.

It was time. I ran the bath and filled it right to the top. I went into my messy room and held Daddy's suitcase in my hand, "I will see you soon, love! I can't wait to hear all your bars." I closed up the suitcase and put on my white Malta coat, gas mask, white hairband, and Steely Dan's. I had a mirror in the bathroom and I slowly took off all my clothes. I was completely naked; and I ran my hands along the sides of my ribs and could feel them protruding.

I took the knife, tablets, and vodka into the bathroom and closed the door behind me. I stepped into the bath and stared at my battered, bruised, and emaciated legs when I lifted them out of the bathwater. I lifted the orange pill bottle, "this is it, Martha; you will be with Daddy soon."

When I had the tablets in my hand, there was a loud boom and my entire flat shook. I hesitated, and instinctively, I half-dried myself and put on my dressing gown and underwear. I looked out the door, and a soldier was running down toward me. He was pointing and roaring at me, "let me in there. Have you any first aid supplies? Move out of my way!"

"What happened? Jesus! I haven't been drinking."

"Explosion in the lift shaft, we have a serious injury. Support Company and medical aid can't move in. What have you got in here?"

Without thinking, "I will come with you; I am a trained first aider with years of experience."

The soldier paused, "Fuck! Get dressed, thirty seconds please, and out!"

"Okay!"

I grabbed my kitbag and threw on the clothes that I had taken off. There were billows of smoke, and people were screaming below. I took off across the stairwell, and my heart was pounding. We didn't know if there would be another bomb, but we went ahead anyway.

A screaming young fella was lying on the ground when we got around the corner. He was no more than eighteen, white as a ghost, and his leg missing below the knee. There was a pink mist of blood and pieces of tissue strewn all over the floor, along with the remnants of his boot. He had taken off his helmet, threw his rifle down, and had to lie there whilst his partner had to come for help.

There was smoke coming out of the lift shaft, and a booby trap tripwire had caught the soldier at the top of the stairwell.

"What is your name?" I said to him.

"Francis."

I held the tears in; another Francis caught in an explosion.

"Okay, Francis, I am going to tourniquet your leg. Bite down on this roll of bandages, and I will put your partner's backpack under the top of your leg to elevate it, okay?"

"Y...y...yes!"

His partner took his pack off and threw it on the ground beside me, and I tied the tourniquet around the middle of his thigh to stem the bleeding. He had a radio pack, and I heard his radio ask if he could be carried down the stairwell to an army ambulance that was on its way down. I agreed. His partner lifted his arms, and I held his intact leg and raised the remnant of his other leg so he wouldn't bleed out. Every step we went down, the lad groaned and cried. His leg spurted blood onto my white coat if we went down too harshly. People were gathering around to see what was going on, and when I reached the fifth floor, I looked Mammy straight in the eye across the balcony.

We got down to the bottom and walked around to block one on Rossville Street, where a green army Pig with a red cross was waiting for us. They had a stretcher ready, and we loaded him onto it. He reached for my hand and said, "thank you, love." The army doctor injected him with morphine immediately, and the Pig roared off.

Loads of other people came down and looked at me in disbelief; I didn't know what to do. To this day, I can't interpret their reaction. Were they disgusted with me? Or were they amazed that I wasn't being a drunken nuisance? Mammy ran over and hugged me; I didn't even see her come down.

"Martha, I am so proud of you! Your Daddy would be smiling now. This is what you were called to do. You needed a calling, love, a calling in life, and this is it."

I agreed with her, and I knew when Mammy and I went back up to her flat for tea that my drinking days were done.

"Mammy, all hell will break loose in here over the next few days. Will you look after me? Please?"

"Of course, I will love."

Twenty-Eight

Concrete Jungle

Jesus Christ, I had Mammy battered on the second day. I nearly tore her hair out at the root, became completely delirious, and she called for the doctor. The tablets he gave me did help a bit, and I was less anxious. Mammy asked a couple of neighbours to move my bed into Daddy's room, as it was where I got the most comfort.

After a week, it stopped, and Mammy had been making enquiries for me to get help. She didn't know where to turn and ended up contacting Marie, who came to visit me. She came into Daddy's room and sat on the bed beside me; other than being happy to see her, I was delighted to have had a bath that morning and washed my hair.

"Martha, there's a group that meets in Queen Street, and it is every Saturday night at six o'clock. We have plenty of our home nursing patients who go and feel they get a lot out of it."

"Aye, but will it be full of drunk old men? I'm an oddball; I will be a wain compared to everybody else."

"I think you will be surprised, Martha!"

I promised her I would give it a go. She even told me that she would come with me to the first meeting. Alcoholics Anonymous (AA) wasn't very well known back then, only for those of us unfortunate enough to become ill with the drink. I thought I would be somewhat excited like I was the first time I went to join the Knights of Malta, but my nerves were wrecked.

Luckily, a wee settler tablet was left, and I took it before I went to the meeting. The tablets were to be taken for two weeks anyway, and I had one left. I still smoked and must have chain-smoked the entire day on the leadup to six o'clock. Mammy, Caroline, and Derek gave me their pep talks on the phone that day, and I felt ready.

Everyone was so welcoming, and I went into the hall where some new members, like me, and a couple more experienced members, were facilitating the group. There are two types of AA meetings: closed meetings, which was the meeting I was going to, and open meetings, where non-alcoholics can come as observers. My first meeting was a closed meeting.

I can't name anybody, so all the following names are little porky pies to protect their privacy. David led the group and gave an overview of the AA. Basically, it is more than just abstaining from drinking; it is a way of life. I felt very lonely, being a drunken nuisance, and it was nice to know other drunken nuisances wanted to stop like I did.

The following are the original twelve steps as published by Alcoholics Anonymous. The religious element isn't as prominent now, as it is opened up to those without a strong faith.

<u>The Twelve Steps</u>

We admitted we were powerless over alcohol - that our lives had become unmanageable. We came to believe that a power greater than ourselves could restore us to sanity. Made a decision to turn our will and our lives over to the care of God *as we understood Him*.Made a searching and fearless moral inventory of ourselves. Admitted to God, to ourselves, and to another human being the exact nature of our wrongs. Were entirely ready to have God remove all these defects of character. Humbly asked Him to remove our shortcomings. Made a list of all persons we had harmed and became willing to make amends to them all. Made direct amends to such people wherever possible, except when to do so would injure them or others. Continued to take personal inventory, and when we were wrong, promptly admitted it. Sought through prayer and meditation to improve our conscious contact with God *as we understood Him*, praying only for knowledge of His will for us and the power to carry that out. Having had a spiritual awakening as the result of these steps, we tried to carry this message to alcoholics and practice these principles in all our affairs.

I had to take the first step in the next meeting. I had to give a testimony and tell my story to the group. I hadn't done any form of public speaking other than to roast somebody if they were cheeky to me. This was a first for me, and the cravings for drink were still very much there. I practised it in Mammy's flat before the meeting.

"My name is Martha, and I'm an alcoholic."

"Welcome Martha," everyone said back to me.

"Whenever I took my first drink when I was fifteen, I felt confident and unstoppable. I found it easier to talk to people and felt very free. I was always shy, and my friend Caroline was always so outgoing. I wished to be confident and brave, like other people around me, and I felt weak. When I drank, I felt strong, and when I felt strong, I wanted to feel strong all the time. I worked in pubs, and when people told me to get one for myself, I took it to make me feel strong and felt that I couldn't say no. I started drinking on my own because I went out to a dance one night and somebody put their hand up my skirt. My Daddy committed suicide when I was nine, my brother moved to

England, and I was always afraid to get close to people after my friend was murdered on Bloody Sunday. I was drinking before all the trouble started."

So many young girls in the town were drinking; it wasn't a rare occurrence. When people think of alcoholics, they think of middle-aged or older men.

Another girl there lived in the flats; she knew me, and I knew her. She told me she had a similar experience. She was older than me, her husband was killed on active service, and she drank when the wains went to bed. She worked in a couple of pubs and said she was also hooked from the first drink. Women were there, and it surprised me — all walks of life.

My neighbour from the high flats became my sponsor, and she still is. I have been sober for thirty-six years, and I still attend weekly meetings. I didn't tell my children until they were all over eighteen. Over the years, I became a stalwart, and when any wee girls came in who had a similar experience to me, I took them under my wing.

I made a wee women's group in the AA called "Martha's Maidens", it has been running for over twenty years and has grown. As the years went on, I facilitated meetings and always had a soft spot for nervous wee girls like me. Even now, I still get cravings for a drink especially when some of the wee girls in my group fell off the wagon or died.

I phoned wee Caroline a couple of weeks before her wedding,

"What about ye, love? You all excited to sign your life away?"

"Awk, there she is! Wee one day at a time."

"What are you on about? You didn't have the craic!"

"And you did?!"

"I had too much craic. Sure somebody threw a petrol bomb at me one time and I drank it."

"I'm proud of ye."

"Awk, thank you, I'm wile happy."

Mammy and I went over to Cardiff, where Joe and Caroline were living, and they had bought themselves a lovely big house. Joe stayed at his parents' house, and Mammy and I stood waiting for wee Caroline to come down. Her family were all there, and we were reminiscing about the good old days. Us all still in our twenties, reminiscing like a bunch of old people with shite memories like me!

She came down the stairs and blew everybody away, the most beautiful bride in the world. I shouted to her, "don't do it! Don't do it!" which brought about a laugh from everybody.

Wee Caroline had to tell us all, "Remember! This is a Baptist Church, folks, no looking for Holy Water."

We all got taxis and cars to the church. I was in a taxi with Mammy,

"Mammy, the church is nice, isn't it?"

"Yes, I suppose so, but it isn't as nice as St. Eugene's."

"Derry woman of the year award goes to Bridie Bradley!"

The taxi driver laughed at that one! Ironically, he happened to be from Strabane and got the joke. We got out of the car, waited for everybody, and walked into the church together. No Holy Water font at the door, and we walked on in. We were brilliant at passing ourselves off as Baptists, walking down the aisle with our chins aloft, not looking for Holy Water. Mammy and I were last. Mammy went in before me, and I let the side down. I genuflected.

All the whisper shouts came over, "fuck sake, Martha!"

"I'm sorry!" I whisper shouted back.

Even Mammy commented, "we fell at the last hurdle. Although you have blown your own cover, you are going to Mass a bit more since joining AA."

I was caught! I was going a bit more. It kept me out of trouble, I suppose. I didn't go every day like a die-hard, but when I wanted a bit of comfort, I made my way up to the Cathedral. I went along with my sponsor from the flats. She loved a spot of mass, and I loved her company. Everybody wins!

Wee Caroline, I love you to death. You have been my best friend for over fifty years, but Jesus Wept. Your wedding lasted hours, not a single flower or candle! Not that our weddings are mighty craic, but your wedding was on par with some funerals I've been to.

They are still married and live in Wales!

***

We returned to the flats, and it was time to sort my life out. I decided to go to the local technical college to do a course that would set me on my way to becoming a paramedic. I met my eventual husband, Mickey, in my tech class and I started returning to the first aid meetings.

The AA give wee coins for significant milestones, saying, "to thine own self be true" on them. I have a nice little collection now. A year, two years, five years, ten years, fifteen years, twenty years, twenty-five years, and thirty years.

Mickey and I were dating a couple of years before we married in 1980. I had been sober for three years and felt confident to move out. We rented this house in Foyle Road for a few years before we bought it from the landlord.

Mammy gave me the leather suitcase I have now, and the day I left the flats in late 1979, I realised that the building and I had been through a lot together. Luxury when I moved in, and the flats deteriorated as I deteriorated. My soul weaved into the concrete, and despite it turning into a rat-riddled, graffiti-strewn shithole, I loved it there.

I was back at the Knights of Malta, and the 1980s were rough too. More riots, hunger strikes, and everything else. I have got the hang of this whole writing thing. If you all enjoy this one, I might write about the 1980s, if the fairies don't take me beforehand! I passed the paramedic exam in 1982, Joanne was born in 1983, and my twins Frankie and Sean-Paul were born in 1986. Marie and I are still great friends, and I have been sporadically volunteering with the Knights of Malta since I joined in 1968.

Mammy and the rest of the resident's association were campaigning into the 1980s to be rehoused and for the flats to come down. They were done up in the early 1980s and looked like a giant Rubik's Cube. Horrendous.

Derek remained in England and nursed Liam until he died of cancer in 1984, aged thirty-two. Liam wanted to be buried back in Derry. Derek always told me that it was "the long goodbye". We reconnected since then, and his taste in music is still shite.

Block one was felled in 1986, and Mammy was still there for a while afterwards. The place looked so strange without block one being there. Mammy got a place at a supported living complex in Creggan in 1987 and couldn't get out of the place quick enough. She was sixty-seven and was going from one flat to another. The girl that didn't want to move into a flat in 1967!

When the rest of the flats were demolished, I drove to the carpark between Abbey Park and Lisfannon Park to watch. The windows had all been removed, and it was a giant tower of hollow rectangular concrete blocks. I could still see some of the last tenants' horrible wallpaper choices. I had a wee cry, I will admit it. I looked up at Mammy's old flat and my own.

When the wrecking ball tore through Mammy's flat, I remember the outro of The Hollies, "He Ain't Heavy He's My Brother", was on the radio. A song that my uncle Damian always said reminded him of my Daddy.

Fancy medical scanners came in at the end of the 1980s and early 1990s, and I had liver scans and brain scans. I had been sober for fifteen years but had developed liver cirrhosis due to taking so many painkillers for migraines, side pains, and so many years of a bottle of vodka a day. Mickey Davidson had stopped caring about me then and assumed I was having surgery for "lady problems" when I went to Belfast for a liver transplant in 1992.

There was a meeting in Pilots Row called in 1992, on the twentieth anniversary of Bloody Sunday. I remember reading about it and being shocked those twenty years had passed. Even now, Bloody Sunday was only a few years ago for those who were there that day. It brought back my memories of Hugh and our friend group at the flats. He could have had a wife and children, owned his own garage and lived a family-orientated life like I was. It made it sore for me that his life was so cruelly taken away from him. I had experienced a lot, mostly bad, but there was some good. He never got to experience that. I threw my full support behind their campaign. Mr and Mrs Gilmour had already passed away at that point. Still, Hugh's brothers and sisters admirably, along with the other families, set out to crush the Widgery Report, have their relatives declared innocent, and bring the Paras to justice.

There was a massive drive in the town after 1998 for those present on Bloody Sunday to come forward for the newly established Savile Inquiry. Hundreds of people did, and it went on for years. So many people wanted to say what they saw was murder and to clear the names of those murdered that day. The Paras dropped to one knee and fired from the hip. The fuckers were born to kill, and they did just that.

In 2010, the report came out, and all got their declarations of innocence. So many turned out, and David Cameron, the Tory Prime Minister, issued a full apology on television broadcast into the Guildhall Square. Thousands turned up on that lovely, sunny June day. The only sad thing was that the inquiry still believed that Gerald Donaghey probably had nail bombs in his pockets. He didn't have fucking nail bombs in his pocket. I suppose the British Government wouldn't give us everything, and one day it will be proven that those nail bombs were planted.

For the surviving Paras, who murdered those men and boys that day, I hope your children and grandchildren know exactly what you did and that they are ashamed of you. I treated every section of society with the Knights of Malta; RUC, Soldiers, Civilians, INLA, and IRA. From my point of view, there were genial people in all those groups; all had different viewpoints. The Paras, that shower of bastards, didn't have an ounce of humanity between them.

Helen and Caroline came over a few weeks ago, they stayed in the town, and I went to meet them and talk to them about writing a book and how my memory is failing. We had tea and visited old friends, which was lovely.

When talking about the days in the high flats, my Alzheimer's disappears. Gilly's friends were so fond of him and gave me lots of things to write to tell his story. He wasn't a rioting lout; he had a caring side that those closest to him remember every day.

Of course, the conversation turned to Hugh when we met Olive, Sarah, and Bridie in Olive and Bernard's house. We were chatting away about him, about how the boys used to fill up that wee car, drive it dry, and push it back again. The laughter that came out of that house that day was like medicine for us all. I wrote it all down just in case I forgot anything. They have pictures of him on their mobile phones and in their houses. Even though he passed so many years ago, the pain of his loss is still with them.

Wee Caroline, Helen, and I decided to go to Rossville Street, and I was prepared for the cold day because I had my big Order of Malta fleece on me. The high flats not being there anymore is still bizarre to me. We were shocked that the "concrete jungle" between Joseph Place and where block two was, is still there. One of the walls that made up the slope to access the walkway between blocks two and three is still there.

My recollections are my recollections. This story gives some sense of what life was like at that time. Back then, Derry was a different place. Different, but the same as it is now. The Bloody Sunday Trust are still fighting for justice for their loved ones; support them! Even if you are young and didn't live through it, we must come together like we always do and see that justice is done.

Young people don't volunteer anymore either. Volunteering saved my life. It made me who I am, and I don't want volunteering to become a dying art. As I have gotten older, community spirit has dampened a wee bit; I think it should come back. I told my wains that they need three skills to survive in life: driving, swimming, and first aid.

The Order of Malta still exists and still recruits volunteers. Join! Contact your local unit. It was the most incredible experience of my life, and many of the Knights of Malta I met from 1968 have remained friends to this day. Just part of that Malta magic. Absolute heroes and the true spirit of Christian charity.

I feel it is important to tell your story, even if it seems insignificant to you. Writing is quite therapeutic. You never know who might be interested in it and become mesmerised by it! Make sure you are all extremely kind in your Amazon reviews too!

Time passes, memories fade, and if we are lucky, The Knights of Malta might even get a monument of their own somewhere in the town one of these days...

Acknowledgements

When I develop an interest in a topic, I throw my heart and soul into it. Thank you to Mum and Dad, my sister Emily, my wonderfully patient son Ethan, and the wider family circle for your constant support throughout this writing journey.

My eternal admiration goes to all the Order of Malta Ambulance Corps Volunteers from the Free Derry period, as well as their family members, who shared their stories with me to greatly influence this work. Thank you to Eiblin Laffery-Mahon, Antoinette Coyle, Attracta Bradley, Martin Bradley, Charlie McMonagle, Charlie Glenn, Majella Cassidy, Maureen Campbell, Alice Doherty, Jim Doherty, Robert Cadman, Kathleen Cadman, Kellie Cadman, Frank Kelly, Kay Byrd, Breidge O'Kane, Hugh Deehan, Cecilia Deehan, Roberta Deehan, Michelle Gallagher, Martin White, Kevin Mac Dermott, Eamonn MacDermott, Paddy MacDermott, Damian McClelland, Margaret Keane, Tony Keane, Winifred Black, Father Pat Day, Stephen Duddy, Lord Lieutenant David McCorkell, Doreen Wray, and Liam Wray. I feel privileged and humbled to have spent time with you all.

Some of the items and personal possessions kept by the first aid group were of incredible value to me. Being able to see medals, uniforms, paperwork, photographs, reports, first aid supplies, gas masks, and lots of other things was an incredible experience and one I will never forget. It's amazing what people have in their attics!

Thank you to the Museum of Free Derry and the Bloody Sunday Trust for their support for this work and putting up with all my visits, emails, and helping me to make connections. Thank you to Adrian Kerr, John Kelly, Mark Hone, Rebecca Brown, Hannah Brown, Noel Doherty, Jimmy Toye, Eoin Yates, Jean Hegarty, Leo Young, Julieann Campbell, and Maeve McLaughlin. I have learned so much from you all and thank you for igniting my passion for local history.

Thank you to the Order of Malta Ambulance Corps CEO John Byrne, The Order of Malta Historical Archive, and the current volunteers who continue to save lives.

For compiling the biography of Hugh Gilmour, my sincerest gratitude to Hugh's family; Olive Bonner, Bridie Nixon, Sarah Murphy, Frankie Murphy, Teresa, Brian, Sandra, Anne-Marie and Ricky. Further thanks to Hugh's close friend group and neighbours, Chris McKnight, Gerry Doherty, Christy Tucker, Peter McLaughlin, Charlie McLaughlin and Jim. Thank you to all of you for allowing me, if only in spirit, to befriend him.

The book *Rossville Flats: The Rise and Fall* by Jim Collins was so beautifully compiled and helped me get a sense of the high flats, and the community there. It is the only real record of the flats, as official paperwork and the original plans for the high flats couldn't be found. Normally if a needle needs found in a haystack, I can find it. Somehow, I couldn't manage to get my hands on plans of three giant sectra-concrete tower blocks that weighed around fifty thousand tons!

Special thanks to Danny McBrearty, for being a great sounding board and friend, not just for this work – but through the years. Thank you Vinny Cunningham for directing me to your documentary of the Battle of The Bogside, which contained a surprise appearance from Hugh Gilmour!

Thank you to everyone else who read the book, gave feedback, and helped to polish and sharpen it to what it is now; Mickey, Sandra, Stella, Sarah, Auntie Nuala, Margie, Grainne-Maeve, Jim, and thanks to Heather Shields for editing and proofreading.

I cannot come up with enough superlatives to thank Kathryn and Geoff, for all their words of encouragement, telling me their stories, and most importantly – teaching me how old money worked. I am forever in your debt, in this life, and the next.

Antoinette Coyle

I joined The Knights of Malta, following in the footsteps of my sister, brother and cousins who had joined them before me. My cousin Eiblin was in the Knights of Malta at the same time as I was. The meetings were held in Ozanam House in Bridge Street. I enjoyed the lessons and practical work. We not only learned the different types of bandages and their uses but also how to make beds and generally nurse someone. It was great for those considering nursing as a career in the days before nursing courses became available through the College of Technology.

Many Knights of Malta members went on to take up nursing on leaving school. The people involved in running the Derry Knights of Malta were Leo Day – the Captain, Johnny Lafferty, Jim McCallion, Joe O'Kane, Mr McKinney, and the nurse Judith Doherty. Dr MacDermott gave us lessons in First Aid. It was a very comfortable group of people. They gave a lot of their free time to train us and we put that knowledge to use through our Order's attendance at Sunday Masses, the annual church retreats, and other church and civil events. We were available to help if anyone became unwell.

We mostly dealt with people who were feeling faint. The big events were the competitions, between the whole of the Knights of Malta in Ireland, which took place each year. I went to one of these with Eiblin who was part of a four-team group taking part in the competition. We went down on the Saturday morning, the competitions took place in the afternoon, and then we were free to go back to our Bed and Breakfast (B and B) to get ready to go out for the night. As far as I can remember now, the Derry teams did well in the competitions, so were in a good mood that night, and we went on to have a lovely weekend.

During my time there several marriages occurred, due to people meeting through The Knights of Malta. By the summer of 1969 riots were occurring and as a result, first aid posts were set up in the Bogside and at the foot of the New Road to help the injured. I worked mostly in the New Road first aid post, which was nearest to my home. There was always a nurse present and we dealt with the effects of CS gas, cuts and things like that.

At that time in Derry there were three groups of first aiders - The Knights of Malta, The Red Cross, and St. Johns Ambulance. Mrs McCorkell was both Red Cross and St. Johns Ambulance, as far as I know. There was some interaction between the Knights of Malta and the Red Cross, and I believe there were times Captain Day and others met with her. I think Mrs McCorkell even worked in the Westland Street first aid post at times during the rioting in 1969. Mrs McCorkell requested The Knights of Malta work at some events that Red Cross members also attended. I remember going to one out at Ballyarnett, Mrs McCorkell's home. I really can't remember when but I think it was about 1969/1970. It was a show-jumping event. We didn't have much to do. I think it was Martin Coyle, Jim Norris and myself went to it as Knights of Malta members. Mrs McCorkell was a lovely woman who invited us into her house, chatted to us, and thanked us for attending the event.

However, the one big event that happened, those of us in the Knights of Malta at that time, was Bloody Sunday. I think most of us, if not all of us were on duty that day. It left a huge mark on us as it did on our city and on our people. I remember our white coats. Up to Bloody Sunday we wore a heavy, grey uniform. It was comfortable and distinctive. We carried a square or rectangular shaped, white, first aid bag that contained some different-shaped bandages and a water bottle. At some time before Bloody Sunday, we were told our uniforms were being changed from our grey uniforms to white coats for use on riot duty.

The uniform was a white nylon type of coat with a pocket on the left-hand side of the breast, and a Red Cross motif in the centre of the pocket. At the meeting before Bloody Sunday, we were told that last-minute instructions given by police were that we were only to walk on the pavements because if we walked in the body of the march, we could be prosecuted for being part of an illegal march.

We met at the Creggan Shops. My cousin Eiblin was also on duty that day, and so the walk began. When it got to the corner of William Street, the march divided into those insisting on walking to the Guildhall as originally planned, and those who decided to just walk to Free Derry Corner and hold the meeting there instead of the Guildhall.

The few Knights of Malta I was walking with decided to go down to the bottom of William Street because if trouble broke out that's where we would be most needed. We arrived at the bottom of William Street just as the army fired loads of CS Gas - a choking, thick cloud that totally filled the air. People were asking us for vinegar, but we didn't have any.

Everyone was running away at this stage to get away from the gas. As we were also choking, we walked down Chamberlain

Street to get away from it, but it was stinging our eyes and we were finding it hard to breathe. A door opened on the right-hand side and, I think it was Jim Norris who said, "in here". We went into the house for a few minutes to recover and then decided to make our way to Free Derry corner to see if anyone needed help.

We were making our way to the high flats when suddenly all these army tanks and cars erupted and came storming up the Lecky Road. Everyone began to run and we did too. I remember a Saracen army vehicle pulled up in front of us and stopped. As it stopped a soldier jumped out, lifted his gun like a club, and as a young woman was running by him he swung it at her. She ducked and it hit her back, she staggered, kept her balance, and ran on.

I remember being totally shocked that not only would he do that to anyone, but that he would hit a woman. I ran on with the crowd and followed them into the high flats and up the stairs, looking to get to Free Derry corner. By this time the level of noise from the firing of rubber bullets, and as it turned out live bullets, was so painful on my ears that to this day it's one of the things that I have never forgotten.

From one of the floors of the flats, I noticed a young person lying at the back of the flats between the High Flats and Chamberlain Street. To this day I can't remember at what stage I saw the young person. Whether it was when I was on the second or third floor. He wasn't moving, so I suspected he could be badly injured. With that in mind, I decided when I got down to the street level I would try to get out to him, to help him.

I made my way from the stairwell to the third-floor apartment corridor of the flats and realised there was nobody about on this level, except myself and a man at the other end. He was sheltering behind a pillar. By this time the noise of shooting was atrocious. I started to run across the balcony towards the other end and as soon as I started to run, I could see something was hitting the concrete at my feet, causing the concrete to chip. I could see the spurt of dust coming out of the concrete. I remember thinking about what could be fast enough and hard enough to cause the concrete to break like that, and realised live bullets were hitting the concrete of the balcony's concrete at my feet as I started along it.

When I reached the other person on the balcony, he grabbed me by the shoulders and pulled me in behind his pillar saying to me to stay in as they were firing live bullets. I told him I had to get to the man lying on the ground at the back of the flats, and I ran on down the stairs to the bottom of the stairwell, but I couldn't get the door to the back of the flats opened so I went out the front to see if there was another way.

By this time, there wasn't anyone lying shot on this side of the flats. I don't remember much at this stage, but have a very vague memory of someone asking me to go into one of the houses beside the high flats, as someone seemed to have back injuries. It was a girl. She had trouble with her legs and told me an army vehicle had hit her. She was in a lot of pain and seemed unable to move her legs.

I told her I was going to get an ambulance for her and told the people not to move her until the ambulance men arrived, who would lift her. By this time the shooting outside was awful, steady and so loud. When I got to the door a man was standing there and said I wasn't to go out as the army was shooting live bullets. I remember saying to him I had to go out to get an ambulance for the girl. He told me to wait and he would check if it was safe. He looked out and told me to go. I ran out and saw Paul McLaughlin, a Knights of Malta cadet, and other people kneeling at the red telephone box at the flats, and I ran towards them.

As I ran I noticed there was a man lying on the ground a short distance from Paul and another man lying to the right. Neither man was moving. As I was running across, Paul started shouting at me to go back. When I reached him, he grabbed me and pulled me into the corner where everyone was sheltering. He told me the army were shooting from the walls. I remember he pointed at the man lying closest to us and said he was dead. This was Barney McGuigan. He told me Barney had gone out to help someone and was waving his white hanky when he was shot dead. He then pointed to the other man and said he was dead and then he pointed up towards a male at the steps to Fahan Street and said he was nearly sure he was dead too.

Up to then, I hadn't noticed there was a man lying up there. There was just one woman in the group sheltering. She was hysterical. Paul told me she had seen Barney McGuigan murdered. I remember looking at Barney's blood seeping out and thinking I just didn't know what to do for someone shot in the head. I remember starting to say the Rosary for them. I also remember that from where we were sheltering, we could see the people at the meeting at Free Derry Corner.

They were all standing around listening to the speaker. I was amazed that they were standing there, unaware that people were dying at the high flats. Then suddenly they began to run and I realised they were now being shot at also. Eventually, the shooting eased. We got up and moved out to the men. I remember it was a very cold frosty day and I stooped over Barney and put my cold hands close to his lips to check if he was dead. I didn't have a mirror, or I would have used that, but there was no breath hitting my hand and so I knew he was dead.

By this time people were walking around and Knights of Malta volunteers, who had been on the march, all seemed to gather at the area where Barney McGuigan was killed. I remember Alice Long, Leo Day, Paul, myself, Sophie Marley, and others. One of them said someone needed to go and call for ambulances to be sent from the hospital. Someone else mentioned there was an ambulance in Chamberlain Street. Alice Long said she would go to get an ambulance and I said I would go with her.

Then others said they would go also. About five or six girls went in the end. I thought it was safer for the girls to go rather than the men. We made our way out the back of the flats (Alice had no bother opening the door to the back of the flats and that's when I discovered I had been trying to open it the wrong way.) We walked over to Chamberlain Street. The soldiers stopped us and wanted to know where we were going. They were so excited and laughing and on such a high. There was an ambulance outside a house in Chamberlain Street but no ambulance men. We told them there were people injured and dead and we needed ambulances and asked where the ambulance men were.

The soldiers told us they were in William Street. We walked across to William Street and looked both up and down but we couldn't see them. As we were walking back across Chamberlain, and not far from the ambulance, we met a woman and asked her if she knew where the ambulance men were. She pointed to the house where the ambulance was parked and said they were in there. The soldiers had deliberately misled us. We went to the house just as the ambulance men came out, along with two of our Knights of Malta members - Majella Doherty and one of the Knights of Malta men. I can't remember who he was now.

They had been called into the house to attend to Peggy Deery, who had been shot in the leg, and had stayed with her until the ambulance arrived. Alice told the ambulance men about the dead and injured, they said they would go round to the flats and would put in a call for more ambulances. Alice asked the ambulance men if they would let us go with them in the ambulance but they said they couldn't as it wouldn't be allowed and they could get into trouble.

We headed up Chamberlain Street toward the flats and the soldiers. The soldiers stopped us again. They were on such a high. I couldn't believe they could laugh and get so excited over people getting shot dead and wounded. We told them we needed to go back to the Bogside. One of them told us we could go but to remember the cross on our white coat pockets made a perfect target for them to hit the heart.

I couldn't believe these soldiers were threatening mostly seventeen- to eighteen-year-old girls. We returned to the Bogside, stayed around a short time longer, and then made our way home. The following week we met up at Ozanam House. Nobody told their story in full. Mostly bits and pieces. We never spoke of Bloody Sunday to one another. A few weeks later we were given medals by the Knights of Malta, for our actions on Bloody Sunday. I couldn't appreciate getting the medal, all I could think of were those who had died and those whom I couldn't help or didn't even know how to help, such as Barney McGuigan. After Bloody Sunday I fell away from The Knights of Malta, going to a couple more meetings and then not going at all.

Eiblin Lafferty-Mahon

I lived on the edge of Creggan and the Bogside, in the area known as free Derry. My family home faced an army post built on the opposite side of Brook Park wall. At no time could anyone enter our front or side door without being seen by the army. The old Rosemount police barracks were up the hill from our home; we had barracks on every side of us. At this time, my dad was a Sergeant in the Knights of Malta.

As a young volunteer in this group, I made many wonderful friends who remain so to this day. One of my first duties as a volunteer was attending mass at St. Eugene's Cathedral and helping those who felt sick during the service. In the summer holidays, I worked at the Bogside Post Office; my spare time was spent volunteering at the first aid post, which took us into the middle of riots, during the troubles - the beginning of a new role with a more serious side. During these times, when the CS gas came over the Bogside, we dealt with it by putting a rag over our nose and mouth. Sometimes we worked from the first aid post when the gas was bad, and we also took the people to the post to get attended to by the doctor.

Little did I know how serious the troubles were to become. My brother Eamonn was shot dead, and my family was left devastated. My heartbroken Mum and Dad were left without their son. I have no words to describe how everyone felt. Our home never emptied, and thousands attended his funeral.

I witnessed pain, sorrow, sadness, and emotions I never knew existed. From then on, I lived from day to day, never expressing my feelings of hurt to anyone. Our family kept together at all times, supporting each other. Great family values from a close-knit family.

The big civil rights March was the next line of duty; it is now known as Bloody Sunday.

First aiders were told to keep to the footpaths, but we were lost in the crowds due to the thousands who attended the march. I wore a white medical coat with a Red Cross on the front pocket at the heart and carried a white bag which contained medical supplies and bandages.

I was in the vicinity of Abbey park when the shooting started. I saw my Dad and Leo Day attend Johnny Johnson. At this stage, everyone was taking cover in people's homes, and I attended a boy called Joe Friel until the doctor took over. As I left this house, I saw a body lying in front of Carr's home in Abbey Park. As I ran forward, I watched the soldier shoot again toward me. The bullet singed the side of my trousers. I grabbed my leg and kept running until I got to the body. At this stage, people came forward, and I was already saying the Act of Contrition into his ear, a prayer for the dying. I was devastated. I couldn't do anything. There was no response, but another Knights of Malta worker came forward.

Moving to Glenfada Park, where I was to witness more bodies, I ran and threw my white bag to the ground and put my hands in the air, shouting, "first aid! first aid!"

Someone pulled me back by my coat, but I ran forward again, arms outstretched, getting in front of the bodies; the soldier shouted to me, "Your white coat is a target, but your red heart is even better."

I kept shouting, "First Aid!", with arms outstretched. My Dad came looking for me and to collect my brother and sister. I sent them home, but I walked around on my own, trying to take it all in. Later I walked home in silence. I will never forget that I witnessed murder: some friends, some neighbours, but all innocent.

In the period that followed everyone was aware that the army was going to make a move to enter Free Derry and Creggan. Many talked about it, and all were on edge. As the days passed, Saracen jeeps and soldiers became more active. The awaited night came sooner rather than later, we awoke to the sounds of engines and soldiers running everywhere. I looked out of my bedroom window, Saracens and jeeps covering the area. I knew then Operation Motorman had begun.

Damian McClelland

I did some of my growing up in Margaret Street, in the Waterside, and attended the Waterside Boy's School which is now Chapel Road Primary School. When I was at school, Master Leo Day was one of my teachers. I joined the Order of Malta just after I left school, and after Bloody Sunday I joined the Order of Lazarus. Relations were good between the Order of Lazarus and The Order of Malta. I joined with one of my closest friends, Alex Wray, who lost his brother Jim Wray on Bloody Sunday.

No matter what, Alex always did his duty, and we treated everybody. Our post was based at the back of the Bogside Inn and it became known as the Bogside First Aid Post (BFAP). Even as we treated soldiers and kneecapping victims, a crowd gathered. Not one person would give us any abuse, everyone knew that was what we did. There were meetings and get-togethers around the country. We would train for weeks to get the marching right!

Alex and I were best friends, and he was my youngest daughter's Godfather. I would like my small contribution to this book to be a tribute to Alex, always ready and willing to help out where he could.

Robert and Kellie Cadman

Robert Cadman

I want to thank Jude for reigniting my memories, from days gone by, in the Order of Malta. There were many happy times, and I have many fond memories. Unfortunately, I buried deep inside me what happened around the days of Bloody Sunday, the 30th of January 1972. There were things that I had never even discussed with my wife and children about some of the scenes we witnessed. When called for the Savile Inquiry, the floodgates opened and only then did I have to revisit the most traumatic time of my life; once again, I tried to suppress it.

After meeting Jude, I feel like I now have permission to remember the people, the characters, and the comradeship we all shared. I shall be forever grateful for that. We were all ordinary folk and just doing what we were trained to do but in extraordinary times.

Kellie Cadman

When Jude approached my dad about contributing his memories to this book, we had absolutely no idea what was about to unfold. Of course, we knew he had been in the Order of Malta, and yes we also knew he had been involved in the Battle of The

Bogside, Bloody Sunday and more. What we didn't know was about his superhero stunts! Like carrying people on his back to get them to the nearest first aid post or ambulance. He was able to tell story after story about his heroics, and all he did was shrug his shoulders and say, "sure we just did what we had to do".

John Robert Cadman was always a hero in my eyes, but it was so amazing to hear the kind words others had to say about him. This has been a huge healing journey for Dad, and I will always be grateful for that.

Lady Aileen McCorkell

Excerpts from Lady McCorkell's memoir, *A Red Cross in My Pocket.* Published by WEA in 1992.

The next day, Thursday the 14th of August, I went back to the Bogside about 10.30am. I met two members of the Order of Malta just as I got to the Post and they asked me to drive them up to Creggan to get the keys of the First Aid Post. On the way we met an American journalist, who had been helping the day before. He got into the car as well. By this time there were many different people from other places gathered in the Bogside. Many Irish men and women had arrived to help from all over the country and there were quite a lot of foreigners too. Many of them had taken part in the French student riots and they knew all about how to make gas masks, etc. The American kept on saying there was no organisation and no leadership. He had obviously been in other theatres of unrest under similar circumstances. We all set to and tidied up the Post, washed everything down and mopped the floor with disinfectant. There was the never ending making of tea which goes on in this country, cups and odd buns mixed up with everything, perhaps that is what keeps us going, and provides that wonderful Irish welcome (p29).

***

A letter which infuriated me appeared in the Irish Times asking where the Order of Malta and the Red Cross were on Bloody Sunday. No one has the right to criticise the Order of Malta in Derry as they were the most highly trained and experienced first aiders in Ireland and they did not fail to do their duty on this occasion.

The modern first aid volunteer does not always wear a uniform and incidents are so numerous that they must be prepared to act quickly on their own initiative, as they go about their daily life. A small metal badge or a crumpled armband may indicate to which organisation they belong. Good deeds seldom make the headlines; someday the true story of the first aid volunteers and all the other volunteers who work in the community for the relief of suffering will be told (p72).

Captain Leo Day K.M. - In Memoriam

Old gentleman – old, gentle man – at last
The last branch is pruned, the last frail
Plant is bedded out, not in solid ground but
In memory seeded to blossom in warmer days.

And tears shall make it root despite the frost
That falls around the bed where roses die
And white fuchsias mourn the evening's loss
Of light and warmth and love – old, gentleman.

And what richer garden could genius plant
Than this mosaic of colour, smell and shape?
What more myriad paths to wander than these
And meet with you, at last old gentle man?

How well that gardened toiled who seven sturdy
Trees left to shade the fragile plot;
How well that sentry stood to guard the acre
Where hawks and harlots savage seedlings by night.

And true to type (for whom "a good type" was better
Than all the earth's riches), your final salute -
Erect in your solid sentry box – has all
The dignity of a soil-close country gentleman.

But closer soil now must you till, till
Garden and gardener at last are one and the last
Acre, Mary's own, is all your own too
To potter in peace and reap at last – last
Old gentleman - old, gentle man.

Anonymous
+RIP: 12 June, 1989.

About The Author

Jude Morrow is an autistic best-selling author, entrepreneur, philanthropist and keynote speaker from Derry, Northern Ireland. Jude travels the world to showcase, through his talks, that autistic children can grow up to live happy and successful lives. Jude's first two books are published by Beyond Words, publisher of *The Secret*. Jude is the founder of Neurodiversity Training International, the world's premier autistic-led training and consultancy to nurture autistic people to thrive in business and embrace their creativity. Jude is also a two-time TEDx speaker and nurtures parents, teachers and professionals to develop a kinder mindset toward autistic people, young and old. Follow and connect with Jude on Facebook, Instagram, Twitter, and Linkedin.

Other Works By Jude Morrow

Why Does Daddy Always Look So Sad (2020) – Beyond Words Publishing

Loving Your Place on The Spectrum : A Neurodiversity Blueprint (2022) – Beyond Words Publishing

Websites and Social Medias - Follow, Share, Tag, Review! :) #TheGhostsOfRiotsPast

https://www.judemorrow.com

https://www.neurodiversity-training.net/

Jude Morrow | Facebook
Jude Morrow | LinkedIn

Jude Morrow (@JudeMorrow10) / Twitter

Jude Morrow (@judemorrow) • Instagram photos and videos

Glossary

Index to some of the commonly used Northern Ireland or Derry-specific colloquialisms, terms and words used throughout this book.

bars
news or story

blootered
drunk

bobo
dummy or pacifier

close
friendly

craic
news, gossip, fun conversation

culchie
someone from the countryside/ rural Ireland

Feis
a festival of music and dancing

"lift"
at a funeral, taking part in the carrying of a coffin

lamps
of a person, eyes

naw
no
skelp
smack, hit a person or child
sore
painful
wains
Derry for children
wan
Derry for one
wee

1. commonly used to mean little, small. 2. also used as a term of endearment or affection

wile

1. very 2. wild

yees
you (plural)